In the Arms of a Highland Warrior

by

Donna Fletcher

In the Arms of a Highland Warrior

Cover art
The Killion Group

Visit Donna's Website
www.donnafletcher.com

Chapter One

Tavia stood in the silence of the forest. She should not be there, but she hadn't been able to resist. She had come here often when she was young. It was her escape, a place to dream, imagine, hope. Her da would scold her, warning her that the forest held beauty, but it also held danger, and she should not venture in it alone. Still, though, he had never stopped her… until the accident.

A sudden sound had her turning and she smiled seeing that a large pine tree had shed some of the snow that had weighed heavily on its branches. The towering tree appeared pleased with itself, its spreading branches no longer drooping, now proudly lifted, finally free of its burden.

If only one could shed problems so easily.

The last few days had been more sun than clouds melting a good portion of the snow that had fallen in intervals for the last week. Not that it was the last of the winter snow, there would be more, but she would not be here to see it.

The sad thought caused her heart to turn heavy and she focused on her surroundings committing the forest she had come to know and love to memory. She went to take a step to walk a bit farther into the woods and a sudden pain struck her leg, causing her to stumble. She could not prevent herself from falling, though she wisely twisted her body so she would land in a snowdrift.

Tavia laughed and sat up, brushing off the snow that had fallen on her. It reminded her of when she was young and would jump or fall, in play, into the snowdrifts. A pain turned her laughter to a wince, stealing the happy memory and reminding her of her limitations. The accident had left her with a limp and the snow and cold made it all that more difficult. She would suffer for her trek into the forest. Her limp would be more pronounced and her leg painful for a day or two. At the moment, she did not care. It was more important that she had this time here and felt as free and carefree as she had—what seemed like not that long ago.

She got herself to her feet with some difficultly and realized the walk back to the keep would be painful, but worth it for this brief taste of freedom. In a few days, it would all be gone.

After a shake of her cloak to rid it of the remaining snow, she took a cautious step and grimaced from the pain that rippled through her leg. The walk back was going to be more difficult than she thought. She would need to take her time, keep her pace slow. It did not help that a chill crept through her, the air having gotten a sudden bite to it and the sun having ducked behind a cloud.

Worry began to take hold, not about her painful return to the keep, she could manage that. Once at the keep, she would rest her leg and apply a warm cloth that would ease her suffering. What worried her more and had since she had first learned of what the future held for her was… what would her new husband think of her limp and the problems that came with it?

Tavia had had little decision in the matter, the marriage arrangement necessary to her clan. Her da had been upset but adamant about the marriage when he had told her about it. Clan Strathearn would not survive if the marriage did not take place. It was her duty to help the clan.

It had only been her and her da, her mum having died giving birth to her and her da never finding another woman he loved as much as he loved Tavia's mum. He'd been a wonderful, loving da, which had made it easier for her to be a loving, obedient daughter. Now she was expected to be a caring, obedient wife to a man she had never met. And a man more Northman than Highlander. But with his clan bordering a small section of her clan to the north, he could provide protection. It also brought much needed help in many different ways to her clan, sufficient food being one of them. With the clan dwindling, it was difficult to provide the necessities. Her new husband, Lord Bhric, intended to infuse the clan with his own people, populating it more and growing it strong once again.

Tavia could not deny her clan such an opportunity, even if it cost her dearly.

She made slow progress through the forest, not something she minded. She cherished this time alone. It had been hectic the last week or more with Lord Cree and Lady Dawn here to help solve a problem plaguing the clan. But it had been settled. At least she hoped it had. There was still concern for the woman, Fia, in the dungeon, but a claim had been made on her and her da was considering it. She had no idea what her husband would have to say about it, or if he would leave it to her da to decide.

It was difficult to imagine bidding her da farewell. She had always been secure in his love and while he would still love her, she would rarely get to see him. How did one manage such an abrupt change? How could it be that one day she was here among those who loved her and the next swept away by a stranger who she was expected to obey without question?

She had been impressed with Lady Dawn's strong, independent nature, even though her husband was the infamous, mighty Lord Cree. She wished she had a small portion of Lady Dawn's strong resolve. At least then, she would not be as fearful as she was in meeting her husband.

A sudden, strong wind had her stopping to pull up her hood, the wind having whipped across her face stinging it. So much had happened in the last week that she barely had had time to comprehend it. She supposed that was why she had needed this time alone in the forest to try and make sense of things, to try and accept her fate, to try and not let her heart break when she bid her da goodbye. She had already bid her cousin Flora, who she had had little time to get to know, farewell. Her sudden and unexpected marriage to Lord Torin and their departure had been rushed after he received a message. The contents or who sent it, he had not shared, only that they would leave immediately.

She shook her head. Life was far more difficult than she ever imagined it would be. She missed the carefree days of when she was young and there was little worry and lots of mischief. She hoped she would be able to give the same to her children.

A shiver ran through her, not from the cold, but from the thought of what it took to conceive a bairn. How was that possible with a man she did not know at all?

Tavia reached the edge of the forest, spying the village not far in the distance. She stopped knowing once she left the refuge of the forest, life would be forever different for her. She could hear her da's voice reminding her again that she had no choice. Her marriage to Lord Bhric of Clan MacShane was beneficial to the clan and it was her duty to see it done.

But wasn't that the lot of a dutiful daughter?

She shook her head again. If she were lucky enough to have a daughter, she would not allow the same to happen to her no matter what the cost to herself. She would see her daughter wed to a good man of her choice, not one forced upon her.

With fortitude born out of necessity, Tavia took a step out of the forest and into the life fate had dictated for her.

The village was a short walk away, Tavia's wander having taken her farther away from the village than she had thought. She took barely a few painful steps when she felt the ground tremble beneath her feet and heard horses' hooves pounding the snow-covered ground, then the mighty sound of a horn filled the air.

Could it be?

"Nay," she whispered and attempted to hurry her steps. She had at least a couple of days before his arrival. *Please. Please, do not let him be early,* she silently pleaded.

She hurried a glance behind her and almost froze with fright at the group of men baring down on the village a few feet away. It was a small troop of men, but every one of them were large especially the man leading them. He was broad beneath the hides and furs he wore, and his light-colored hair was long with two narrow braids hanging along each side of his face. Even from a distance his features were striking and intimidating. He exuded confidence in the powerful way he sat his horse, in the way he held himself erect, in the way his eyes remained focused in front of him as if he feared nothing. But then the numerous weapons that hung off his horse's sides attested to his many skills as a warrior.

Tavia pressed her hand to her chest, her heart beating so rapidly she thought it would burst. Fear captured her, an intense fear she had never felt before this moment. It ripped through her, squeezed at her, threatened her. How would she ever be wife to such a powerfully intimidating man?

The group was baring down on her fast and she barely had room to avoid them, though if she could run, she could at least make it to a small clearing up ahead where she could avoid being trampled by them.

Tavia raised the hem of her garments, gritted her teeth against the pain that would strike and rushed her steps. Tears threatened her eyes from the pain that shot through her leg, but she ignored it and pushed forward. A few more steps, just a few… her leg gave out without warning, and she went down hard.

She tried to roll out of the way of the horses but

wasn't fast enough. The powerful, black horse reared up near her and a string of oaths flew from the rider's mouth as he fought to control the animal.

Instinct had Tavia squeezing her eyes shut tightly against a death she hoped would be quick and painless. They sprung open when she was suddenly hoisted off the ground and slammed to her feet. Pain shot through her as she gazed into the darkest blue eyes she had ever seen before she collapsed in a faint, falling against the large man.

***

Tavia woke with a start an icy cold racing through her to find snow being rubbed over her face.

"What is the matter with you, woman? You need to move fast when you see horses bearing down on you, especially when you are nothing more than a wee bit of a thing. Have you no sense?"

Tavia stared at him, shocked to find herself in his arms and seeing his features up close. He possessed more than fine features. He was a handsome man that could easily capture a woman's breath and heart all in one look, but not so Tavia. His deep, angry voice and his dark blue eyes filled with even more anger was enough to heighten her fear of him.

He dropped her down on her feet, though held on to her arm, and she bit back against the pain that gripped her leg.

"Stay out of the way," he ordered and released her arm.

As soon as he did, her leg gave out from the pain,

and she went down but never hit the ground. His arm was swift to coil around her waist, keeping her from collapsing.

"You've gone and hurt yourself," he accused.

That he faulted her fired her ire and without thought, she said, "You ride without care."

He placed his face close to hers. "Watch your tongue with me, woman, or suffer for it."

She silently admonished herself. What was she thinking speaking to him like that? She could jeopardize the marriage… unless he wasn't her husband.

"Was the woman hurt, Lord Bhric?" a man asked, walking up to them.

Good Lord, he was her husband. Her legs grew weak, and she thought for sure she would collapse. He must have felt it too, his grip tightening on her.

"She is a weak one. We will get her to the village and let her people tend her," Bhric said. "Hand her up to me, Sven."

The man he called Sven was tall but did not reach Bhric's height or his width. He was slimmer and leaner. He had good features and long blond hair with several braids in it. He took hold of her arm as Lord Bhric released her and mounted his horse, then he scooped Tavia up and placed her in front of Lord Bhric.

"I hope your wife is a lot stronger than this helpless one," Sven said with a grin and a nod at Tavia.

"May the gods help me if I am straddled with such a weak one," Bhric said and Tavia's stomach roiled.

Sven kept his grin as he offered reassurance. "Your mother would not do that to you. Surely, she has chosen a strong woman for you."

Tavia held her tongue, not knowing what to say, though more afraid to say anything. He had not yet met her and already she could tell he would not be pleased with her. Hadn't her da been truthful with his mum? Had he convinced the woman that she was a good match for her son? And why hadn't the woman come and met Tavia herself before agreeing to any marriage?

"I will bring you to the keep and let Chieftain Newlin decide what to do with you," Bhric said, surprisingly caught up in the softness of her blue eyes that appeared far too caring and her lovely face that certainly captured a man's eye. However, she was far too petite for him. He preferred tall women, strong in body and mind. Someone who would fight beside him if necessary. Someone with strength and courage.

Tavia kept her hood covering as much of her face as possible when they entered the village, fearful someone would call out her name. Though from what she did spy, everyone seemed too shocked by Lord Bhric and his sizeable men to do anything but stare, many with their mouths agape.

Lord Bhric lowered her gently to the ground once they stopped in front of the keep and when he saw she tilted some once on her feet, he hurried to dismount and take hold of her arm.

"You hurt yourself," he said. "You need your healer."

Her da emerged from the keep just then and smiled broadly. "Lord Bhric, I have been looking forward to your arrival, and how wonderful that you have already met Tavia, your wife."

Chapter Two

Bhric stared down at the woman who barely reached his chin. What had his mother done marrying him to a woman that a good wind would blow away and who had not the sense to move out of the way of approaching horses and who injured easily? The wee woman was far too weak to be his wife.

"Why did you not tell me who you were?" he demanded, though the reason was obvious. She was too frightened to admit it. How would he ever deal with a wife who frightened so easily? He shook his head, not caring to hear her excuse and looked to Chieftain Newlin. "She suffered an injury of her own doing. Have your healer tend it."

Newlin hurried down the three stairs to his daughter.

"It is nothing, Da," she assured him, letting him know not to say anything about her permanent limp and took his arm so that Bhric would release her other arm, and he did.

"She can barely walk. Summon your healer," Bhric ordered, his annoyance clear in his snappish tone.

"Fetch the healer," Newlin ordered to one of his warriors standing nearby and, with a firm arm around his daughter's waist, helped her to slowly mount the first step.

Tavia cried out in shock as she was ripped from her

father's grip after barely taking a step and hoisted up once again into her husband's arms.

"Only three steps and you can barely make the first one." Bhric turned a glare on Newlin. "Hurry your healer. I will not see my wife suffer through her injury even though it was her own foolish fault."

"It is easier to blame me than to take responsibility for your poor riding ability," she said, her response, as courageous as it was, was also foolish for speaking without giving it thought.

Bhric stopped abruptly. "I will not tolerate a sharp-tongued wife. Do it again and see what happens."

His threat frightened her since she had no idea what he would do. Men could strike their wives without fearing any consequences. Was he a man of brutish nature? Would he raise his hand against her when displeased with her?

She cast a glance at his hands as he continued carrying her. They were large and could do much damage if he ever struck her. She closed her eyes against the image of his sizeable hands swinging at her face and it sent a shiver racing through her.

"Have you no strength to you, woman?" Bhric asked with disgust upon feeling her shiver.

Tavia was spared a response, not that she had one, since he deposited her quickly on a bench near the fireplace in the Great Hall and walked away.

"Drink!" Bhric ordered when he turned to Newlin, trying to contain his annoyance.

He yanked his fur cloak off his wide shoulders and tossed it to a nearby bench. How could his mother ever think this petite woman would make him a good wife?

How could she ever bear him children, let alone take him easily between her legs?

Bhric shook his head and downed the tankard of ale, a servant handed him, in little time, then he turned once again to Newlin. "Did my mother meet, Tavia?"

"Aye, she did," Newlin said, dreading the question that might follow.

"How long ago?" Bhric asked.

Newlin kept his smile though wondered if it appeared more a cringe since he was fighting to maintain it. "A few years or more."

It must have been more than a few years since Tavia did not recall ever meeting Lord Bhric's mum.

"Look at me," Bhric ordered and pounded his wide chest before stretching his arms out from his sides, the height and width of him more than impressive. "Now look at your daughter. Do you think us a good match?"

Newlin's chin went up. "My daughter may be petite, but she has a strong nature and more importantly she has a kind heart."

"A kind heart does me no good. I need a wife who is almost as fearless as I am and strong enough to bear me many sons and daughters." He pointed to Tavia. "Tell me she can deliver a brood of bairns without difficulty."

"No one can tell you that about any woman."

Bhric turned to see a woman of fairly good height, slim, and with plain features. The gray in her dark hair and the wrinkles that pinched at the corners of her eyes spoke of her many years.

"I am Auda, the clan's healer, my lord," she said, introducing herself. "I have seen large women have trouble giving birth and bairns slip out of thin and petite women with ease. No one knows how a birth will go until the time comes."

"Did you attend Tavia's birth?" Bhric asked.

"I was in attendance, but it was the healer before me, Eartha, who saw to the delivery."

Bhric looked to Newlin. "Tavia is your only child?"

"Aye," Newlin said again, nervous about the question that was sure to follow.

"Why?" Bhric demanded.

"My mum died giving me life," Tavia called out from where she sat.

Bhric mumbled several oaths beneath his breath. He was going to have a serious talk with his mother when he returned home.

"You can always wed again, a stronger wife next time," Sven said, filling Bhric's tankard with more ale.

Newlin and Auda stared at the two men, too shocked to speak, not so Tavia. The words had struck her like a slap in the face that she should be thought so little of, but they also emboldened her to speak up.

"Aye, he can do that just as I can wed again if he is so foolish to die in battle."

Complete silence fell over the room, the servants halting in mid-step.

Bhric slammed his tankard down on the table, then walked over to Tavia. "A sharp-tongued wife doesn't make a strong wife. I'm going to teach you other things to do with that tongue that will dull it."

"As you say, my lord," Tavia said with more mettle than she felt, for she wondered what those things could be that he would teach her.

"See to her wound," Bhric ordered the healer. "You and I will talk, Newlin, while my men eat. Bring the men here, Sven."

Sven nodded and donned the rest of his ale before he took off.

Newlin gave rushed orders to the servants, and they began hurrying about, preparing the tables with food and drink.

"Help me to my bedchamber, Auda, where we can have some privacy," Tavia said, and the woman nodded and helped her to her feet.

Bhric watched his wife as he spoke with Newlin. "More of my men along with carts filled with needed supplies are a day behind me. We will discuss what is to be done here before I take my leave."

"I am grateful, Lord Bhric," Newlin said.

"It was made part of the marriage agreement and I keep my word when an agreement is made," Bhric said, watching his wife take obviously painful steps. "My men will also provide protection since Torin told me of the difficulties you had with Lord Ivan and a supposed demon." Bhric shook his head not able to watch his wife any longer and a rash of oaths left his mouth as he went to her.

This time Tavia saw him coming and rushed her hand out to stop him. "I do not need your help."

Bhric shoved her hand away and scooped her up for a third time. "I did not ask if you needed it. Now show me where to take you."

She did not want to be in his arms any longer than necessary. Though, it annoyed her that he carried her with such ease, not even needing a spare breath as she directed him to her bedchamber. Though he frightened her, oddly enough, she felt a sense of safety in his arms, but then he was a large man who could easily protect her.

Bhric placed her on the bed. "We will talk later."

"As you say, my lord," Tavia said, since what else could she say.

"Why do I think you placate me with those words?" he asked annoyed and not bothering to wait for an answer, he turned and left the room.

Tavia stared at the door after Auda closed it.

"I bit of advice," Auda offered.

"I will take any and all I can get."

"Be careful. Most women learn to manipulate men out of necessity to survive unwanted coupling or the repeated sting of a hand. Lord Bhric is not a man who can be manipulated. You would be wise to obey when necessary and stay clear of him when you can."

Tavia's shoulders slumped in defeat.

"I know that is not what you wanted to hear, but it is better to face the truth of your situation and prepare as best as possible for what will be. Now let's rest that leg and get some warmth on it so the pain will ease."

Tavia thought on Auda's advice. Had she truly and foolishly expected more from the marriage? After meeting Lady Dawn and Lord Cree and seeing what a loving and wonderful marriage they had, she had harbored hope that she could possibly find the same with Lord Bhric. If only it could be so, but Auda was right. It would be unwise of her not to face the truth of her marriage. She would find no love with Lord Bhric, though she did hope that they would at least become friends and, if nothing else, learn to tolerate each other.

***

Bhric purposely took slow steps down the stairs. He was annoyed to find he had a wife who was the complete opposite of the type of woman he preferred. Though, he had wanted one easy on the eyes and she was that. There was a loveliness about her face that caught the eye. Maybe it was her soft blue eyes and the long, dark lashes that framed them or the slight blush to her cheeks or the faint splatter of freckles across her nose that could only be seen up close. Whatever it was it would not be difficult to look upon her face.

However, her body was another thing. She was a wee one. He could crush her if he hugged her too tight. What really troubled him was joining with her. He liked to give a woman a good pounding and he could not see doing that to her. He'd probably break something in her.

He shook his head. What had his mother been thinking? Had she agreed to the marriage because it would grow the Clan MacShane holdings? Or had she accepted the first offer, his father having made known she had been gone from him long enough and she was to return home.

A smile surfaced thinking about his parents. He did not know anyone as much in love as his parents or anyone whose love had lasted and had even grown stronger through the years. They had had six bairns together, three lads and three lasses, he the oldest. He enjoyed coming to maturity with so many siblings and hoped to have a wife who would give him at least six bairns.

His smile faded. He could not see such a petite woman giving him even one bairn. Would Tavia be like her mother, too weak to survive childbirth? He shook his head. This was not a dilemma he expected to face. He had hoped to claim his wife this night and plant his seed deep inside her. He no longer saw that happening, at least not tonight.

Their marriage had not been consummated yet which meant he could negate the marriage agreement if he wanted to. But he could not believe that his mother had chosen Tavia in a rush to see a marriage arranged for him. She had chosen Tavia for a reason and he knew it had to benefit him in some way or his mother would have never entered into the agreement. He would disappoint her if he chose otherwise.

So, did he trust his mother and accept the woman she had chosen to be his wife, or did he refuse her choice and search for a wife himself?

He had no answer right now and there was more he needed to know about the Clan Strathearn before he made any decision.

"Newlin," Bhric called out when he entered the Great Hall. "Time to talk."

***

Tavia woke snuggled in the warmth of the wool blankets. She had not expected to fall asleep, though she should have since the valerian brew Auda had given her always made her sleepy as well as easing the cramping pain in her leg.

She glanced at the fire that had dwindled which meant she had slept for at least a couple of hours, perhaps more. She cuddled deeper in the warmth of the blankets or was she hiding, afraid to face what awaited her?

"You are a coward, Tavia," she whispered.

She recalled something Lady Dawn had explained through gestures, having been mute since birth, that she should grab courage and keep it close. She supposed Lady Dawn was right. People might encourage, but no one gave you courage. It was something you had to find and grab for yourself. But how?

She shook her head at the answer that came to her. *Fear.*

Did fear birth courage?

Tavia struggled to understand the strange thought when another thought interrupted. She knew someone whose steady companion was fear… or was it courage?

She eased herself out of bed, placing a light pressure on her leg as she sat on the edge of the bed. The pain had subsided leaving in its wake a dull ache. A bit more rest and she would do well, but first she needed to pay someone a visit.

She took cautious steps to the hearth and sat on the small bench that she kept close yet a safe distance from the fire. She rested a moment, after slipping on her shoes. Then remaining cautious and slow in her movements, she added more logs to the dwindling fire one by one. The room would be toasty warm by the time she returned.

After grabbing her warm wool shawl off the chest by the door and wrapping it around her, she grabbed the door latch and made her way slowly to the stairs. She stopped, a sadness creeping over her recalling how she used to rush down the curving stone stairs. She missed those days of feeling whole, free of worry, free of pain.

She shook her head. "Keep yourself in the present. It is now that matters."

Loud voices mixed with laughter and shouts reached her ears before she reached the bottom of the staircase. She was not accustomed to such raucous behavior. Meals in the Great Hall, even when celebrating, had never been as boisterous as her husband's warriors.

The rich scent of meat pies and ale drifted her way letting her know that the evening meal was underway. She had no desire to join the rowdy group and quietly made her way to the kitchen, realizing she was in need of a hot brew and food.

The kitchen was busy, all there working at a frenzied pace.

"My lady," Cora, one of the cooks, said with a bob of her head.

Tavia stepped close to Cora to whisper, "Was Fia fed?"

Cora's eyes went wide. "Lord Bhric and his men have kept us busy. I did not know men could eat and drink so much."

Tavia scooped up a basket and filled it with food, then grabbed a small jug of warm apple cider. And before anyone could offer her any help, she left the kitchen and headed for the dungeon.

The ache in Tavia's leg warned her to take the curving stairs down to the dungeon slowly. They were damp and often slippery.

"Fia," she called out as she neared the bottom and grew worried when she saw no candle glowing in the one occupied cell out of the three the dungeon contained.

The torch in the bracer on the wall wasn't sufficient to light the inside of the cells but it gave Tavia enough light to see where she stepped.

"I am here, Tavia," a woman's voice responded.

Tavia was relieved seeing a figure emerge from the dark depths of the cell and walk to the metal bars of the cell door. Her eyes lighted when she spotted the jug and Tavia quickly handed it to her.

"I have neglected to look after you," Tavia said, feeling guilty.

"Nonsense," Fia said after taking a substantial swallow of cider from the jug. "You have done well by me, sneaking down here with food and drink against your father's orders. "You are a brave woman."

"Nowhere near as brave as you," Tavia said. "I cannot imagine the horror of being called a demon or witch with calls to be burned at the stake when you have done nothing wrong."

"Many would not agree with you once it was learned that I cut open a human heart," Fia said and eagerly took the meat pie Tavia passed through the bars to her.

"You are a healer and curious and brave to attempt such a thing to gain knowledge, knowing if caught you surely would be condemned."

"And you are courageous in trusting my word when none do," Fia said and fetched the small bench in her cell to sit by the iron-barred door and talk with Tavia as she ate.

Tavia fetched a bench as well and sat to enjoy her meat pie as she talked with Fia.

"Your husband has arrived," Fia said.

Tavia was not surprised that Fia knew Bhric was here. The woman had a knowing about things without being told and was able to see things before they happened. It frightened most people, thinking it the devil's doing, but having come to know Fia in the few weeks she had been held prisoner here, Tavia had come to understand that she was a good woman… different but good.

"He is a powerful man and fears little." Fia grew silent, staring off, then spoke. "He respects strength, show him nothing less."

Tavia asked about her earlier thought. "Does fear birth courage?"

Fia smiled. "Fear is part of living as is joy, sadness, laughter, pain, tears, love. Living is what births courage. Do not be afraid to live, Tavia. Allow yourself to experience it all and you will live a good, courageous life."

"But do I have the strength to do that?" Tavia asked more of herself than Fia.

"You will never know if you don't try," Fia warned.

***

Bhric had delayed long enough in speaking with his wife. He did not plan to talk long with her. He would have his say and let her be until… he was still trying to make sense of why his mother had chosen Tavia to be his wife. He had planned on leaving in a day's time, wanting to get home and begin a life that had been planned for him and one he had been trained for but did not know if he wanted. Meeting Tavia made him question even more what was right for him. Was he duty bound to remain here on this soil his grandfather had insisted he be born on? Did he lead a clan that was foreign to him yet in his blood? Or did he return to the life he knew well, loved, and missed?

He climbed the stairs to her bedchamber wanting done with this chore. He did not bother to announce his entrance with a rap on the door since she was his wife and there would be no door that would keep him from entering wherever she may be.

He swung the door open ready to speak, his mouth open, staring at an empty room. He got annoyed. If she was well enough to leave her bed, then why had she not joined him for supper?

He took the stairs down two at a time, his annoyance growing with each step. Was she purposely avoiding him? Did she think not to consider her own husband?

"Where is she?" Bhric demanded of Newlin when he returned to the Great Hall.

Newlin looked puzzled, then worried. "Tavia is not in her bedchamber?"

"Nay, she is not. And if she is well enough to leave there, then why did she not join her husband for supper?" Bhric asked, his temper flaring. "Where do I find her?"

"Her solar," Newlin said relieved and waved at a nearby servant lass. "Go fetch, Lady Tavia."

"Nay, I will go speak with her there," Bhric said and caused the servant lass to jump with his demand. "Show me!"

The lass hurried to lead the way and gave Bhric a wide berth when the solar was found empty.

"Newlin!" Bhric called out, returning once again to the Great Hall. "I will know now where my wife is."

The room grew silent, his warriors' hands going to the hilts of their knives tucked at their sides, ready for his command.

Newlin shook his head, not sure where his daughter had gone.

Bhric, out of the corner of his eye, caught a young servant lad sneaking to hide himself in the shadows of a dark corner.

"You lad!" Bhric yelled, and the servant froze. "Step forward and tell me what you know of my wife."

The lad did as he was ordered, his skinny body trembling. "I saw Lady Tavia in the kitchen gathering a basket of food."

Bhric turned to Newlin, fury swirling in his dark eyes. "Who does she go to meet?"

Newlin was hesitant, knowing as soon as he heard that his daughter had gathered a basket of food where she had intended to go.

Bhric fisted his hands at his sides as he stepped in front of Newlin. "Does she go to meet a man?"

Newlin's eyes popped wide. "Nay! Nay, my lord.

She goes to see the demon witch."

Chapter Three

"Your husband knows you are here," Fia said.

Tavia sighed. "I cannot run. I will not run."

"Courage is your ally. Keep it with you always," Fia advised softly.

"TAVIA!"

She cringed at the strength of her husband's shout. He exuded power not only in his commanding voice but his impressive size as well, and she did not know how she would ever deal with him.

Strength. Whether she felt it or not she had to stay strong.

"I am here," she called out.

He seemed to take up the width of the stairs when he reached the bottom or perhaps it was her fear of him that had her see it that way.

"If you think to get some curse or spell to put on me from this demon witch, know now it will not work," Bhric said, standing beside her, his arms crossed over his chest as he glared down at her.

"You are right. It would not work on you. You are much too tenacious for anything to penetrate that thick head of yours," Tavia said and almost gasped at her own audacious response.

Her bold response surprised him and annoyed him as well, and he was quick to warn, "I'll not tolerate a sharp-tongued wife."

"So you have told me, and I will do my best to remember that, but you would do well to remember that Fia is no witch."

His large hands were at her waist in a flash, and he launched her to her feet with one swift lift. He was surprised she grabbed hold of his arms when he did, and he did not fail to see her slight cringe. That she was still in pain was obvious and he kept a firm grasp on her.

"This woman is not a demon or witch then? She has no powers to cast spells?" he asked, though wondered how she could be so certain or so foolish.

"As I said, Fia is no witch or demon. She is a wise healer."

"Or so she has you believe," he challenged. "You know not what truth or lies she tells you."

Tavia saw no reason to argue with him. He thought one way and she another. "As you say, my lord."

Bhric took hold of her chin, raising her head to look at him. "Your father told me that Lord Varrick is on his way here to collect this woman. I have agreed that he should surrender her to him. Until we take our leave, I forbid you to come here and speak with her."

Tavia's anger spiked, and her heart pounded in her chest. That this man, whose hands found their way upon her far too often when only meeting him, would reign over her telling her what she could and could not do, did not set well with her. She had been a dutiful daughter, but it had been easy with a father who had not been overly demanding and would at least hear her out. This man demanded without any thought to how she felt or what she, herself, thought.

She bit her tongue from lashing out at him and responded as she had done since meeting him. "As you say, my lord." That it annoyed him was obvious and she felt a sense of victory, small as it might be.

"You are done here," he ordered sharply and scooped her up in his arms.

"I am capable of walking," she snapped, staring into his dark blue eyes that swirled with a bite of anger.

"And yet you keep a firm hold on me which tells me your leg still causes you pain," he said and started climbing the stairs.

"Take care, Fia, I will pray for you," Tavia called out more concerned that she would have no chance to see her again than respond to her husband who had been right about her leg.

"She will need it once the legendary warrior arrives," Bhric said.

"Are you so afraid of her that you would not look upon her or say a word to her?" Tavia accused as he climbed the stairs with her in his arms with ease.

"I will give no demon or witch a chance to have any power over me. I rule with a strength I will not see challenged and you would be wise to remember that."

He sat her on the bed once they entered her bedchamber.

"Rest," he ordered with a harsh bite and turned to leave.

The words were out of her mouth before she could stop them. "You will not stay the night with me?"

He turned. "Until I determine for certain that I will keep you as my wife, I will not seek your bed."

While she was relieved to hear that he would not

seek her bed, she was shocked and worried that he questioned whether he would remain in the marriage. She had not expected that. This marriage had to succeed, her clan depended on it.

"The documents have been signed," she reminded as if nothing more needed to be discussed.

"But until the marriage is consummated, you are not officially my wife," he reminded.

"My clan needs this marriage," she said and disliked sounding as if she begged.

"Mine does not, though when, if it should," —he made sure to clarify— "it is consummated, I will fully commit to it. Never will we part," he said and left the room.

Tears flooded her eyes, and she brushed them away. She had not been wise in dealing with her husband. She allowed anger and her own disappointment to interfere with her duties. This marriage was not about what she wanted or hopes of love, it was to benefit her clan. She needed to remember that when dealing with her husband. She had to make the most of this marriage whether she wanted to or not. Dreams of finding love with the man she wed was just that—dreams.

Tomorrow was another day, and she would do her best to secure this marriage so that her clan would prosper.

***

"Are you keeping her or not?" Sven asked the next morning, snow flurries falling as they walked through the village.

"I do not know," Bhric said, having slept little last night, the thought heavy on his mind.

"She is a pretty little thing," Sven said.

"She is that, though as you said… little. I could squash her with one arm." Bhric recalled how light she was to carry in his arms. It was as if he carried nothing at all.

"That is true," Sven agreed.

"She has no strength to defend herself and I cannot be with her all the time."

"Also true," Sven agreed again. "I know Ingrid can easily defend herself. She has done so against me when I have drunk too much, or I have become too demanding with her."

Bhric laughed. "I have seen the results. Your jaw was bruised for a week. Besides, that is what you get for marrying my sister. She is a true Northwoman, strong and proud."

Sven laughed as well and rubbed his jaw. "That she is, and I deserved what she gave me, and I have not done it since, especially now with her being with child. I would hate myself if I hurt her or the bairn, I mean *rind*." He shook his head. "We have been friends so long that I use your language instead of Norse."

"I do the same," Bhric admitted. "Does Ingrid mind living here or does she wish to go home."

"She goes where I go and makes no protest. Would your wife do the same? Even join you on a visit to our motherland?"

"A good question," Bhric said and wondered over it. Would Tavia be a dutiful enough wife to follow him anywhere without protest?

"There is quite a bit of work to be done around here, but I have no doubt Birger will see it done," Sven said. "He was a wise choice to lead the task."

"Birger is a good man and large enough that no one will defy him. He will see it all done."

"What of this demon witch Torin told you about that sends tongues wagging and instills fright in the people?" Sven asked. "And that has your wife visiting her. That will not rest well with our people."

"The witch is not our worry. Newlin confirmed the message Torin sent me. Lord Varrick is on his way here to claim her. She will be his problem."

Sven wrinkled his brow. "What does the legendary warrior want with a demon witch?"

"I do not know. She will be his problem not mine. I have ordered Newlin to give the witch to Lord Varrick. With his infamous reputation, the witch should fear him more than any other punishment she would face."

"I hear he is a ruthless man."

"He must be since failure is not known to him, his battle skills beyond believable" Bhric said.

Sven lowered his voice. "Perhaps he is in league with evil and he wishes the witch to help him gain more power."

"Time will tell," Bhric said. "We will keep watch on the situation."

"And what of those we are meant to take with us?" Sven asked.

"A couple and two children. It is to protect them from Lord Ivan of the neighboring Clan MacVannan. Several children he had paid coin for fled his home after brutal treatment. Some of Newlin's people helped them and he fears they are in danger from Lord Ivan if they remain here. Torin took some, and others went with Lord Cree. Lord Ivan had demanded the witch as payment for his loss, but Lord Varrick had already sent word he would claim the witch."

"This Lord Ivan has not held the title long from what I recall. He arrived here six months after Lord Bennett's death claiming to be his nephew and sole heir to Clan MacVannan. With supposed documents to prove it, no one disputed his claim. See that Birger keeps a watch on him. Now tell me that all will be done so we can leave tomorrow."

Sven was hesitant to say, "The day after would be more likely."

"I thought the same, though did not want to admit it," Bhric said and looked to the sky. "I hope the weather holds for our departure."

Sven laughed. "Snow never stopped us."

"But it could take its toll on my wee wife."

***

Tavia lingered in bed the next morning, hoping the extra rest would help her leg. She was pleased when she finally was up and dressed, and while her leg ached it was nothing she could not bear. It had taken time to become used to the pain that lingered now and again. Mostly, though, she was able to deal with the limp and even found herself getting around much more easily after adapting to her new gait.

She rubbed dried mint in her long, dark hair, then brushed it thoroughly before plaiting it. She then scrubbed her face fresh with a wet cloth until her cheeks blossomed pink. She was determined to do what was needed to see that her clan had sufficient food for winter and that it prospered.

With a soft smile, she entered the Great Hall.

"Your leg still pains you?" Bhric asked upon seeing that she still limped.

"Nothing I cannot abide, my lord," she said, fearing what he would say when he discovered her limp was permanent. Would he end the arrangement? He could not do that if the marriage was consummated. Did she make sure to couple with him before he discovered the truth and seal the agreement?

Bhric was glad to hear that and also that she was up and about in spite of her injury. Perhaps the woman was stronger than he had first thought. Or was it wishful thinking?

"We will be ready to leave the day after tomorrow for home, no matter the weather," Bhric said, making it clear there would be no delays.

The question was would he take her with him or terminate the marriage? She had to couple with her husband so there would be no chance of him ending their marriage before it even started, and she had only one night to see it done.

"Hertha wanted a word with you," Newlin said. "I will have her fetched. She waits in the kitchen."

"I will go to her," Tavia said and went to turn, her husband's sharp command stopping her.

"You will wait here. She will come to you."

"As you say, my lord," Tavia said, already tired of hearing herself say that to him, but held her tongue, too worried that she would make matters worse if she objected to his command.

"A word in private, my lady?" Hertha asked once in the Great Hall."

"You will speak here in front of me or not at all," Bhric ordered, turning a glare on the plump lass.

"It is of a private nature, my lord," Hertha said.

"What do you wish to hide, Hertha?" Bhric demanded.

"Nothing, my lord, nothing," Hertha hurried to say. "It concerns a woman's nature I wish to speak to Lady Tavia about."

Tavia waited, seeing her husband was giving it thought and she feared he would make Hertha speak of it in front of him and her father.

"Then go and be done quick," Bhric ordered.

Tavia hurried Hertha a distance away where whispers could not be heard.

Hertha kept her voice low and remained close to Tavia so she would easily hear her. "I lied, my lady."

"I assumed so," Tavia said, "but it matters not. What do you wish for no one to hear?"

Hertha hesitated.

"We do not have much time, tell me," Tavia urged.

"Word spreads that Lord Bhric is disappointed in his new bride and that he may break the marriage agreement and take his leave. The clan worries what will happen to them, while I worry what will happen to Doritt and Edward, the two children who suffered under Lord Ivan and are meant to accompany me and Hume to their new home at Clan MacShane. He will surely demand their return and without Lord Bhric's protection, Chieftain Newlin will have no choice but to surrender them. Please tell me it is nothing but gossip."

"I cannot," Tavia said softly, "for I do not know for sure."

"What do I tell the children. They are so frightened."

"Tell them all will be well."

"But it might not," Hertha said, a tremble of worry in her voice.

"Fear not, I will see that it is." Tavia tried to assure her but saw the doubt in her eyes. "Trust me, Hertha. We will leave here with the children."

"I hope you are right, my lady," Hertha said, tears stinging her eyes as she hurried from the keep.

Tavia worried for her clan and the children if her marriage failed. There was far too much to be lost if the marriage agreement faltered. She could not let that happen.

Her husband had said that if he fully committed to the marriage it was forever. They would never separate. The only way she could see that done was to see their marriage consummated tonight. But how did she do that when he avoided her bed?

"Is everything all right, Tavia?" Bhric called out, seeing his wife had not moved since Hertha had taken her leave.

Tavia turned, hoping her smile did not appear forced. "Everything is well, husband."

It startled him, though he did not let it show, that she referred to him as her husband. While he had referred to her as his wife often upon his arrival, she had not called him such until this moment. It sounded pleasant enough coming from her, but he had yet to decide what to do with her and he could not delay in making a decision. She would leave with him, or he would leave her behind.

He felt a tug of sorts when he thought of leaving her behind, but why? He did not know her enough to have any true feelings for her, though she did feel good and fit well in his arms. He also favored the pleasing, light scent of mint that drifted off her and she also had a pleasing smile. Those were qualities he could not deny, but were they enough for him to keep her as his wife?

"Your husband and I will be busy in the village. See that you are ready to leave with him tomorrow," Newlin said with a pleasant smile to his daughter.

Bhric did not comment. There would be time enough to tell him whether he would accept Tavia as his wife, the decision continuing to trouble him. His mother could be a formidable force and no doubt it would be easier to simply commit to the arrangement agreed upon. He trusted his mother, that would never change, and yet he could not help but continue to question her wisdom in this situation. And it irritated him that he did. So, what did not set right with him about it?

"There are still things that need to be done before then. I must make sure that Hertha, Hume, and the children are ready as well." Tavia bobbed her head to her husband, "My lord, I will see you later."

Bhric watched her walk away, glad to see her limp not as pronounced, though it still lingered. Had her injury been worse than he had been told?

"My wife is healing well, is she not, Newlin?"

Bhric asked, the man following him to the door.

"Aye. Aye, my lord," Newlin assured him. "She heals nicely."

Tavia heard them from where she had hidden in the shadows and her worries grew. Things would not go well once he found out the truth about her leg. He would surely end the arrangement when he discovered her limp was permanent and she could not let that happen.

She kept alert, making sure no one saw her make her way to the dungeon. She would not be long. Her question would be quick. She had no time to linger. This had to be done and she could not waste time thinking of the right or wrong of it. It was the only thing left to her.

***

Bhric caught sight of his wife talking with Hertha, the woman who had spoken with her in the Great Hall not long ago. He was told that Hertha was a healer, a young one, but her skill would be welcomed as would the man Hume who he had been told was wise in the properties of plants. He would see the two children housed with the pair once at the clan.

Hertha kept nodding as his wife spoke to her. Was she agreeing with what his wife had to say or was she agreeing to something entirely different? He wondered if he would have to keep an eye on Hertha. After all, she would be loyal to Tavia, and loyalty brought all types of possibilities with it.

He caught the look of surprise on his wife's face when she spotted him. It turned quickly enough to a pleasant smile, and she waved, acknowledging him. Then she took off, though not with haste. Her limp kept her pace tempered and she avoided heavy areas of snow. She would never be able to handle the snow in his homeland even without the limp. She would sink and be lost in a snowdrift with no strength to get herself out.

Did the thought of her buried in a snowdrift make the decision for him? The only thing in her favor was that he found her pleasing to look upon, though he did favor her scent, and he had to admit he had given thought to what it would be like to bed her. The image had aroused him, but he never finished it in his mind, too fearful of hurting her and that definitely would not do.

He knew what he had to do. What was best. He would compensate Newlin by making needed repairs in the village and see Clan Strathearn was provided with food for the remaining winter.

"A moment, Newlin," he said. "I wish to speak with my wife." He called out to her. "Tavia."

She stopped and turned, her cheeks rosy from the cold as well as her lips and he was suddenly struck with the unexpected thought to kiss her and to his surprise he grew aroused.

"We need to talk," he snapped annoyed that his shaft responded so easily to the thought. "Later and in private."

"No one will disturb us in my bedchamber," she said.

His tongue remained snappish since her innocent invitation aroused him even more. "We will speak after supper."

"I will await your arrival, my lord," she said.

"Go!" he ordered harshly.

She bobbed her head and walked away.

His arousal remained, but as he watched her limp away, he knew he had made the right choice. She would not make him a good wife. She lacked strength. It was only right he tell her before he told Newlin. He would see to it tonight and it would be done. His mother would have to start the search for a wife for him once again.

Chapter Four

Tavia paced her bedchamber. She had to do this. She had no choice. She had told herself that repeatedly after Lord Bhric had told her that he wished to speak to her. She knew what he intended to say… he would not honor the marriage agreement.

Her heart fluttered wildly in her chest and her stomach churned as badly as tumultuous waves in the sea. She had to make sure this worked. She could not fail. Too many were counting on her. And she had only this one chance. She looked at the two goblets filled with wine, one more potent than the other, sitting on the small table against the wall. She had followed Fia's directions precisely. The bedding was drawn back, the sheets freshly scented, and she wore only her nightdress.

The plan had come to her in haste and out of desperation. She prayed it would work. It had to.

She jumped when the door opened without a cautionary knock, and her husband entered. She feared he might snuff the fire from the hearth, his dominate presence and size overpowering the room. Or was it her own fear that stirred the image?

"This will not take long," he said, seeing her ready for bed or had she hoped to entice him into her bed and seal their vows?

"A glass of wine. It is excellent wine. My da gets it

from a traveling merchant," she babbled nervously as she stepped toward the table.

"Nay, Tavia. I will be quick," he said, knowing the news would disappoint her and not wanting to linger over it. "I have come to tell you that I have decided I cannot agree to our marriage arrangement, though I—" He stopped when he saw her face break out in a huge smile.

"Thank goodness," Tavia said dramatically, her hand suddenly pressed flat against her chest. "You are right. We are not suited at all. You have brought me great relief." She hurried and grabbed the two goblets of wine. "A toast to what is surely the best thing for us both."

Bhric took the goblet from her, shocked by her response. He thought she would break down in tears and here she was celebrating that she would not be his wife. He should be relieved, but he was annoyed.

He downed the wine quickly and held the goblet out to her. "More."

She refilled his goblet with only wine and recalled Fia telling her that if he drank more wine after taking the mixture it would work faster. She handed it to him, happy he had asked for another.

"You do not want me as a husband?" Bhric asked, still surprised by her response and still bothered he was annoyed with it.

"As you said, we are not suited. I am sure you will find a woman that will suit you far better than me," Tavia said and sipped her wine.

Bhric downed half the goblet. "I need a strong woman with height and weight to her and who can give me many bairns."

"Aye, I agree," Tavia said and saw him sway slightly.

It was working. She walked over by the bed and sat on the edge hoping he would follow, and he did. Though, he wobbled on his feet as he did, and he plopped down ungracefully to sit beside her, tilting toward her.

He was blunt with her, though why he could not say. "I like to pound a woman when I couple. You are not strong enough for that. I would cause you pain and I would not want to do that. Though, you are fair enough to look upon." He reached out and ran the back of his hand slowly down her cheek. "And I like the scent of you."

She maintained her smile, though a flutter hit her stomach when his large hand touched her so tenderly. Could her husband, as large as he was, have a tender touch? She forced the thought aside, concentrating on how he slurred his words. The potion was working and faster than she had thought, the extra wine helping it along. It also was not lost on her that he at least thought her fair enough to look upon.

He yawned. "I am tired. I need to go."

She could not let him leave and collapse somewhere in the keep. "I do not know what you mean by pound a woman." It was a lie. She knew well what he referred to thanks to her talk with Lady Dawn.

"That's right. You are a virgin. You know nothing of coupling. I would have taught you well and gone easy with you until you grew accustomed to it… to me." His head lolled to the side closer to Tavia's. "You have lips that beg to be kissed."

"I know nothing of kissing," she said truthfully, his warm wine-scented breath fanned her cheek and sent a strange tingle through her.

"Let me show you," he said and brought his lips to faintly touch hers.

His lips touching hers sparked the tingling sensation in her and sent it racing through her. His faint kiss turned more powerful and caused her to want to feel more, explore more of the titillating sensation, but she had no time. She had to keep her mind clear. She had to see this through. Her plan had to succeed. She daringly met his demand, her lips pressing eagerly to his in hopes he would linger in the kiss, linger there beside her until the potion accomplished its task.

His hand went to the back of her head, tangling his fingers in the waves of her soft, dark hair. He thought he caught the scent of mint as he took tight hold of the soft strands to keep her from escaping him as he eagerly deepened the kiss.

She tasted far better than he ever imagined, a sweetness of sorts to her as well as a bit of hesitancy and inexperience. His shaft tightened at the thought that no other lips had touched hers but his. He had marked her as his. Could he let her go now?

His hand went to her breast, and he was annoyed the nightdress, thin as it was, kept him from feeling her breast naked. Its full size rested comfortably in his large hand, and he gave it a squeeze, then teased the nipple between his fingers. He felt the tremble that rushed over her. She had known no hand there but his. Had he been too hasty in his decision to abandon this marriage?

Could she be more perfect for him than he had first thought?

His hand roamed down to rest between her legs and even against the material he could feel the wetness there. She aroused easily. Could marriage to her be more enjoyable than he had questioned?

More sparks ignited in her when his hand went between her legs, and he gripped her lightly there. To her surprise, she found that she did not abhor his touch. She quite liked it. She let herself enjoy the pleasurable sensation until… his hand fell away and his lips left hers as he collapsed back on the bed.

Tavia stared at him a moment, her lips left aching from the loss of his kiss, and she shook her head. There was no time to waste and no time to question why his kiss and touch had surprisingly felt so good.

She got busy. His boots were the first to go, then she got to work on his plaid and shirt, glad he had worn them, rather than the many furs and hides he had first arrived in. It took several exhausted pushes and rolls until finally one last roll, and it would be done. She went to roll him to his side and her hands slipped and she found her breasts planted firmly against his chest. She hurried a glance at his face expecting his eyes to open, but they didn't. He was dead asleep.

She took a moment to look at his face. He truly was a handsome man, his face unmarred with the slightest scar and his lips evenly shaped with just enough fullness to them. Was that why his kisses had felt so good?

A spark ignited in her suddenly sending the same tingle between her legs and it had her rushing off him, though she stood beside the bed to glance over him.

He was thick with muscle and his manhood large, even flaccid as it lay draped against his leg. She shook her head not wanting to think of how it would feel inside her when enlarged, and the sensations she had experienced when he had touched her returned with a shock. She shook her head again to clear it. She could not waste her time on such thoughts and yet they lingered, making her wonder if they could share a good marriage since she did not mind his touch.

"Be done with this," she reminded herself on a whisper.

It took work to try and get him where she needed him in the bed, his size and weight not easy to maneuver. She was breathless by the time she finished and though he was not quite where she wanted him, it would suffice.

Once done, she stripped off her nightdress, threw it on the floor by his garments to make it seem like they had both hastily shed them and grabbed the small bowl of blood from under the bed. Fia told her too much blood would make him fear he had hurt her and might spark doubt. She spilled what she hoped was a sufficient and unquestionable amount.

With a quick rush to the hearth, she dropped the remaining blood and small wooden bowl in the fire waiting until the flames consumed it. She added more logs so that more ash would cover any evidence of what she had done.

She blew out the few candles and afterward stood by the side of the bed for a moment. Once she crawled in beside him, her fate would be sealed, but there was no other way for her. This was her duty, and she must do it. She slipped in beside him and pulled the blankets up over them, then inched closer to him. The warmth of his body startled her chilled skin as she settled against him, and she found herself inching closer as his heat began to chase the cold away.

Sleep was something she did not think she would get this night, for she worried what the morning would bring when the servant she ordered to wake her early found her and her husband naked in bed together. She shut her eyes exhausted, praying for sleep or her endless thoughts would invade her mind and she would question the deceit she had perpetrated on her husband.

Deceit.

Never had she been deceitful in her life, and it did not set well with her now that she had been forced to do so. But what choice had she? And what price would she pay for it?

Her endless thoughts continued to haunt her, and she feared she would not sleep at all, but her body could not fight her exhaustion, and worry and sleep soon claimed her.

Chapter Five

A slight hammering in his head stirred Bhric awake, though he did not open his eyes. He had drunk himself into oblivion once years ago—never again. He had learned his lesson, having almost lost his life on the battlefield the next day. After that, he never did it again. He drank but never to the point he was not in control. He always wanted to be prepared to fight, to protect those he loved and his home.

So why did he feel as if he had drunk too much?

He let himself drift, enjoying the naked warmth snuggled against him. His hand explored, silky soft, toasty warm, and a slender curve.

His eyes shot open, and a pain stung his head for a moment. It was nothing to the jab he felt in his chest when he saw his wife planted snug against him… and she was as naked as was he.

"Bloody hell!" he said and jumped out of bed just as a knock sounded at the door and it opened.

"Lady Tavia—" The servant lass froze at the imposing sight of Bhric naked.

Tavia held the blanket to her chest when she sat up, at first confused, having woken with a fright when her husband yelled, until she realized her plan had worked.

"GET OUT!" Bhric yelled at the servant, and she almost fell in her haste to obey him.

"What did you do?" Bhric demanded, fighting his

rising fury as soon as the door closed behind the fleeing servant.

"We must have drunk too much," Tavia said, knowing full well he would never believe her.

"You deceive me, woman," Bhric accused, his hand going to his mouth, his memory of last night returning some. He had kissed her, touched her, and he had enjoyed it.

"We both drank," she said, as if it was explanation enough.

"Get out of bed NOW!" he ordered harshly.

Tavia kept the blanket covering her chest as she moved to do as he commanded.

"Leave the blanket. You should have no qualms about being naked in front of me if we were intimate enough for you to sleep naked next to me," he demanded.

Tavia did her best not to tremble, not to show her fear, but it was difficult with him standing there naked. His powerful strength was on full display. His one arm alone, the muscles so thick, could squash her like a pesty bug. And the fury in his eyes made her fear that he just might do that.

She could not stop the tremble that ran through her body as he walked over to her and almost sighed with relief when a knock sounded at the door before he could speak.

"LEAVE NOW!" Bhric shouted.

A quivering voice called out, "I am sorry to disturb you, my lord, but Chieftain Newlin requires your immediate presence. Lord Ivan has arrived and is causing a problem."

Bhric leaned down and whispered harshly, "You have much to answer for, wife." He stepped away from her as he shouted, "Tell Newlin I will be there shortly.

"Aye, my lord," the servant lass said with relief.

Bhric snatched his garments up off the floor. "Get dressed. You are coming with me."

Tavia hurried to fetch her garments, feeling far too vulnerable naked in his presence.

As soon as Bhric finished dressing, he went to the goblets and sniffed both, but could detect no different scent in them. He turned and that was when he caught a spot of blood on the bed. He went and threw the covers back and when he saw the blood stain, he strained his memory to recall if he had coupled with her. If he could remember the kiss, the feel of her——the weight of her breast in his hand returning to him—surely he would remember coupling with his wife… unless it was unmemorable.

Tavia knew what his question would be as soon as he saw the bloodstain and already feeling guilty over the mounting lies, she said, "You did not hurt me."

Not sure what happened between them last night left him with little choice then to keep her as his wife.

He went to her and grabbed her chin. "Never would I have hurt you knowing it was your first time. I would have been gentle with you. Now I no longer have to worry about that. From this point on I can pound you as hard as I want." He released her chin and turned away from her, annoyed she had trapped him.

What was there for Tavia to say? She could not admit the truth. She would suffer for her lies, but at least the children would be safe and so would her clan.

She was not sorry she did what she had done, especially with Lord Ivan's unexpected appearance. His presence did not, nor had it ever, bode well for her clan, but with her marriage to Lord Bhric solidified there was no worries. He would defend the clan.

She went to plait her hair and Bhric ordered, "Leave it. Let all see that we were disturbed while in the throes of coupling, since by now the servant will have spread the news that our vows have been consummated and once the blood on the bedding is seen…" He glared at her. "How then can it be denied?"

His words stung and warned that he did not believe they had coupled, that he knew she had trapped him and that he was not happy about it. If she thought there could have ever been at least a friendship between them, she knew now that her deceit had ruined any chance of it.

Bhric stopped abruptly when he reached the top of the stairs, Tavia relieved she had kept a safe distance behind him, or she would have collided with him.

"There was one thing above all I wanted in a wife, one thing I will never have with you." His dark blue eyes narrowed when he turned to look at her. "Trust. Never will I trust you."

If a heart could break, Tavia's did at that moment. Her decision had cost her dearly and she would spend the rest of her life paying for it.

***

"I have told you repeatedly it is done, Lord Ivan," Newlin said annoyed with the man. "And do you forget

I denied your request months ago."

"That matters not. I demand to see Lord Bhric now," Lord Ivan said, slamming the tankard he held down on the table, the ale splashing over the sides.

"Make another demand in the home of a clan I protect, and I will see you never speak another word again," Bhric threatened when he entered the Great Hall.

He could tell from one look that the bald, dark-bearded man thought himself important. His good height and thick body warned he could be a formidable opponent, though not for Bhric.

"Lord Bhric," Ivan acknowledged without a respectful nod. "I am here to help you. I learned that you are unsure of whether to keep the marriage agreement made between you and Tavia. I will gladly take her off your hands."

"And why would you do that?" Bhric asked and could almost feel his wife tense beside him.

"You are a great warrior, and a great warrior should have a woman worthy of being his wife. Tavia will never have such a worthiness or strength to fulfill such an important position, her permanent limp making her less of a capable woman."

Tavia stood strong beside her husband, not moving, not blinking an eye, not so her da. He cringed and Ivan saw it.

Ivan grinned as if he had just received a most cherished gift and he spoke with a boldness that had Newlin cringing again. "You did not tell Lord Bhric that his wife suffers a permanent limp? That it will never heal? That she is incapable of doing certain things and will always need care?" He then turned to Bhric. "I suppose you were told it was a recent accident that caused her limp—such deceit." Ivan shook his head. "Much like the deceit they perpetrated on me, believing ungrateful children instead of believing an honorable man."

Tavia could take no more. "You are far from an honorable man. You are a liar, and you are cruel. And never, ever would I wed such a horrible man."

Ivan took a hasty step toward Tavia, appearing as if he would strike her.

Bhric took a quicker step in front of his wife and gave Ivan a powerful shove in the chest, sending him tumbling back and fighting to stay on his feet.

"If you ever dare lunge at my wife again, I will kill you," Bhric cautioned in such a ferocious tone that it had Ivan taking several steps back though he was already a good distance from Bhric. "Unlike you, I am an honorable man and the marriage arrangement to Tavia remains and has been officially sealed. She is my wife and will remain my wife." Bhric took a step toward Ivan and the man's hand went to the hilt of the knife tucked at his waist. "Listen well, Lord Ivan. I have no want to make an enemy of you and your clan, but if you persist in causing the Clan Strathearn any more trouble or bring harm to the people in any way, I will rain a war on you with my Northmen that you will not live to regret. And one other thing you need to remember—when my hand goes to my weapon I do not haste to use it."

"I will take my leave now," Lord Ivan said.

Bhric waited until the man reached the door. "Lord

Ivan!"

Ivan stopped but did not turn.

"Do not make me regret I let you live today," Bhric said and when he got no reply, he knew it would not be the last he heard from the man.

"My apologizes—"

Bhric raised his hand, stopping Newlin from saying any more. "I did not expect such deceit from a man my mother thought honorable. The more I learn about you and your daughter makes me wonder why my mother ever thought to trust you or to believe your daughter would make me a good wife."

Newlin collapsed down on the bench, shaking his head. "It is easily explained."

"Tell me, for it has puzzled me greatly," Bhric said.

"Your mother, Lady Orianna, and my wife, Margaret, were more like sisters than close childhood friends. Margaret was present at your birth at Clan MacShane. Orianna promised she would attend Margaret's first birth as well. When it was obvious that Margaret would not survive the birth, she begged your mother to look after Tavia, and keep her safe. Orianna reminded me of the promise she had made to Margaret when she approached me about a marriage between you and Tavia. She told me that with Tavia married to her son, she could fulfill that promise. And she also told me that Tavia was much like her mother and would make her son the perfect wife."

"You never told me that, Da," Tavia said, stunned by the news.

"I promised Orianna I would say nothing, but

things have gone so poorly since Lord Bhric's arrival that I thought it best the truth was finally made known," Newlin said.

"My mother knew of Tavia's limp?" Bhric asked.

"Aye, she did." Newlin nodded. "She assured me it would not bother you in the least, but I saw that you thought differently that first day and worried you would reject Tavia. Forgive me for the lie, but like your mother, I wanted Tavia protected. And seeing how you handled Lord Ivan, I know your mum was right. You will protect my daughter."

Tavia walked away from both men to stand nearer to the heat of the hearth, a sudden chill turning her cold. It seemed as if everyone thought her incapable of protecting herself, even from the smallest threat. Did she appear that weak to people? Did the accident not only leave her with a limp but had stolen her confidence as well? And if so, why had she let it?

"Continue to implement the changes Lord Cree was having you make, Newlin, and those we discussed. Birger will oversee the work and send reports to me on the progress," Bhric said, making it clear with a change of subject that he would discuss the other matter no more. "Tavia. Tavia!" he called out again when she failed to respond to his first summons.

"Eat and be ready to leave by mid-day," he ordered and left the room.

Newlin went to his daughter, his arm going around her to ease her away from the hearth to sit at one of the tables.

"This has all been a nightmare, Da, and I wish I would wake up." Sadness engulfed her eyes and her heart. “You should have confided the truth to me from the beginning. Lies and deceit serve no one well.”

“Lord Bhric would have never agreed to the union,” Newlin said.

“Because I am not what he looks for in a wife. I do not suit him and now we are stuck with each other. What future is there for either of us?”

“You will find your way through this marriage, Tavia. Orianna was right. You are much like your mum. There is courage and determination in you, and both surface when needed. And I hope and pray Orianna is right and that someday you and Bhric come to love each other.”

“That will never be, Da, for there can be no love where there is no trust.”

Chapter Six

Bhric refused to look back and glance at his wife since they left the keep hours ago. He was furious with her. She had lied to him and tricked him, and he felt a fool for it.

"Are you going to stop scowling and accept your fate or spend the rest of your life a miserable wretched soul no one wants to be around?" Sven asked.

"She tricked me," Bhric muttered, annoyed that he had not even given thought that she would be capable of it.

Sven disagreed. "She saved you."

"You are a bigger fool than me."

"You said your mother knew your wife's mother, best friends they were just like you and me, and that she knew of the limp. If that is so then she made no mistake in her choice of a wife for you, though it may seem so. Make the best of it as all couples who know little of each other have no choice but to do."

"That is easy for you to say when you wed for love," Bhric said.

"I am not the eldest son of a tribe leader or the grandson of a powerful clan lord. You have a duty and forget your mother and her fury when she learns that you even considered reneging on the marriage arrangement. What would your father, an honorable and respected tribe leader, think? And think of the courage it took for your wife to do what she did."

"Be deceitful?"

Sven shook his head. "She is a wee one and add to that her debilitating limp and the question that no doubt plagued her… who else would wed her? It was you or Newlin might not have had any choice but to wed her to Lord Ivan. She was brave enough to recognize it and seize the moment."

"Or selfish enough if what you say is true," Bhric continued to argue, though the thought of Lord Ivan touching his wife fired his anger.

"You will not find out if you keep your distance from her."

Bhric's scowl deepened. "Did I ask for your advice?"

"Nay, but I give it to you freely anyway," Sven said with a grin and, with a laugh, turned his horse away to join the two men in the distance who traveled ahead to keep watch if anyone should approach.

Bhric mumbled several oaths before he turned his horse around and rode to come up beside his wife's horse. He was about to ask her if she did well, but it was not necessary. He could see with the tight set of her face and the tiredness in her soft blue eyes that she struggled with pain.

"Your leg troubles you."

That it was not a question made Tavia realize there was no point in denying it. "Riding has been difficult for me since the injury to my leg. When we camp later, rest will help it."

Bhric waved one of his warriors over. "Hold the reins of her horse."

Tavia turned a bewildered look on him and in the next moment his hands were at her waist and with a swift lift, she was on his horse to sit crossways in front of him.

With a nod from Bhric, the warrior rode off with Tavia's horse and after tucking his wife in the crook of his arm, he proceeded to wrap her cloak over and around her legs, then he yanked his own fur cloak across her as well.

The cold left her, whether from the heat of his body or the fur cloaks she was not sure and she did not care. The warmth would do much to help her leg and she allowed herself to settle comfortably against him.

Bhric expected her to remain stiff in his arms and was pleased when her body lost its rigidness, but then she was tired and in pain, and her body gave her no choice. And that thought annoyed him.

That annoyance fueled his question. "I did not hurt you when we coupled, did I?"

"Nay," she said, realizing what he was doing—trying to get to the truth, but for what reason? Did he think to prove her a liar and evade their marriage?

"Did you enjoy it?" he asked.

She rested her head on his chest, fearing he could see the lies in her eyes. "I fear I drank too much leaving me with little memory of it."

"Then I failed you, wife, for there is not a woman I poked that did not enjoy and remember it fondly."

Not sure how to respond to that Tavia chose to remain silent.

Bhric gripped her chin and lifted it so she would meet his eyes. "Next time, I will make sure it is memorable."

Feeling he expected a response, she said, "I look forward to it."

"As do I," he said and for some reason he could not comprehend, he leaned down and kissed her lightly. Her eyes held his when his lips left hers and he felt a sudden jab inside him, not a painful one but a pleasant one. "You like my kisses?"

Why had he asked her that? He had never asked a woman that. He was a Northmen. A Northmen would never ask such a question of a woman let alone his wife.

He hurried to correct himself. "It matters not if you do, I will kiss you when I want."

"As you say, my lord, but I do not mind your kisses," Tavia said surprised that she did and glad for it since marriage to him would not be pleasant if she abhorred his kiss or touch.

Anger jabbed at him when his shaft gave a salute to her response. What was it about this wee woman that stirred him so fast?

"I will be a good wife, if you will let me," Tavia said, hoping he would consider her words.

His shaft gave a sturdier salute as a sudden image of her spread naked on his bed helped it along.

"You will be a good wife regardless," he snapped. "I will tolerate nothing less."

"Aye, my lord," she said, having no desire to anger him or argue with him.

She was grateful for the yawn that surfaced, and she turned her face into his chest away from the cold that stung her cheeks and closed her eyes. If he thought she slept, he would say no more to her, hopefully.

Bhric watched his wife's eyes flutter closed, his annoyance twisting at his gut. With so many questions to ask her, he had asked her the least important ones. Or were they more important to him than he had thought?

***

They camped as the sky turned to dusk. Two campfires were set and the food that had been packed for them at Clan Strathearn distributed throughout. Bhric settled Tavia by a campfire and draped a fur around her, covering her, and saw that she had food and drink.

Her eyes caught on Hertha and Hume busy tending the two children, Doritt and Edward. They talked and laughed together. The constant fear she had seen in the children's eyes was gone. They felt safe and would feel safer the farther they got from Lord Ivan.

She rested her hand to her stomach, thinking what it would be like to grow round with a bairn, to hold the precious bundle in her arms, to give him or her all the love she had to give.

Tavia startled when her husband suddenly sat down beside her.

"You have not touched the food I gave you," he said.

She snatched up a piece of cheese to appease him, though she felt no hunger.

"You watch the children. You wish a bairn of your own?" he asked curious, not that it mattered since it was her duty to give him heirs, but he had hoped for a wife who would be as good and loving a mother as his mum was.

"Aye, several," she said with a soft smile.

"Was your mum like you, small in size?" he asked, fearing if she was then his wife might meet the same fate as her mum… dying in childbirth. The thought surprisingly upset him.

"Aye, from what my da has told me I am much like her," she said proudly of the woman who gave her life, but she never got a chance to meet. It was obvious what he thought for he had voiced his opinion about her chances of giving birth without difficulty. "I am stronger than I look."

"That remains to be seen," he said.

"Are you strong, my lord?" she asked, with a tilt of her head, her eyes searching his blue ones.

Her question sparked his ire. "What kind of foolish question is that?"

She responded with another question. "Should I doubt your strength, my lord?"

"Another foolish question. What game do you play with me, wife?" he demanded, wondering what trick she might pull on him again.

"If my question is foolish, then is not your response foolish as well? I tell you I am strong, but you do not believe me. You tell me you are strong, yet I am to believe you without hesitation."

He smacked his chest. "Look at me and look at you and you will have your answer."

"Strength does not always come in a large size," she said softly.

"Northmen would debate that," Bhric said.

She would not argue the point since she felt he failed to see it.

"You will have ample opportunity to prove your strength as my wife—childbirth is only one of them. Now eat or there will be nothing left of you."

Tavia nibbled at the cheese and bread to make it appear that she ate more than she did, but she doubted she fooled her husband. She saw how he kept a keen eye on everything going on around him. Even when his glance strayed to the campfire flames, she could tell he listened to what went on. He was a man who observed and absorbed all that went on, a trait of a fine leader.

"We leave at dawn," Bhric called out and shortly after that the camp grew quiet and all began to settle into sleep.

She did the same, stretching out on the blanket beneath her to lie on her side. She was grateful when her husband draped a fur over her and surprised when he crawled beneath it to rest against her and tuck her back tight against him.

"We will keep each other warm," he whispered in her ear.

His warm breath sent gooseflesh running over her neck along with a shiver.

"Do I tempt you, wife?" he murmured, feeling her body respond to their closeness.

She almost faltered and told him she knew nothing of temptation but caught herself. If they had coupled she would not be ignorant of what he had made her feel.

"Aye, as you did last night," she said softly.

"How did I tempt you last night?" he asked, though warned himself he was playing with fire since he already felt passion poking at him planted so firmly against her.

"With your kisses and intimate touches," she whispered, recalling them and how she had found them more than pleasant.

"You remember them?"

The truth fell from her lips. "I cannot forget them."

"And I can remember only little of them," he said.

"Then we shall have to make new memories that remain with us always."

An image rushed into his head of her naked in his bed, her legs spread invitingly, and he suddenly wondered if she would have a trick waiting for him as she had done last night.

"Go to sleep, wife," he snapped, annoyed that trust would be an issue with his wife and one that would not be settled soon enough.

The morning brought gray skies and a light flurry of snow. The camp was quickly dismantled, everyone mounting their horses, the two children each sharing a horse with Hertha and Hume.

Bhric hoisted his wife up onto her horse. "You will ride the morning alone and with me after mid-day. We reach home early tomorrow morning."

She nodded and took her place in the procession of horses as he went and mounted his horse and rode up ahead, watchful as ever. She found herself looking forward to riding once again with her husband. She was pleased with how comfortable she felt in his arms and how easily they spoke with each other. She hoped it was the start of at least a friendship that would endure.

It was just before mid-day when they came upon a

merchant and his wagon stopped along the path they traveled. Tavia recognized him immediately and brought her horse to a stop when she reached him.

"Kevin," she said, excited, and he turned and smiled broadly.

"Tavia," he called out and went to her horse to reach up and help her off it. "I was headed your way. I found some ribbons I thought you would like… but what are you doing with this group," —he lowered his voice— "of Northmen?"

"I am wed to Lord Bhric of the Clan MacShane who is part Northman," she explained, her smile strong, happy to see him.

They had been friends since the first time he had stopped at Clan Strathearn. It was like they had always known each other. They could chat endlessly never faltering for conversation. He had been good to her after the accident, visiting with her, encouraging her, and bringing her little trinkets.

"This pleases you?" he asked concerned.

Tavia spoke the truth. "It is my duty."

He nodded understanding. "Come and let me show you the ribbons I have that will suit you perfectly before the procession leaves you behind."

"I have no coin," she said and felt shameful to admit it. She had run her da's keep and knew what coin there was to spend so there had never been any need for her to ask permission to purchase anything from Kevin. Not so now.

"A wedding gift since the color is perfect for you," Kevin insisted and hooked his arm around hers to walk her to his wagon. "Your leg is well?"

"A bit painful from riding all morning, but nothing I cannot bear."

"You are a strong one, Tavia. I could have never done what you did, let alone survive it," he admitted and left her to lean against the wagon while he rummaged through a sack.

"You are far braver than me traveling these roads alone." She always worried for him. The roads and woods were too dangerous to travel even for a group but more so for a lone traveler.

"The road is my home and I know it well and avoid the danger that lurks there," he assured her. "Ah, here they are."

"Oh, Kevin, they are beautiful and such a lovely pale yellow," she said excitedly and took the batch of ribbons from him.

"Perfect for your lovely dark hair," Kevin said.

Tavia gave no thought when she rushed to give him a hug. She had done so many times when he had stopped at the clan. She imagined it was like hugging a brother since he often told her she was the sister he never had.

"You show affection to another man?" Bhric bellowed and flew off his horse, his hand reaching out for Kevin.

Tavia quickly stepped in front of Kevin, hearing the anger in his voice and seeing the murderous look in her husband's eyes made her fear what he might do to him. His large hand intended for Kevin latched onto her throat.

His grip that had quickly stolen her breath eased and his hand fell away. "You dare protect him? Who is he to you?"

She coughed lightly as her breath returned to her and said, "We are longtime friends nothing more." She held up the ribbons. "He gave me a wedding gift."

Bhric ripped the tied batch of ribbons out of her hand and threw it at Kevin and he caught it. "My wife needs no wedding gift from you, and if I ever see you with your arms around my wife again you will not live to see another day."

Tavia gasped. "He is a friend, my lord, no more than a friend."

"Aye, my lord, Tavia and I have been friends for years," Kevin said.

Bhric took a fast step toward him and though it was a meager and useless attempt to stop him, Tavia hurried her hand out along with a plea. "Kevin has called me Tavia since we first met."

Kevin was quick to offer an apology. "I am so sorry, my lord. I did not think." He turned to Tavia. "Please forgive me, Lady Tavia, I meant no disrespect."

"Of course, you didn't," Tavia assured him, though she hoped it reassured her angry husband. But from the vicious scowl on his face, she did not think it had.

"Leave now and do not let me see your face ever again," Bhric ordered with a stinging sharpness.

"You cannot mean that. He is a friend of mine," Tavia argued.

"It upsets you that you will not see him again?" Bhric asked with an accusatory tone.

"Of course, it does. He is a good friend, and it would pain me never to see him again," she said, hoping he would understand. The questioning look in his eyes made her realize he did not trust her word. Worried for Kevin's safety, she turned to him. "You should go now."

"A wise decision, wife," Bhric said.

"I am sorry," Kevin said.

"Go and be safe," she said, and felt him slip the ribbons into her hand and smiled. She hid them in the folds of her cloak until she had a chance to tuck them away and keep them out of her husband's sight, then turned to him.

He grabbed her arm roughly. "You tricked me once before, wife. I will not have you trick me again."

"I tell you the truth, husband. Kevin is nothing more than a friend to me."

"A friend you hug," he accused. "And kiss as well?"

Tavia shook her head, sad that he should even ask that. "Your lips are the only ones that have ever touched mine."

"How can I be sure when you have deceived me not once but twice already?"

His accusation stung, but he was right. She had deceived him about consummating their marriage and about her limp.

All she could say was, "I do not lie about this."

"We shall see and know now if you deceived me again, the consequences will be harsh," he said and hurried to lift her onto her horse.

She was shocked to even consider what her husband had insinuated that she and Kevin had been intimate, but she saw it in his accusing glare. The thought pained her and the only solace she had was that she knew the truth while he would need to learn it for himself.

Chapter Seven

Tavia looked with curious eyes on her new home as they entered the village on the morning of the third day of travel. It was far larger than she had expected. She had been surprised by the many crofts they had passed on the outskirts of the village and all well-kept. Even with snow on the ground and the flurries of snowflakes that now fell, people were busy outside tending to chores or talking in small groups. Children ran about laughing in delight, pups running along eager to play.

Tavia noticed that many of the people were dressed differently than her and it was then she realized that the majority of those there were Northmen and women. Were there no people left from the Clan MacShane?

She was already missing the only home she had ever known and the sudden realization that she was with strangers in her own homeland made her glad that Hertha and Hume had come with her. At least she would not feel entirely alone, something she had felt yesterday when her husband ignored her after the incident with Kevin. The day and night spent with him before then had given her a shred of hope that things might go well between them. It no longer seemed that way.

Her present problem, though, was not her husband, it was her leg which had grown stiff and sore from endless riding. Her husband had avoided her after the incident with Kevin, so she had spent the day on her horse alone. However, she had been glad that he had joined her by the campfire that night, once again wrapping himself around her to share the heat of their bodies and the fire, though he had not spoken a word to her.

While she found no fault in hugging Kevin, she could see how it might look to her husband, who did not know of her innocent relationship with him. She should have thought better of her actions, but she had been so pleased to see him.

Her leg cramped and she winced. She had found through trial and error that if she did not overdo walking or riding that her leg would not trouble her, leaving her limp far from pronounced and leaving her to suffer little to no pain. Thankfully, Hertha had helped Auda attend her, and the woman knew what to do to help her when the leg gave her trouble.

Her musings faded as her eyes caught sight of the keep not far ahead. It loomed large almost like a bird of prey ready to sweep down and devour the village. The Clan MacShane was a powerful clan, Lord Donald had been a respected and influential man. When he had grown ill much began to change and he had wisely sent for his daughter and grandson. Bhric had managed to keep Clan MacShane powerful. The clans in the area had soon learned that Bhric was not a man to trifle with or make an enemy of and it seemed that Tavia had done both.

Tavia's stomach churned as she rode toward the keep. Bhric's men turned Hertha, Hume, and the two bairns in a different direction. She had spent time with Hertha and Hume while traveling here and was grateful for their company and grateful that their presence gave her a small sense of home and had eased her growing apprehension. Now that they were no longer with her, the weight of her true situation grew heavy… she was on her own.

She followed along with the warriors, Bhric in the lead. They came to a slow stop and Bhric dismounted as did his warriors. Tavia wished she could dismount without assistance but that was not possible and so she waited. Her husband approached her and, without meeting her eyes or saying a word, he reached up, his hands finding their way beneath her cloak to grab at her waist and lifted her off the horse and placed her on her feet.

With an abrupt snap of his hand, a woman hurried down the keep steps.

"Marta will see to your care," he said and walked away.

Tavia fought the pain nagging at her leg. She had been astride the horse too long and was suffering the consequences. She smiled as pleasantly as she could, but the woman did not return her smile. Instead, she stared at Tavia oddly. She was a good head taller than Tavia, her plain face pinched taut with dislike or annoyance, she could not be sure. Wrinkles, many of them, and gray hair braided tightly defined her advanced age.

"I will show you to your quarters," Marta said and preceded up the stairs.

That she did not address her properly or even

welcome her pleasantly left Tavia feeling uncomfortable with the woman.

Tavia took a fortifying breath, lifted the hem of her garments and ascended up the stairs slowly. After three steps, she stopped, the pain tightening her leg. She looked to where Marta waited at the top, her face more pinched than before if possible, and the distance seemed insurmountable. How would she ever make it?

She took two more steps and cringed, sucking in the pain with a deep breath.

Suddenly, she was swept off her feet and into her husband's arms, his face a mask of anger.

"You cannot even climb the stairs," he said, taking the stairs two at a time annoyed at himself for leaving her to ride her horse as long as she had. She suffered because of him, and it annoyed him even more that he had been struck with a fiery sense of jealousy when he had seen her in the arms of another man. But how did he trust her when she had tricked him once already?

She thought to say something, but what good would it do. Still, she found herself unable to hold her tongue. "I do not need your help, nor do I want it."

Bhric stopped mid-way up and placed her on her feet. "Then finish the steps yourself and the ones that will take you to your bedchamber. And make sure you are ready to join the celebration of our marriage tonight in the Great Hall." He pointed up the remaining stairs. "Go!"

Tavia's glance followed where he pointed. Several stairs awaited her before she entered the keep and how many stairs would she need to climb to reach her bedchamber? More climbing would only add to her discomfort. How then would she ever be able to attend the celebration tonight if she were not wise enough to accept help now.

"You may not want my help, but you need my help," Bhric said. "You not only have a limp that limits you, but you also have a tongue that speaks before thinking, a fault that can prove foolish."

Tavia tilted her chin stubbornly, hoisted her garments and took careful and slow steps up the stairs. Tears soon brimmed her eyes, every step more painful than the last. She reached the top and stood gaining her strength to continue.

Once again, she was scooped up into her husband's arms. "Your foolishness is unwise."

Exhaustion took hold and she cared not what he thought. She laid her head on his shoulder relieved to be off her leg. And as much as she did not want to admit it, he was right. Foolishness was unwise. She was limited to what she could do to a certain extent especially when her leg pained her. It did her little good to think she could change that. It was better she accepted it and worked around it, which she had been successfully doing until her husband had arrived.

Bhric remained silent as he carried her through the keep and up the stone stairs. It bothered him to see his wife in pain. She might not be the wife of his choice, but she was his wife and he protected and cared for what was his. Though, how this marriage could prove fruitful was another matter when there was little trust between them.

He took the numerous steps quickly and entered a bedchamber, his broad shoulders pushing the door that stood ajar open all the way.

"These are your quarters," Bhric said after placing her on the bed. Mine are through that door." He gave a nod to a wood door not far from the fireplace. You will not enter there without permission."

Feeling the need for the same privacy, she said, "And you will not enter mine without permission."

"I need no permission to enter any room in this keep and I never knock," he warned.

His glare was intense almost as if he could peer into her mind and know her deepest thoughts. She crossed her arms over her chest offering herself some minor protection.

She did not know why she called out what she did when he turned and walked away, perhaps a beginning of sorts if possible. "We need to talk, husband."

Bhric turned. "It will not be talking we do when I enter this room next."

She had no reply for him, too shocked by his words, and his rapid departure.

Marta stepped forward. "I will help you refresh yourself, then you will rest so you are ready for the festivities tonight."

Tavia spied the bucket of water and stack of cloths by the hearth. She had what she needed to see to her leg.

"I appreciate your help, but I have no need of it. You are dismissed," Tavia said, feeling uneasy with the woman's obvious dislike of her.

"I have been ordered to tend you," Marta said defiantly.

Tavia felt a fright as the woman approached and

instinct had her pointing her finger at the woman and speaking with authority. "I have given you an order. Take your leave now."

The woman hesitated, casting Tavia a strange look, and appeared as if to argue with her when a knock sounded at the door.

"It is Hertha, my lady, I have come to tend you."

"Let her in," Tavia ordered, and Marta went to the door.

Hertha did not wait for permission to enter, she pushed past the woman, and went straight to Tavia.

Marta appeared ready to protest.

"Take your leave," Tavia ordered again.

The woman hesitated a moment, then without so much of a nod left the room.

"I got here as soon as I could. I knew your leg would need tending. Now let me help you get all but your shift off so you may rest comfortably," Hertha said, taking things in hand.

Her familiar soothing voice and kind nature brought Tavia much-needed comfort and as the young woman worked, she talked which made Tavia relax even more.

"Hume and I were surprised when we were taken to a nice cottage with Doritt and Edward and told it was ours and we were expected to do our share. In all Doritt's six years and Edward's eight, neither had seen, let alone lived in such a fine place. They both began to cry, and Edward bravely stepped forward and said he was ready to see to his chore." Hertha wiped at her own tears. "The warrior nodded to me and Hume and told Edward that that was his mum and da's decision. I have never seen the two bairns so happy. I hope the other children who Lord Ivan mistreated have found as good a home as we have."

The news brought great relief to Tavia, for it made what she had done worthwhile. And when Hertha settled the warm, wet cloth on her leg, she rested her head back on the pillow the young woman had braced behind her back and sighed with relief. She closed her eyes and listened to Hertha talk as she worked to brew a drink near the hearth that would help with the pain.

"I cannot believe after almost three days of travel there will be a celebration tonight. These Northmen have great stamina. I hear there will be much food and drink. Already they light more campfires throughout the village and food has been cooking on spits for hours. There is a joy in the air that I have never felt before and it is quite invigorating. Everyone talks of the lord's new wife and how soon news will not only be heard of an heir to the Clan MacShane but also an heir to the mighty Thrubolt tribe. It is a special night for sure."

Tavia opened her eyes. "A night I cannot miss."

"Aye, my lady," Hertha said and handed her a tankard. "This will help you rest and ease the pain. Sit as much as you can tonight. I will return in the morning and tend your leg again."

"I am grateful, Hertha, and relieved you are with me," Tavia said. "I ask that you let me know all you hear and see so I am not blind and ignorant as to what is said around me."

"You unselfishly made sure the clan and those who helped the children remained safe. We all owe you much. So, have no fear, my lady, Hume and I will watch out for you. Finish the drink and rest. I will return later to help get you ready for the celebration."

Exhausted from two days of travel, sleep came quickly to Tavia, but it was not Hertha who woke her later. It was Marta.

"Wake up!" Marta snapped.

The unfamiliar voice startled Tavia and she hurried to sit up, wincing as she did, having disturbed her leg with her sudden movement.

"You must prepare for the celebration," Marta ordered. "I will help you dress in the garments of our people."

Tavia followed the woman's eyes to several garments draped over a chair.

"They will keep you warm unlike the light wool garments you wore here," Marta said.

Tavia kept her garments light on purpose, having discovered heavier material weighed on her causing her leg discomfort. Besides, this was her homeland, and she would not wear foreign garments here.

"You may leave, Marta. Hertha returns to help me," Tavia said, wanting the woman gone.

"It is my chore to help you not hers," Marta argued. "I sent her away. I was tasked with a chore by Lord Bhric, and I will see my duty done."

Tavia wanted to get to her feet, but she could not rush out of bed and if she went slow she feared it would show weakness. She sat up straight, lifted her chin, and pointed to the door. "Get out and send Hertha to me now!"

Marta looked ready to argue.

Tavia's stomach twisted nervously, and her tongue

surprised her when she issued sharp orders. “Not another word. Get out!”

The woman turned and fled the room.

Tavia eased her legs out of bed and stood slowly. Her leg felt better and would be much better tomorrow if she rested the remainder of the night, but with the celebration tonight that was impossible. She walked over to the hearth, glancing at the garments she was meant to wear as she did. They were well-made garments and looked to be of fine wool, but she worried if she dressed in the foreign garments, she would lose herself entirely.

The door flung open startling her. Her husband filled the doorway, and she took a step back. He appeared an angry Northman ready for attack dressed in leather and furs.

“I rule here in my home. The people obey me. Marta is to tend you. I will hear no more about it,” he commanded and turned to leave.

“NAY!”

Bhric turned around at her sharp retort. “That is not something you will ever say to me again.”

That seemed unlikely to Tavia, but what point was there in arguing with him? She did, however, need him to understand she was not comfortable with Marta.

“I find myself uneasy with Marta, I would prefer Hertha to tend me.”

“Hertha will help the healer. Marta will tend you and I will hear no more about it,” he said and turned to leave once again.

“Please,” she found herself saying and she was relieved that he turned around. “I need time to adjust to my new home, the people here, and to you. I ask that you at least allow Hertha to share my care with Marta so I may grow accustomed to her." That he stood staring at her and not immediately denying her request gave her hope.

Bhric walked over to his wife. "This is your home now. These are your people, your family. And I am your husband whether you like it or not. If you were strong, you would accept your fate and do whatever was necessary to be a good wife. And you would have never kept your weakness from me let alone trap me once I told you I would not honor the agreement. Or fling yourself into the arms of another man making me trust you even less. So, I care not if you adjust, I only care that you obey."

He turned away from her and Tavia was glad he did, for she trembled not from fright but from anger. She bit her tongue to keep hold of it, though what did it matter? He cared not about her, so why should she worry what she said to him?

She called out at him. "You know nothing about me."

He spun around. "I know you are weak, you lie, and I cannot trust you."

"And you are far from honorable when you decided to end the marriage arrangement not only agreed upon in good faith, but the documents signed. As for your strength… it is also your weakness, for you cannot see beyond it."

"You spew nonsense with a sharp tongue that I will not tolerate just as I cannot tolerate your presence. Keep a silent tongue around me, suffer coupling with me and

I with you until you are with child, then we will see little of each other. But we will not couple until after your monthly bleed. You made a point of leaving blood on the bedding. And after seeing how you were with the merchant, I know not if it was to make me think I took your virginity or if it was to hide the fact that you have been with another man and carry his bairn." He nodded at the garments on the chair. "You will wear my peoples' garments for the celebration. Unfortunately, they will not be worn with honor."

Tavia rested a hand to her chest as her husband turned and left the room, then sank to the bench nearby. His words were like a knife to her heart. She never imagined him thinking that of her. How he must hate her. How did she share a life with a man who hated her? How did she couple with a man who hated her? How did she survive this marriage?

Tears ran down her cheeks. Her father had spoken often of her mother and the love they had for each other. He had painted such a beautiful picture of their love that it was a dream of hers to find the same someday. More tears fell as she felt her dream slowly die.

"Tears will do you no good," Marta snapped when she entered the room.

Had the woman heard what Bhric had said to her? Would she share the news with others? What then would people think of her?

Tavia was tired of defending herself. It was all she had done since arriving here only a few short hours ago and it had left her drained. She wanted no more of it. She would sit quietly like an obedient wife tonight and retire to her bedchamber as soon as possible.

She wiped at her wet cheeks. "Tears will also do me no harm."

"Bah," Marta said as if scolding. "Time to wash and dress."

With a sense of defeat washing over her, Tavia allowed the woman to tend her.

Marta gave her a light washing from a fresh bucket of water, her hands a bit rough except when she got to her leg.

"What happened to your leg?" Marta asked.

"It does not concern you," Tavia said, having no intention of discussing it with her.

The woman turned an odd look on her and appeared as if she might demand to know, then stopped and continued with her task.

Tavia wondered about Marta. She did not seem a pleasant woman. Or was she unpleasant because of the task Bhric had assigned her? Or was she set upon Tavia to spy on her? Had she been made aware that Lord Bhric was not pleased with his new wife? If that was so, she surely would not be able to trust the woman or make any friends here when they were all faithful to Bhric.

Marta helped Tavia into a gray linen underdress, then began applying layer after layer until Tavia felt weighted down from the various wool garments. A lovely woolen shawl was the last garment Marta added, tying the ends in a knot at her chest.

"Now for your hair," Marta said and got busy.

Tavia cringed at the tight braids Marta fashioned in her hair then coiled around her head and secured with bone combs. She was stunned to see the woman smile when she finished.

"Now you look like a proper Northman's wife."

Tavia did not agree. She had wed Lord Bhric, ruler of the Clan MacShane, not a Northman, but she said nothing.

"The festivities have probably started. I must go see that all goes well. Come, I will see you to the Great Hall," Marta said, stretching her hand out.

"I need a moment to myself. I will be down shortly."

"Do not take long," Marta ordered. "All wait to meet you."

Tavia nodded and after Marta left, she stood staring at the door. Her feet would not move for her but then she did not know who she was, this woman in strange garments, her hair styled so foreign to her. She felt robbed of her identity.

"Go and be done with it," she encouraged herself with a whisper.

Still her feet would not budge.

This was not who she was. This was not who Bhric had wed.

Without hesitation, she turned, pulling the combs out of her hair.

Chapter Eight

Bhric walked from table to table talking and drinking with his warriors and the wives of those wed. There was endless talk and laughter, words of congratulation, and teasing about how fast the new bride's stomach would grow. He only wished he could feel the same enjoyment. He had had hopes for this marriage, his mother insisting she would find a woman for him who he would come to love.

He had been disappointed when arriving here to find his mother had left for home. He had wanted to know if what Newlin had told him was true. If she had been good friends with Tavia's mother, why then had she not told him of her intentions to wed him to her best friend's daughter?

"It is done. Enjoy bedding her," Sven advised with a grin and a friendly slap on Bhric's back. "It is not as if she is hard to look upon, a bit tiny, but pretty."

Bhric could not argue with that. His wife was more than pretty, she had lovely features that stirred him whenever he looked upon her. But that could be because he had not been with a woman in a while. Why then hadn't other women he looked upon since meeting her stirred his loins as she did? The thought annoyed him though it shouldn't. At least it would not be hard to bed her.

"I want more," he whispered, not expecting Sven

to hear him.

"Don't we all," Sven said with a hardy laugh.

"What have you said to my brother to put such a foul scowl on his face?"

Sven turned and with a quick arm around her waist pulled his wife against his side and rested his hand on her rounded belly. "He pouts like a woman."

Ingrid jabbed him in the side and shook her head. "Your mouth has a daring tongue when you drink."

"I will show you how daring my tongue is later tonight," Sven said and nibbled at her neck.

Bhric cringed. "I do not want to hear that."

"What? How do you think the bairn got in her stomach?" Sven asked, laughing.

Bhric cringed again. "I wish all daughters on you."

Sven cringed this time. "Do not curse me when I but tease."

"All daughters sound just fine to me," Ingrid said.

"Bite your tongue, woman," Sven warned. "You can have all daughters after you give me a strong son."

"I will hold you to that," Ingrid said.

Sven kissed her lips quick. "And I will enjoy giving you every single daughter."

Bhric shook his head. "I do not know how Mother and Father let you wed him, Ingrid."

"Love! I love him with all my heart, and Mother never says no to love."

Bhric never felt envy, never had the need to but at that moment he did. He was not only envious of the love his sister and Sven shared but how happy they were with each other. But looking at them one could see they were a good fit. His sister was of good height.

Sven did not have to bend down to kiss her. She had fine features, and her hair was as golden as Sven's. She had a strong nature and the skills to stand beside her husband and fight if necessary. Their combined strength would produce many strong bairns. He pushed the thought from his mind. It reminded him too much of what his wife lacked. He spotted Marta and she nodded at him, and he returned a brief nod.

Sven caught the exchange. "So, Marta got her to wear the garb of a Northwoman."

"My wife was ordered to wear it," Bhric said. "I will have her show respect to the Thrubolt Tribe for this celebration."

"I think she failed to understand," Sven said, as his glance settled across the room.

Bhric turned and while anger rushed over him, he could not help but be captivated by his wife. She looked beautiful in a Clan Strathearn plaid artfully wrapped around a deep gold underdress intricately embroidered at the neck, wrists, and hem of the garment. Her dark hair appeared to glitter in the light as it fell in waves, free of any confinement, and her cheeks were tinged pink.

She stared at him anxiously and Bhric realized the room had turned quiet, all eyes on him as he stood there silently looking at his wife. A wife who had blatantly disobeyed him.

"Has she injured herself, she limps?" his sister whispered.

And so it began, the endless questions and no doubt surprise that he had wed a woman with an affliction. Bhric went to her and took her arm to wrap around his. He looked out over the room and announced with as much enthusiasm as he could muster, "My wife, Lady Tavia."

The room erupted into a cacophony of shouts, whistles, applause, and the banging of tankards on the table.

He kept his voice low as he escorted her to the table on the dais where Sven and Ingrid sat. "You will answer to me later, wife, for your neglect in obeying me."

Tavia remained silent, keeping a pleasant, yet forced smile on her face.

"You have been injured?" Ingrid asked before her brother could introduce her.

"At one time, my limp is what is left of it," Tavia said, seeing no reason to hide it.

Ingrid raised her brow as she sent her brother a quick look.

Bhric ignored the questionable look and introduced Ingrid. "This is my sister Ingrid and Sven's wife."

"Be careful you don't squash her. She is a wee bit of a thing," Ingrid said to her brother before looking to Tavia. "Welcome to the Thrubolt Tribe."

Tavia turned a confused look on Ingrid.

"The Thrubolt Tribe in the north is where we were raised, Bhric and I and two other brothers and sisters. That tribe is as important to us as is our mother's Clan MacShane."

Tavia gave no thought to the tribe but instead focused on the fact that Bhric's mum had given his da six bairns. She wondered if she would be able to give him just one.

"I see," Tavia managed to say and sat, her husband and Sven separating her from Ingrid.

Bowls, platters, and trenches of food filled the tables and ale and wine were endlessly poured. Tavia did not understand how so much food and drink could be consumed, but then the men were large as were the women. They were giants compared to her.

"Eat," her husband snapped, causing her to jump and he lowered his head close to her face. "Wipe that fear off your face. They watch you."

Tavia had no stomach for food, but she took a small piece of bread to appease her husband.

Bhric kept himself from shaking his head and speared a sizeable piece of meat with his knife and placed it in the trencher in front of his wife. "Eat!"

Her stomach churned at the thought, and she was glad he turned away from her to continue talking with Sven. The night wore on and she grew tired. She wondered if it would be acceptable if she excused herself or must she wait to retire with her husband.

Tavia poked at the meat in front of her while she nibbled at the bread, hoping it appeared as if she was eating more than she was.

The noise in the room suddenly lowered and Tavia was surprised to see an older woman, tall, slim, her gray hair braided and tightly coiled on either side of her head walk with the help of a tall staff toward the dais. Her features were sharp, and wrinkles marred a good portion of her aged face. That everyone eyed her with respect and awe warned Tavia that she was someone of importance.

"I have come to congratulate you and your bride on

your marriage and to bless you with a fruitful union," the old woman said.

"I am grateful, Greta. This is Tavia, my bride," Bhric said, turning to face her.

"I am pleased to meet you," Tavia said, and an unease ran through her at the way the woman's glance slowly examined her. When she finished, Tavia was not surprised to see disappointment on her face.

"If you need anything, I am here to serve you, my lady," Greta said.

"I am grateful," Tavia said and unexpectedly added, "but my healer came with me."

The soft chatter vanished in an instant and she did not dare look at her husband, knowing she would see disapproval in his eyes. Though, she was forced to when he turned to her.

"Greta is an exceptional healer. She will see to your care when necessary." That it was an order was undeniable, his voice raised and his tone commanding.

She had meant no insult, but she feared that was how everyone saw it.

"I have met, Hertha, your healer," Greta said. "She is an extremely pleasant and somewhat knowledgeable young woman. I will teach her much and I look forward to helping you birth your first of many bairns."

Cheers and shouts rang out and fists pounded the tables in joy.

Greta stepped closer to the dais. "We will talk, my lady."

"Join us," Bhric offered.

Greta nodded and Sven stood and pulled out the chair beside his wife for the healer.

Bhric leaned his head down toward Tavia once again. "Greta is revered in our tribe. Do not insult her again."

"I meant no insult, my lord," Tavia said. "I feel more comfortable with Hertha that was all."

"Comfortable or not, Greta will tend you when necessary."

Tavia acknowledged him with a nod and turned to stifle a yawn.

"You are tired?" he asked.

"I am, your lord," she admitted with hopes he would allow her to retire.

"You have slept and yet you are still tired." He shook his head. "Find some strength, for we are meant to leave this celebration together and it is far too early for us to do that."

He turned away from her before she could acknowledge his command. She looked around the Great Hall. She was a stranger here and she worried that she might always be a stranger in her new home. Unless, of course, she found a way to change that, but how? She had kept herself busy at home though if she were truthful with herself, she would admit that after the accident and forced isolation while she healed and the pitiful glances once free to walk about had forced further isolation on her. And she had allowed herself to grow comfortable with it.

She did not think it would be wise to do the same here.

"My lord," she said softly to get his attention and when he did not respond, she hesitated to rest her hand lightly on his forearm, but fearing it was her only way since she was not prone to raising her voice, she laid her hand on his arm and tried again. "My lord."

He turned with an angry scowl and Tavia quickly removed her hand.

"What is it?" he snapped. Her gentle touch had startled him and sent a stirring through him, and he had gotten annoyed, the reason for his abrupt retort.

"I was wondering my duties here in the keep," she said. "So that I may see to them without delay."

"Marta sees well to the keep."

"Then what am I to do?" she asked, surprised since running the keep was a wife's duty.

"Your one and only duty is… me. Make certain you see to it wisely."

His dark blue eyes reminded her of the dark depths of the sea and how one could not see what lay deep beneath the water. She wondered that now. What lay buried deep down inside him?

Her hand went of its own accord to rest on his forearm once again and words tumbled out of her mouth without thought. "I will make you a good wife."

Bhric stared at her, her words slipping inside him to squeeze at his heart. How did she do that? How did she sneak past his defenses so easily and touch him where he least expected it?

The night wore on without further incident until Sven stood and raised his tankard. "It's time for Lord Bhric to take his wife to bed."

Tavia had to keep herself from cringing against the cacophony of cheers and fists pounding on the table.

Bhric stood after swallowing the last of his ale and held his hand out to her. She stood, turning her head slightly so no one would see her wince from the pain, though she failed to realize she squeezed her husband's hand. She had sat too long.

Bhric made a show of scooping her up in his arms and planting a firm kiss on her lips and more cheers rang out.

No words passed between them as they climbed the stairs and when he went to his bedchamber instead of hers, she turned a raised brow on him.

"You sleep with me tonight."

"I thought you said—"

"Aye, I did say I will not touch you until after your monthly bleed, but others must think differently. Marta will find us naked in bed tomorrow and she will spread the news that our marriage bed was put to good use."

Naked.

That was all she heard. She had slept naked with him already but that had been different. He had not known they slept naked together until morning. Not so now. He would get in bed naked of his own volition.

He set her on her feet as soon as they entered his bedchamber and began disrobing once he closed the door. Not so Tavia, she hesitated, then realizing he would be naked well before her and have nothing to do but watch her disrobe, she hurried out of her garments. Once she was naked, she took hasty steps to the bed and slipped beneath the blankets with relief.

Needing to keep her eyes on anything but her husband stripping off his garments, she glanced around the room. It was a good size as was the sizeable, sturdy wood bed taking up a good portion of the room. A multitude of chests, some piled three high, sat braced against two walls. A small table sat against another wall with two benches beneath. Two chests hugged either side of the bed. A sizeable, flickering candle sat atop the chest on the opposite side from where she lay and beside it lay a dagger.

Her eyes accidentally landed on him as her glance took her around the room. He was a fine built man, all muscle and strength that could do her damage if he so wished. And while he warned and threatened her often enough since meeting him, he had not once shown a propensity for raising his hand to her or causing her any harm—except.

He did mention pounding her when they coupled since he believed her no longer a virgin.

She wanted to blurt out that she had never been with any man. That his lips had been the first she'd ever felt. But that would be admitting the lie she had perpetrated to seal their marriage agreement. She could not chance admitting the truth until after their vows were sealed.

He extinguished the various candles before walking to his side of the bed, stretching back his shoulders with a wince, then extinguishing the candle on the chest before getting beneath the blankets and settling himself beside her, his body so close that she could feel his heat drifting off him.

Tavia lay stiff beside him, not moving the slightest, and gripping the blanket high on her chest. Her heart hammered wildly, and she did not dare close her eyes. She hoped he would fall asleep fast only then would she feel safe.

She almost jumped when he turned on his side to

face her.

"Your actions forced this marriage and now we are stuck tolerating each other, something I hoped to have avoided in a wife."

"What did you want from your wife?" she asked.

"A good, strong woman who knew the wisdom of being obedient when necessary and one I could talk with and could offer me good counsel when needed, and one who would bear me strong sons and daughters. A wife I could share the perils and the pleasures of life with, a wife I could trust, I could count on without question."

It was much of what Tavia wanted in a husband, though she would add love to it, for she believed love was what helped bind a relationship. Love would not have her husband look at her limp as weakness or her small size an obstacle. He would love and respect her for who she was and not who he wanted her to be. Could there be the slightest chance they could share a good marriage together. She had to ask.

Bhric pressed a finger to her lips when she went to speak. "Do not offer what you cannot give, for I will hear no more lies spill from your lips. Now sleep and let the morning bring news and rejoicing that all is well with the lord and his lady."

Chapter Nine

Bhric walked through the village as he did every so often making himself available to anyone who wished to speak with him and to keep an eye on everything that went on. The Clan MacShane people were beginning to blend well with his people, though some still held animosity toward him. A few felt he had no right to rule the clan, but he was the rightful heir to the clan, and it was now his to rule over.

All had settled well over the last three days since his arrival home with his new bride. At least he made it seem that way to everyone. He treated his wife well when in her presence while avoiding her most other times. He was annoyed with the whole situation especially waking the morning after the celebration to find her snuggled against him and his arm snug around her. He had lingered, keeping her there tucked close and enjoying the feel of her soft, warm skin. It was as if she had always been there beside him, as if she belonged there.

He had left the bed with haste when the gentle stirring he had felt turned to a hard arousal and far too rapidly. He would not chance coupling with her until he knew for sure she carried no other man's bairn. And that was the problem. He could not trust her to keep a truthful tongue. She had not told him upon meeting him that she was his wife and she had allowed him to believe that she had suffered an injury rather than confess the truth about her limp. And that she tricked him into their marriage bed so he would have no choice but to honor the agreement made him wonder what more she hid from him.

"She's a small one and that limp limits her."

Bhric turned to Greta. Her slow and soft gait often had her sneaking up on people. He looked to where her head was turned and saw his wife talking with Hume.

"Too small?" he asked, knowing she would understand his question.

"That will not be known until her delivery time comes," Greta said and turned to him. "What happened to her leg?"

"I have yet to find out," Bhric said, having wondered the same.

"You should know if it is an affliction that can be passed on to bairns or if your wife is prone to foolishness that can bring her harm or if someone failed to protect her, something I fear her small size will warrant much attention."

"An accident I believe," Bhric said but wondered if that was a lie. He had not considered her limp could be hereditary, though she had tried to hide it from him. The possibility troubled him. "Is there talk of her limp already?"

"It was inevitable, and many assume, understandably so, that she is not strong enough to be your wife."

"My mother believed differently," Bhric said, watching the way his wife's face lit with a smile as she spoke with Hume. Did she fancy the man? Had she brought him here to be close to him?

"I learned over the years to respect your mother's wisdom. Perhaps she knows something we do not."

A scream pierced the air, catching everyone's attention and everything happened so fast there was little time to react, though his wife did not hesitate.

A large elkhound was growling and nipping as he chased after Uta, a young lass, barely five years. It was one of the war hounds, trained to hunt and kill, and he was almost on top of the lass. If his teeth sank into her, she would not survive.

Bhric stared in shock as did all the others in the area when his wife ran limping far faster than he believed her capable of and placed herself in front of the lass to boldly raise her hand and command the hound to…

"STOP!" Tavia ordered, pointing her finger at the hound and when the beast of a dog stopped, she then commanded, "SIT!"

To everyone's shock and amazement the hound sat. They were even more amazed that the lass had fastened herself to Tavia's leg and when she peeked her head from behind her, the hound growled and Tavia commanded him once again.

"Quiet!" Tavia ordered, shaking her finger at the hound and he turned silent.

A large man came running toward them, calling out, "Uta! Uta!

Uta peeked her head out from behind Tavia once again but would not step past her.

"I just wanted to hug him. *Faðir*," Uta called out.

Bhric reached his wife before Harald reached her

and his daughter. Uta gripped Tavia's cloak, tucking it around her as if trying to disappear in its folds.

"You have been warned to stay away from the hounds, Uta," Bhric said firmly. "They are not playthings."

Uta's slim bottom lip began to quiver. "Bones looked lonely."

"Uta! How many times have I told you not to go near Bones?" the large man scolded as he stopped next to the hound.

"He's lonely," the little lass insisted.

"You need to teach her to stay away from the hounds, Harald, before there is a serious mishap," Bhric ordered and noticed how the hound kept focused on Tavia.

"He's grumpy because he's lonely," Uta said, keeping herself buried tight in the folds of Tavia's cloak.

"Bones does look lonely," Tavia said and went to step toward the hound.

Bhric went to grab his wife to yank her back and Harald went to hurry around her. They both were too late.

Tavia's hand had reached the hound's mouth and he sniffed at it. "Are you lonely, Bones?' she asked softly and with a gentle hand rubbed his neck. The hound leaned into her touch, wanting more and she drew closer to give him a proper rub. "Come, Uta, rub him so he knows you are no threat to him and he will not chase you again."

The little lass did not hesitate. She scurried around Tavia.

"This is Uta, Bones, and she wishes to be friends with you," Tavia said and Uta's hand rushed out to touch the hound. "Gently," Tavia cautioned and Uta's small hand disappeared into the hound's fur to rub lightly. "

"Can I hug him?" Uta asked and before either man could object, Tavia said, "It is best you start with a gentle rub until he comes to know you better and trusts you."

"I love you, Bones, I love you," Uta said in a singsong voice as she rubbed him, and the large hound leaned against her. She gave a glance at her father. "See, Bones was lonely. Now he will play with me."

Bhric turned a scowl on Harald. "The war hounds aren't meant for play."

"Aye, my lord," Harald said. "Come, Uta, Bones must return to his pen."

"After we play, *Faðir*," Uta said and turned to speak in her singsong voice to the hound. "Come on, Bones, we'll play together." She skipped off and Bones followed alongside her.

"That hound was one of our best. He is no good to us anymore if he goes off so easily with a bairn," Bhric said.

Harald shrugged. "I do not know what happened. Could be that your wife has a gentling touch."

That she does. This morning her hand had drifted close to his manhood, soft and gentle, and the unexpected results had been the reason he had vacated the bed so fast, and the thought annoyed him.

"See that the hounds are kept hounds and not playthings for your daughter," Bhric ordered harshly.

"Especially Fen. He has been nasty, snapping and growling at anyone who goes near him since he last saw battle with my father."

"Aye, my lord. Fen stays much to himself these days, the other hounds not going near him," Harald said, then hurried off after his daughter.

"You, wife," Bhric said, turning to her.

Tavia waited for the reprimand that was sure to come.

"Will not do something so foolish ever again."

And there it was. "Aye, my lord," she said and went to leave, disappointed that in three days' time, he had barely spoken to her and when he did it was usually telling her what she should not do, what she had to do, what he expected her to do.

Bhric grabbed her arm, stopping her. "You smile often at Hume."

"He gives me reason to smile," she said, without thinking since conversations were always interesting with the young man.

Bhric leaned his face down close to hers. "And why would that be?"

A puzzled expression crossed her face. "He has a bright mind and is witty."

"So, you think highly of him?"

"Aye, I do just as I think highly of the woman he loves… Hertha," Tavia said.

"Are they wed?" Bhric asked.

"Aye, they were wed the same day Flora and Lord Torin were wed."

"Something else you failed to tell me?" he accused.

She tilted her head slightly and a small crease

appeared between her eyes. "I did not think it would be of interest to you, my lord."

Truthfulness. That was what he saw in her eyes. It was difficult to miss, it sparked so bright, and that annoyed him even more. Had it been there before and had he failed to see it?

Tavia looked around for Hume, fearful for him though there was no reason she should be. It was the look in her husband's eyes that worried her but why talk of Hume should anger him puzzled her.

"Anything that concerns my wife concerns me." He saw that people were watching and with a firm grip on her arm he hurried her toward the side of a cottage.

Tavia felt the pull to her leg as soon as he yanked her, and she stumbled from the quick jab of pain.

"You cannot even stay on your feet," he reprimanded.

His words not only hurt but they also angered her. "I could stay on my feet just fine if it was not for your thoughtlessness."

His head snapped back as if she had slapped him. "You dare to chastise me?"

"When you deserve it," Tavia said, her anger sparking her courage. "I have a limp and it slows me, and nothing will change that no matter how many times you yank me to keep pace with you."

That she was right, frustrated him. He refused to admit it, but he wished she did not have a limp. He wished she could match his powerful strides, keep pace with him as he walked through the village, and run if necessary. How would she ever run if she needed to? But she had not allowed her limp to stop her from keeping Uta from being hurt as foolish as it had been for her to do so.

Tavia kept her voice low. “I am sorry I am not the wife you wanted, but I will make you a good wife if only you will give me the chance.”

“What happened to your leg?” he asked, taking advantage of the moment to confront her about it. Besides, her gentle tone made it seem that she spoke the truth and perhaps she would make a good wife if given the chance.

“An accident,” she said.

“Tell me about it,” he said.

“I do not like to recall it,” she said, having locked the memory away.

“I want to know. Tell me,” Bhric insisted, wondering if her reluctance to tell him was due to a lie. Had she been born with the limp? Accidents did happen, but too often it was the person’s own fault. Did she not want to admit her fault?

“I fell from a tree,” she said, the memory returning swiftly.

“What were you doing climbing a tree?” Bhric asked, wanting clearer answers, wanting to believe her.

She said the first thing that came to mind. “Why not climb a tree?”

Again, she avoided details. “You slipped?”

She heard the crack ring in her head as loudly as she had the day it happened. “A branch broke.”

“You did not test the branch before stepping on it?” he asked.

“I was new to tree climbing.”

He got an image in his head of what might have

happened. An impetuous lass pays no mind to possible danger, climbs a tree for the first time and falls, leaving her leg permanently damaged and her with a limp. Did he believe her when she had given him such little detail? Or was it the truth and should he be relieved it was not an affliction that could be passed on to their bairns?

"A fault of yours… not thinking reasonably before doing something like petting a hound trained to kill. Bones' name fits him. He enjoys latching onto bones and tearing the meat from them whether the creature is alive or dead."

"Then it was a woman's gentle touch and love that Bones craved and not her flesh."

Was her touch so gentle and loving that it could actually calm a beast? Could she possibly calm the unrest that stirred in him? He did not know what brought him such unrest and it had only begun a year or more ago. It lingered in him as if waiting, but for what he did not know. It had left him feeling unsettled. He had thought that just the idea of his move to Clan MacShane had caused the unrest and that it would dissipate once here, but it hadn't.

He did not know what made him ask or snap at her the way he did. "And do you crave love, wife?"

"I do, which is probably why Bones obeyed my commands. He sensed a kindred spirit looking for what he desperately wanted… to be loved."

"You look for love?" he asked, not sure if she was saying what she thought he might want to hear or if she spoke the truth and was truly hoping to find love.

"Everyone looks for love, at least those with good

hearts do," she said. "Those with cold hearts could care less. Is your heart cold, my lord?"

"Bhric! Come, we hunt!" Sven called out.

He ignored her question, not having an answer for her. "No climbing trees and no touching hounds," he ordered his wife before turning away from her. When he heard nothing but silence from her, he turned back around. "Did you hear me, wife?"

"I did, my lord," she said with a bob of her head.

"Did I fail to hear you say, 'Aye, my lord?'" he asked, his expression stern.

"You could not fail to hear what I did not say, my lord."

He stepped closer to her. "You refuse to obey my orders?"

"How can I agree to obey when I do not know if I would be able to? Though, I doubt I will be climbing a tree, I would not fail to protect a bairn from a hound again if necessary."

"You will do no such thing, I forbid it," he commanded with a biting snap.

"Instinct is a higher commander than you, my lord. It forces one to respond without thought, therefore, I cannot obey when I know instinct will force me to do otherwise." Tavia continued before her husband could respond. "I speak what you ask of me… the truth."

Bhric glared at her. "Then hear my truth. Disobey me again and suffer the consequences." He turned and stormed off. His wife could be vexing at times. Or was it that she strived to do exactly what he had wanted… speak the truth to him? Once again leaving him wondering if she might make him a good wife after all.

Tavia stood watching him walk away, his strides so powerful they left deep tracks in the snow.

"How did you command that hound to do your bidding?"

Tavia turned to see Ingrid approach her. She was beginning to feel that she lived amongst giants, Northwomen almost as tall as their men. Ingrid also had lovely features making Tavia think that Bhric's da and mum were exceptionally fine-looking people.

"I do not know. I simply responded to the situation," Tavia said.

"Foolish when you did not know what the hound would do."

"I knew what I would do. I would not let him reach the bairn," Tavia said, feeling the need to defend herself.

"Foolish courage," Ingrid said with a grin. "Be careful the next time you might not be so lucky. And be wise when it comes to my brother. He will tolerate only so much."

"Ingrid!" a woman shouted and waved her over.

She hurried off without another word to Tavia. She watched the two women bend their heads in talk and glance her way a couple of times. That they spoke about her was obvious and that they did not hide it hurt. She had thought Ingrid and her might become friends but since the evening of the celebration when they first met, her sister-in-law had not spoken to her or made any effort to seek her out. Others seemed to ignore her as well. Every walk she took through the village had been met with stares, sometimes a bob of a head, but rarely did anyone speak with her.

"Are you all right, my lady?"

A sigh of relief welled up in Tavia, though she contained it, she was so happy to see a familiar face. "Hertha, I am pleased to see you."

"Hume hurried to tell me what happened, then I saw Lord Bhric talking with you, then his sister, and well, you look a bit dazed, standing here alone."

"I feel alone, Hertha. It has not been easy to get to know people here," she admitted. "They seem to shy away from me."

"We should walk and talk so you can stretch your leg," Hertha said and hooked her arm out for Tavia to take.

Tavia took the young woman's arm, her leg feeling stiff. She stumbled two steps before righting herself and caught the disapproving glances from those around her.

"They think me not fit to be Lord Bhric's wife," Tavia said softly as they fell into a slow stroll.

"They do not understand that your limp is a badge of honor you carry for your bravery."

"Our clan did not think so. They avoided me after the accident."

"Because of guilt," Hertha said. "You did what none of them would, what none of them could. And you did not hesitate to do it just as you did not hesitate today to help the lass. Do not do what you did at our clan because you believed people shunned you. Do not lock yourself away no matter what people think, or they will never get to truly come to know you, see your strength, and be touched by your kindness just as you touched that hound with kindness today."

"The North people think I am not a strong enough

wife for their leader," Tavia said.

"In the few days we have been here, I have come to realize the Northmen and women revere strength and courage. At first I feared they might view Hume as weak since he appears as if he has a meek nature, but when they learned that he went searching for me in a snowstorm, they accepted him as a fine warrior and they treat him with respect."

"Yet I am thought foolish for helping the lass," Tavia said, shaking her head.

"Or are they embarrassed because no one responded as fast as you did?" Hertha suggested.

"I wish we could talk more often, Hertha. It does me good to talk with someone from home, someone I trust."

"I request daily to see you, but Greta denies me time to slip away. When Hume came and told me what had happened, I slipped away since Greta was not at the healing cottage to stop me. I feel as though Greta and Marta conspire to keep me away from you."

Tavia wondered why they would do such a thing and it made her trust the two women even less than she already did.

"Does Greta teach you much?" Tavia asked.

Hertha lowered her voice to a whisper. "I feel more a servant than a student. Hume and I continue to prepare what plants we know in case you and our people need them. And I ask questions of Greta to learn what I can since she tends some illnesses differently than I am used to."

"Hertha, why are you not tending to your chores?"

Tavia stopped, though kept hold of Hertha's arm as

she turned her head to Greta. “She is walking with me. We have not visited since arriving here.”

“She has chores to see to. Now be off with you,” Greta ordered.

“Nay, Hertha stays with me until I say otherwise,” Tavia said, her voice strong, though her stomach churned as it always did when she gathered courage to speak.

“I command what Hertha does,” Greta argued.

Tavia saw they were drawing attention from people around them and though she felt a slight tremble she stood her ground. “No longer. Hertha is from my clan and follows my word above all else.”

“Lord Bhric commands all here,” Greta said.

Tavia caught several heads nodding in agreement. Still, she remained not only determined but calm in nature and in her words. “Hertha will remain walking with me until I say otherwise. You can raise your objection with my husband when he returns. Until then, Hertha obeys me, not you.”

The whispers started and Tavia was sure that when her husband returned her confrontation with Greta would be relayed to him quite differently.

“I will take this up with Lord Bhric,” Greta said.

“Please do, Greta,” Tavia said and turned her head to continue walking with Hertha, her stomach already churning nervously over the inevitable confrontation with her husband.

Chapter Ten

Tavia was returning to the keep after she finished talking with Hertha when a woman slowed by age approached her.

"My lady, a moment, if you please."

Tavia walked over to her and took her arm, seeing that walking was not easy for her and knowing the feeling all too well.

"I am Wilona, my lady, born to the Clan MacShane. I want to say that I and others in the clan are happy and relieved that you are Lord Bhric's new bride. Many in the clan worried he would wed one of his father's own. It is good to see he wed a woman of this land and the blood of our homeland will continue to run through your bairns, future leaders of our clan."

"Have the Northmen treated any Clan MacShane people cruelly?" Tavia asked eager to learn all she could about the clan.

"Nay, they have not been cruel, but neither do they bother much with us. They have their ways, and we have ours and we have yet to blend. They think otherwise since there is more of them than us, which is why we are so pleased to see one of our own. You are one of us. You know us and understand us, our beliefs, customs, our love of this land. And we are proud of your courage in wedding Lord Bhric."

"I am grateful you told me this, Wilona, for I was

feeling as though I was in a foreign land with so many Northmen. It is good to know my people are still strong here."

"We are, my lady, and we stand strong with you."

"If there is anything you need, Wilona, please do not hesitate to let me know. Also, the young woman I brought with me, Hertha, who has been assigned to help Greta, the Northmen's healer, is a healer as well. She knows well how to tend the ills of our people."

Wilona's face brightened, her aged skin appearing as if it plumped from her wide smile. "I am so pleased to know that as will others."

"You will like Hertha. She is pleasant, always smiling, and wise in the way of healing."

Tavia continued talking with the older woman as she walked with her to her cottage.

"It has been an honor to have spoken with you, my lady," Wilona said once at her door.

"The honor was mine, Wilona, and I hope to meet and speak with more Clan MacShane people. And we will speak again and perhaps next time share a hot brew together."

Wilona's face brightened again. "I would be honored, my lady, and I will let others know how pleasant you are and how eager you are to speak with them."

Tavia turned away from the door once Wilona was inside and continued her walk to the keep. Hertha had been right about not locking herself away. The Northmen might not welcome her warmly, but her own people would, and she would see that she got to know them.

She felt much better than she had this morning when she woke not looking forward to another day. She had faced a struggle the last three days since arriving here, feeling more alone than she had ever felt. She was beginning to wonder if misery was all that awaited her in her marriage. Her husband certainly was not giving her a chance, avoiding her as he did and as he had done the morning they had woken in bed together. He had jumped out of bed so fast after she had woken, snuggled comfortably against him, that she had assumed he could not stand the touch of her. But that made no sense after giving it thought, since he had already kissed her and touched her intimately and seemed to have enjoyed it like she had done.

Tavia shook her head as she entered the Great Hall and sat by the fire after discarding her cloak to the bench. She stretched her legs out to the heat, relishing its warmth especially the feel of it on her leg.

A young servant lass approached her. "A hot brew, my lady?"

"That would be most welcoming. Thank you…" Tavia tilted her head in question.

The lass seemed unsure as to what Tavia silently asked.

"Your name?" Tavia asked with a smile.

The servant looked surprised but responded, "Shea, my lady."

"Thank you again, Shea," Tavia said.

"Fetch the brew, Shea, now!"

The servant jumped at Marta's commanding tone and hurried off.

"The servants are not thanked for doing their

chores," Marta reprimanded.

"Perhaps you do not thank them, but I do," Tavia said and let loose with a command of her own before she could stop herself. "Never reprimand me again, Marta."

Marta stared at her a moment, then sneered as she went to speak.

"Is there anything else you wish to say, Marta?" Tavia snapped, a warning of sorts that she would brook no argument from her.

Of course, the familiar churn of her stomach after speaking up before giving it much thought and wondering too late if she overstepped her bounds took hold. But then she was not the servant, Marta was, and not only did she need to remember that, but Marta did as well.

"You should rest your leg before supper tonight, my lady," Marta said, keeping her hands clasped snug in front of her.

Tavia did not know if she and the woman would ever get along, but she did not want an unbearable situation born of an already uneasy one. It would make life in the keep far too unpleasant. So, she chose to speak kindly to her as she had to Shea.

"Thank you for thinking of my leg, Marta. I will let you know what I decide to do."

Marta bobbed her head and took her leave.

Tavia was almost finished with the brew when a few servants hurried through the Great Hall, worry on their faces, and out of the keep.

A few minutes later, Marta followed after them.

"What's wrong, Marta?" Tavia asked when she

saw the woman had no intentions of stopping and alerting her to a possible problem.

"A hunting accident," Marta said.

Tavia got to her feet. "My husband?"

"It is not known yet. One returned before the others so the healer will be prepared to tend the injured."

Tavia grabbed her cloak.

"You should wait here," Marta advised.

"Why? My husband could be hurt," Tavia said, swinging her cloak over her shoulders.

"Precisely, he could be the one hurt and we do not know how badly," she said.

"All the more reason for me to be there when he returns," Tavia said and preceded the woman out of the keep.

With having rested her leg, she was able to walk through the village without difficulty. A light snow was falling, and she followed along with others, stopping abruptly when an agonizing scream ripped through the air.

Tavia could not help but pale, fearing it was her husband who had fallen to a severe accident.

"It is not Lord Bhric. He would never scream like that no matter how bad the pain," Marta said.

A shiver ran through Tavia at the thought of such strength. She had not been that strong when she had suffered her leg injury. The pain had been unbearable, and she had not been able to hold back her screams.

Tavia cringed, the screams growing louder as she drew closer. She was relieved to see her husband standing to the side with some of his men. It was then she noticed that those of the Clan MacShane stood by a man on the ground.

"Wild boar got him," she heard someone say.

"Didn't know what he was doing," said another.

"Not good hunters,"

Those words were untrue, and it annoyed her to hear them. Knowing her husband was not injured she went to see if there was anything she could do to help the injured man.

Greta was being helped to her feet after having examined the wound. "It is beyond repair. From the knee down needs to come off or he will die."

Shouts of "NAY" filled the air.

Tavia felt a hand on her arm and saw it was Wilona.

"Lath is my sister's son. Please help him. Please do not let them take his leg," Wilona pleaded.

Bhric gave a commanding nod, and his men went to approach the injured man to carry him off to have his leg cut off.

"WAIT!" Tavia called out.

Her husband glared at her.

"I will have a Highland healer look at it," Tavia said and waved Hertha forward before her husband could deny her.

Tavia was glad Hume joined her and together the three squatted down beside Lath and while Tavia placed a comforting hand on his shoulder and spoke softly to him, assuring him all would be well, Hertha and Hume looked him over.

"Can you stitch it?" Tavia asked.

"It will take a multitude of stitches and an experienced hand," Hertha said, "and much healing time without any promise that…"

Tavia knew what Hertha left unsaid… without any promise that Lath would survive.

"I beg you, my lady," Lath said, grabbing hold of her hand. "I would rather die than lose my leg."

A memory gripped Tavia, her da shouting, "*You will not cut off her leg You will heal it.*"

Tavia squeezed Lath's hand tight. "We will not cut off your leg."

"Your leg will come off! And let go of my wife's hand!"

Tavia looked up to see her husband standing over them, a stern and determined look in his eyes.

Lath released her hand mumbling apologies while keeping a pleading eye on Tavia.

She stood. "We can save his leg."

"We?" Bhric asked.

Hertha stood then. "Lady Tavia is an exceptionally skilled stitcher. Her talent is needed to sew the wound closed."

"Impossible," Greta said, shaking her head. The leg is too damaged. It is beyond repair. Besides, either way he will die."

"Then what difference does it make if we try?" Tavia asked, her eyes on her husband.

"Hertha will stitch his leg," Bhric ordered.

"She is not skilled enough. I will do it," Tavia said.

"I forbid it," Bhric commanded.

Tavia's chin went up and her courage came from deep down inside. "I am a Highland woman and I stand with my Highland brethren. I will do what I must to save them as you would with your Northmen tribe. You have a foot in both worlds. Will you stand this time with your Highland brethren?"

A tremendous roar went up from those in Clan MacShane, chests expanded, voices rang strong, even Lath managed to join in as painful as it was. Highland pride was heard and felt, not so the Northmen, anger sparked in their eyes.

Tavia worried that once again she had spoken without thought and may have overstepped her bounds. But the words had been spoken and could not be taken back. Besides, her husband had Highland blood running through him and his people here needed to know he was one of them.

Bhric kept a scowl on his wife. She set forth a challenge and a difficult one at that. He could not lose face in front of his tribesmen, yet he also could not alienate his Highland brethren, either way the consequences of his actions could cause strife.

Tavia could see that she had placed her husband in a difficult position, something she had not meant to do, and would not bode well for her. Words came quick and unexpected as they had done of late and she wondered if it was from having gotten to know Lady Dawn and her cousin Flora, both women confident in strength and courage that had her speaking up when normally her tongue would remain silent.

"I will obey your word, my lord," Tavia said with a respectful bow of her head. "But I beg of you to please allow me to help my brethren."

She kept her eyes on her husband and, therefore, did not see the swell of pride on the faces of the clan members that she should beg for one of them, but Bhric saw it. And bloody hell if he did not admire the bravery it had taken her to do so. Was there more to his petite wife than he first believed?

"Greta says either way he will die, so I will allow you to try while we prepare a grave for him," Bhric said, appeasing his wife and his tribesmen who believed Greta knew better.

"Thank you, my lord," Tavia said with a slight bob of her head.

Clansmen stepped forward ready to move Lath.

Tavia looked to her husband. "An empty cottage, my lord?"

He nodded and looked to Marta. "Take him to one closest to Hertha and Hume's cottage.

After nodding to Lord Bhric, Marta looked to the men. "Follow me."

Tavia took hold of Lath's hand. "Stay strong."

"Your courage gives me courage," Lath said, and their hands parted as one of the men handed him a stick to bite down on to keep him from crying out as they lifted him.

Bhric walked over to his wife and kept his voice low for her ears alone. "Never challenge me again."

"Even if you need to be challenged." Again, the words slipped from her mouth before she could stop them. She shook her head. "Forgive me, my lord, you were gracious enough to grant my request. I mean no disrespect, but you are not only a Northman but a Highlander as well. If you wish to succeed here, have your heirs accepted and respected, then you and your fellow tribesmen need to become part of this clan and not simply rule over it."

She offered sage advice and that she did, annoyed him. But didn't he want a wife that could help guide him when necessary? A wife who would speak up to him without fear as his mother did with his father.

"I cannot linger, my lord. I must go see to Lath," Tavia said when he did not respond to her.

"I will go with you," Bhric said and took hold of her arm.

"It is not necessary, my lord," she said, unnerved by the task ahead and his presence would only make it that more unnerving.

"Necessary or not, I go with you," Bhric said, making it clear she had no choice.

The cottage was two cottages down from Hertha and Hume's home. Lath had been settled on a table, Hertha preparing him for the stitching.

Bhric left his wife at the door, seeing the cottage was too small to hold them all. "Hume, you will keep me abreast of what goes on."

Hume bobbed his head. "Aye, my lord."

"I will watch," Greta said, making her way past Bhric.

"I will have no interference from you," Tavia snapped and bit her tongue too late after seeing her husband turn an angry glance on her. But she had had enough of the healer's commanding way, and she certainly did not need her interfering now.

"A fool fails to listen to wise words," Greta said.

"On that we agree," Tavia said and turned her attention to Lath.

Bhric had enough. He would leave the two women to battle it out. "I will be outside."

Tavia did not acknowledge his departure. She set her mind on the task ahead, combing through Hertha's healing basket to gather what she needed.

"What are you giving him?" Greta asked as Hume helped Lath drink from a brew he had made.

"A brew made from henbane seeds," Hume said.

"That will kill him," Greta argued.

Lath turned frightened eyes on Tavia.

"Worry not, Hume knows what he is doing," she said. "Given in an appropriate amount it will keep you from feeling the pain and let you rest more easily."

"You know this for sure?" Greta questioned.

"Aye, I am certain," Tavia said, recalling how it had helped her.

When everything was set, Lath groggy, barely able to speak, they finally began.

"I am going to tell you a story, Lath, as I stitch you. It is a story about a young lass who suffered as much as you do now. Listen well so when all is done you will know what awaits you. But I will have your word and the word of all here that this story is never repeated to anyone."

Lath nodded and mumbled, "My word."

Hertha and Hume said the same as unnecessary as it was for they were familiar with the story she was about to tell.

Tavia turned her head to Greta.

"My word, my lady," Greta said with a nod.

Tavia began the tale, speaking for several minutes before digging the needle into the torn flesh. "Snow had recently fallen and the gray clouds that day promised more. The forest was quiet, animals remaining in their shelters knowing a storm was brewing, a storm that would bring far more pain than anyone imagined."

***

Bhric paced outside, after spending hours sitting on the ground.

"You punish yourself waiting out here in this lightly falling snow," Sven said, joining him.

Bhric laughed. "I have sat, slept, and battled in far worse snow."

"You forgot coupled," Sven said with a laugh. "You forget I caught you that day with that woman in a snowdrift."

"We were both cold," Bhric said with a smile recalling the pleasant liaison.

"You warmed up fast enough, melting that snow beneath and around you, perhaps she would have made you a good wife."

Bhric winced. "Ilka availed herself of as many men as she could. She would never be a faithful wife."

"And this one can be?" Ingrid asked, joining her husband and brother.

"Mother believes so or she would have never arranged the marriage," Bhric said, defending the union he had intended to nullify.

"I am baffled by Mother's choice," Ingrid admitted.

"Your mother is wise," Sven said. "She knows what she does."

"She can be stubborn," Ingrid argued, snuggling into the crook of her husband's arm to be yanked tight against him.

Sven grinned. “A trait her daughter inherited.” He laughed at the jab of his wife’s elbow to his side.

“It is done,” Bhric said, “and I will make the best of it.”

“Still, she is a strange one,” Ingrid said. “Quiet and demure one minute, challenging and demanding the next. Do you know she kept Hertha from Greta earlier today and that she and Marta sparred?”

“Maybe you have a hellion on your hands,” Sven said with a teasing grin.

Bhric looked to the door, the image of his wife coming to mind. He had been a fool for not getting to know her. Something he intended to rectify.

The door opened and he expected to see Hume emerge as he had done twice thus far to let him know all was going well. It was not Hume who emerged from the cottage. It was Greta and with dusk having fallen the flickering light from the campfire cast just enough light to see tears glistening in her aged eyes.

“He is dead?” Sven asked, seeing the sorrow on the healer’s face.

Bhric saw her sorrow as well, something Greta rarely showed. She had dealt with much illness and death through the years, and she had remained strong for everyone. He could not fathom why this man’s death, a stranger, would move her to tears.

Greta stopped by Bhric. “There is more to your wife than you know. Waste no time in finding out about her. The warrior lives and rests peacefully. I have never seen such skilled hands.” With her hand leaning heavily on her staff, she groaned. “I go rest.”

Bhric had no chance to ask her what she meant, she walked away, disappearing into the night that was overpowering the fading dusk.

"What does she mean?" Sven asked. "Does she warn you about your wife? Or has her opinion of her changed?"

"It seems Greta wants Bhric to find out for himself?" Ingrid said.

"Why? Make it easier on him and just tell him," Sven argued.

"Why should anything be easy?" Bhric said, shaking his head.

The door to the cottage opened again and Hume stepped out and approached Bhric. "Lady Tavia is almost finished."

"Has she been standing this whole time?" Bhric asked.

"Nay, but she has been in the same position too long. Her leg will give her some trouble, not that she will admit it," Hume said.

"And the fellow, Lath?" Bhric asked, when his thought was more on his wife and what she would suffer for helping the man.

"Time will tell, my lord, though Lady Tavia did an amazing job stitching the leg. She found flesh where I thought none was left. If the wound does not turn putrid or fever sets in, he has a good chance of surviving," Hume said.

"Go see that my wife finishes, so she may finally eat and rest," Bhric ordered and turned toward the campfire.

"At least she has a talented stitching hand," Ingrid

said.

"Leave me," he ordered them both.

Ingrid went to say something, and Sven shook his head at her and with his arm around her, he did as Bhric ordered and left him alone.

His wife stepped out of the cottage a short time later. Her gait was slow, though steady, and exhaustion marred her lovely face. He went to her.

Tavia hurried to thank him again, pleased that all had gone well, and Lath slept with no unrest. "Thank yo—" She gasped when he scooped her up and planted her tight against him.

"You will eat and rest," he commanded as he walked through the village as if he carried nothing more than a lightweight sack.

"I have no argument with that," Tavia said, a yawn slipping out.

"Rest your head," he ordered.

"Do you always command?" she asked and stifling another yawn laid her head on his shoulder, finding it most welcoming.

"Mostly," he said, following the torch lit path through the village. Her body softened against his and he was pleased she found no unease in his arms.

"It still snows," she said, feeling the flakes drop on her cheeks.

Bhric saw that her hood had fallen away from her face and stopped a moment. His cheek brushed hers as he brought his head down to capture the edge of her hood with his teeth and draw it up over the side of her face. His lips faintly caught hers after he finished, and the slight touch sent a shock coursing through him to grab at his manhood.

She seemed not to notice, but he was wrong. A strong tingle scampered over her and settled between her legs.

"Food and drink, my bedchambers," Bhric called out to Marta after entering the Great Hall and not stopping.

He deposited his wife gently on her feet once in his bedchamber and he barely had her cloak off when Marta entered with servants carrying a tray of food and drink.

"I will not be disturbed tonight, Marta," Bhric ordered.

"Aye, my lord," Marta said and hurried the servants out.

Tavia was surprised by her hunger but then she had no time to think on it. Her only thought had been on making sure Lath's leg could be saved.

Bhric poured her wine only to refill it, she drank it so fast.

"I would tell you how things went, but I am too tired," she said in between bites of food. "If you have questions for me, I would appreciate it if they could wait until morning, and I will gladly answer them then."

Bhric could see she would not last long, her eyes too heavy with sleep. "You need say nothing tonight. We will talk tomorrow."

Tavia was grateful and continued to eat until she looked to the bed. She took a few more mouthfuls and that was it. Exhaustion had taken hold as well as relief that all had gone well and, God willing, Lath would survive along with his leg. Right now, all she wanted was to sleep.

Tavia went to stand and found her strength had completely waned. Her husband was at her side before she could reach out to him for help.

"You need to sleep," he said and warned himself to leave her to undress on her own, not strip her completely naked or himself for that matter. He did not heed his warning. He stripped off his garments then hers, without protest from her. Then he scooped her up, enjoying the feel of her soft skin against his, the way her full breasts tucked firm against his chest and the way her round bottom warmed against his arm.

Bloody hell if he did not find his naked wife appealing.

He placed her in bed, slipping in beside her, intending to take her in his arms, aching to press the length of her against him. He was surprised and pleased that she turned and buried herself tight against him as if she could not get close enough. She settled comfortably when his arm went around her to hold her snug there. And the next moment, her breathing fell into a steady rhythm… she was asleep.

He feared sleep would not come to him tonight, an overpowering desire to couple with his wife jabbing at him endlessly, and his shaft swelling considerably to prove it.

If he were not careful, he would give his wife a good poke before he discovered any lies she may have told him. And what of Greta's words and tears? Did she warn him away from Tavia or had she discovered something that would prove Tavia a good wife?

He had a lot to learn about his wife and he intended to start tomorrow.

Chapter Eleven

Bhric woke with a smile, his hand roaming over a soft backside and giving it a tender squeeze. He turned slightly, just enough for the leg draped over his to slip between his two and settle against his aroused shaft. He tried to recall what woman he had taken to his bed last night before opening his eyes, so her name could spill from his lips before he kissed her.

Tavia... his wife!

His eyes sprang open to see her lovely, sleepy face warm with a smile. He did not hesitate, he jumped out of bed and rushed to don his garments.

"I will see you downstairs for the morning meal," he said, running his fingers through his hair after he finished dressing and racing out of the room once his boots were on.

Tavia sat up staring at the closed door that trembled, her husband had closed it so hard and fast. Why did he rush away from her? He had shown no objection when she had cuddled against him last night looking for warmth. Yet this morning he seemed to evade her closeness. She smiled, believing she understood. He desired her more than he cared to admit. Or cared to allow himself to, preventing him from doing what he desired when he had sworn not to touch her until he knew if she carried another man's child?

That thought grew her a soft smile. He had seen to

her care last night after she had tended Lath, seeing that she ate then rested… in his bed.

What had made him keep her in his bed when she could have easily slept in her own?

She would have liked to linger in thought on it, but she shook her head. She had no time to waste. She needed to see how Lath was doing. She hoped her effort and his suffering had not been in vain and that he was doing well.

Tavia grabbed her garments and hurried to her bedchamber to give her long, dark hair a good combing after scenting it with dried mint, then plaited it into a single braid before she scooped up a handful of chilled water from a bucket to clean the sleep from her face. The splash of cold water served her well, brightening her skin and mind. A quick donning of her garments and boots, rather than her shoes since she would be outside, and a snatch of her cloak off the wall peg, and she rushed out the door.

Her husband was engaged in a conversation with Sven, and Ingrid was busy talking with Marta. With everyone occupied, Tavia draped her cloak over her shoulders and headed to the door.

"TAVIA!"

Her husband's powerful voice felt as if it shook the rafters in the Great Hall and it brought her to an abrupt stop.

She turned, knowing why he stopped her. "I go to see how Lath does."

"You will eat first, then I will go with you to see him," Bhric said.

She shook her head. "It cannot wait that long."

"Aye, it can, and it will," he commanded.

Her feet took flight as she called out without giving it any thought, "I think not."

Bhric stood staring as his wife fled the room without glancing back at him.

"She has more courage than you thought," Sven said with a laugh and heard his wife chuckle as well.

Several Norse oaths flew from Bhric's mouth as he swiped his fur cloak off the bench and chased after his wife.

Snow had fallen during the night leaving several inches on the ground which caused Tavia to be more cautious with her gait. She heard her husband shout her name and while she could pretend not to hear him, she did not think it wise. She stopped and turned.

She did not wait until he was upon her, she kept her voice strong for him to hear as he approached. "If I wait to see how Lath does until after the meal, I may have no stomach to eat. A quick visit and I will be done."

Bhric stopped directly in front of her. "Continue to disobey me and we will have a problem."

"A problem that can be solved easily enough," she said with a sweet smile.

"And how is that?"

"Stop expecting me to obey your every word." Did that just come out of her mouth? What was she thinking? Again, she spoke. "I but speak the truth, my lord. There are times I fear I will disobey you, fail to agree with you, and follow what I feel is the right thing to do. I am not a foolish woman, and I am not prone to foolish ways. A brief visit with an injured man I stitched should not require your permission, unless circumstances warrant it."

There she was making sense again which of course annoyed Bhric.

"Permission is mine to determine and notifying me of your intentions is your wifely duty," he reprimanded.

Tavia winced. "You are right. I should not have left without speaking with you. There is no excuse for such rudeness, and I am sorry."

Her quick and sincere apology caught him off guard. He thought she might argue, but he was beginning to see that his wife had no difficulty in accepting her wrongdoing and apologizing for it. Something he never did.

"I will go with you to see Lath, then we will share the morning meal," Bhric said and took hold of her hand.

His large hand engulfed her small one. His grip was strong and determined, letting her know he would not let her go until he chose to. It was a possessive hold as well as a protective one, but then he was her husband, and she should expect no less. What she could not grasp was why her body seemed to flutter all over as if in anticipation.

"With no word from Hertha or Hume, I would assume Lath does well," Bhric said.

She was relieved he disrupted her thoughts, concerned where they may have taken her. "True, but I would like to see for myself how the wound does."

"Your leg gives you no trouble?" he asked, her limp not as pronounced as he had expected.

There was no point in evading the truth. She had a

limp, and it was not going away. "As long as I pay my leg heed, it gives me little difficulty, though the winter's cold can trouble it if I am not careful."

He wanted to know more about the accident that caused her limp but not now. There was time enough for that. He also decided there was no point in making constant reference to it. He could remind her to pay her leg heed at given times, but no more. If she was not prone to foolishness as she claimed, then she would be wise to tend her limp properly.

Seeing Greta speaking with Hertha outside the cottage was not unexpected. Whether she prayed for Lath to live, or die was another matter since Tavia was not sure if the woman would take offense if proven wrong and Lath survived. But if she were a true healer it would not trouble her. She would want Lath to live.

Greta nodded to Tavia as she and Bhric drew close. "Lath does well."

"Surprisingly, he had a most restful night and bears the healing pain well," Hertha said.

Tavia felt hopeful with the news. "I am so pleased to hear that."

"He asks for you," Hertha said. "He says he owes you much."

"You both are the healers," Tavia said, including Greta to the older woman's surprise. "You do far more for him than I did."

"Your skilled hand saved him," Greta said. "The stitched wound is tender and red but looks to be healing well."

"More good news," Tavia said, relieved that so far things were going well for Lath. "I will take but a moment to speak with him, then let him continue to rest."

"I will wait here," Bhric said, releasing her hand slowly.

As soon as Tavia entered the cottage, Bhric waved Hertha away and spoke in a whisper to Greta. "What did you mean yesterday when you said there is more to my wife than I know?"

"That, my lord," Greta said, leaning on her staff as she turned, "is for you to find out."

Bhric wanted to command her to tell him but knew it would do little good. Greta was a respected and wise healer and not one to take to commands, and he would not disrespect her position in the tribe. Hertha, however, was under his command. He turned to her.

"I gave my word, my lord," Hertha said, knowing what he would ask having heard snippets of his and Greta's conversation. "Besides, it is best Lady Tavia tells you herself… in her own time."

***

Hume nodded when Tavia entered the cottage. "My lady."

"She is here?" Lath called out anxiously from the bed.

"I am, Lath," Tavia said and went to him.

Lath reached out his hand. "I owe you far more than I can ever repay you."

Tavia took hold of his hand. "Nonsense. I did nothing more than help family."

Lath smiled. "Aye, you are family now, part of the

Clan MacShane and we are lucky and grateful to have you."

He winced as he spoke, bearing the pain as best as he could, though with help from one of Hume's mixtures. Tavia knew such pain, but unfortunately there had been no mixture to help ease it.

"Healing will take time, the pain easing more and more each day," she said, the memory of her own healing still fresh in her mind.

"If the young, brave lass in your tale was able to do it when her leg wound was far worse than mine, then so can I," Lath whispered, keeping true to his word that he would not utter a word of what he had heard.

"I am confident you will," Tavia said. "Now I leave you to rest. It is the best thing for you and will help you heal fast."

"Then rest I shall," Lath assured her.

"I will visit again," Tavia said.

Lath sent her a weak smile. "I appreciate that, my lady."

"You saved him and his leg," Hume whispered, walking with her to the door.

"I gave him a chance. He does the rest," Tavia said and greeted her husband with a smile after leaving the cottage. "Now I am hungry."

Bhric found himself smiling as well. "As am I."

Their hands joined. Bhric was not sure who had reached out first or if they both had reached out together. But it mattered little since he found himself eager to hold her hand again, to connect with her, to feel her small hand disappear into his large one, to feel close to her.

Close.

Why suddenly did he wish to be close to her? Granted he wanted to learn about her, see what he may have failed to see in her, but close? Exactly how close did he wish to be with her?

Several barks and a squeal of delight had them turning their heads to see Uta running around playfully with Bones, the large hound.

Bhric shook his head. "That hound is ruined."

"They make a happy pair," Tavia said with a brief chuckle.

"He is a war hound, bred for battle, bred to kill," Bhric argued.

Tavia fought back the laughter that wished to erupt, seeing what fun the pair were having together. "Maybe one time, but no more, perhaps he never was. Perhaps Uta freed him."

Harald approached them shaking his head. "I do not know what it is, my lord. It is as if a spell has been cast on the hound. He wants nothing more than to be with Uta."

"Whatever it is do not let it spread to the other hounds," Bhric ordered.

"Aye, my lord. Bones no longer resides with the other hounds," Harald said.

"Where does he reside?" Bhric asked.

Harald cringed fearful to speak.

"Never mind I do not want to know," Bhric said, shaking his head.

Harald looked relieved and hurried off, Uta and Bones trailing after him, laughing and barking in play.

They barely took a few steps when Wilona

approached them.

"My lady," Wilona said with a respectful nod. "My sister is most grateful that you saved her son's leg. She makes food now for him and Hertha and Hume in appreciation and she has begun stitching garments to gift your first born."

"That is generous of her. Please tell her I am most grateful," Tavia said, wondering what everyone would think when she failed to get with child as soon as everyone believed she would.

Bhric still wondered if a woman as petite as Tavia could carry and deliver a bairn safely. Or would she be like her mum and die in childbirth? The thought unexpectedly sent an ache to his heart. He would not want to lose her, yet he feared it could be her fate.

"I go to visit Lath. Again, thank you, my lady," Wilona said and left them to continue walking.

They walked in silence both lost in thoughts until a Northman warrior approached them.

"An old couple seek rest and shelter here, the husband is not well," the warrior said.

"How ill is the man?" Bhric asked.

"He can barely stand," the warrior said.

"He needs help," Tavia said. "We must offer them shelter and food so he may heal."

"Sickness can spread if not careful," Bhric warned.

"They can be isolated in a cottage," Tavia said.

"They can shelter with the animals," Bhric ordered.

Tavia gasped. "It is cold. The man needs heat. You cannot be so cruel."

"I know not what ails him and I will not have him spread anything to my people," Bhric said and shook his head wondering why he was explaining himself to his wife.

"I can speak with him and see if he poses any risk to the clan," Tavia said.

"You will do no such thing," Bhric said.

Tavia had no intentions of giving up. "At least give the couple a chance to speak with you and judge for yourself if they should stay or go."

"And I suppose you wish to be with me when I do this," Bhric said, having every intention of taking her with him and seeing what she thought of the couple.

A smile lit her face. "I would love to accompany you, my lord. Thank you for including me."

His wife had a quicker mind than he first thought. He had focused only on her limp when meeting her, nothing else, though her lies had not set well with him. But why had she lied? Did he look for excuses to dismiss them? How could trust be born of lies?

"Something troubles you," Tavia said a sudden scowl marring her husband's fine features.

"We will talk of it another time," he said, after he had learned more about her.

They walked to the edge of the village.

Bhric went to inquire about her leg and stopped himself. As she had said herself, if she paid her leg heed she had no trouble. He would leave it to her, for now.

The old man sat on the snow-covered ground and his wife stood beside him, her frail hand on his shoulder. Both were thin and appeared weak, the man more so than the woman. Their garments were worn, their cloaks threadbare offering little protection against the cold. Their aged faces betrayed the harshness of their life and Tavia's heart ached for them.

"A few days of food and shelter is all we ask, my lord," the woman said, a tremble to her voice.

"How ill is your husband?' Bhric demanded.

"He is weak from barely having food to eat and trying to do work better left to the young to keep us from starving," the woman said, the tremble in her voice extending to the hand on her husband's shoulder.

"A day of rest, my lord, and I can work for our shelter and food," the man said, raising his head slowly.

Tavia turned to her husband and kept her voice low. "We must help them. They are too weak to continue walking and they have nothing to protect them against the cold."

His wife had a caring heart and he a skeptical one, but he would not turn the aged couple away. He turned to his warrior. "Take them to Bowen's cottage, he needs it no longer, having moved in with the widow Olga. See a fire is set for them and food brought to them."

The old woman looked about ready to collapse with relief.

"Bless you, my lord. Bless you," she said, her eyes tearing.

"We are grateful," the old man said.

The Northman warrior offered his support to help the old man walk after a nod from Bhric.

"That was generous," Tavia said.

Bhric said nothing, as he continued walking with his wife. He had not offered the couple shelter out of generosity. He had done so because he wondered what brought them here. Why had an old couple shown up in the dead of winter at his home at this particular time? Instinct had him cautious and he would see if he was right in paying it heed.

Chapter Twelve

Bhric found sleep difficult. He rolled back and forth on the bed not able to find a comfortable position, the blankets twisting around him and causing his annoyance to flair. He could not get his wife off his mind, having spent a pleasant day with her. They had not lacked for conversation. He had found himself telling her of his plans to extend the planting fields in the spring and add a longhouse for his warriors where they could gather.

He played the conversation again in his head.

"My warriors would appreciate a longhouse where they can gather to talk and drink."

"And the MacShane warriors? Where will they gather to talk and drink?" Tavia asked, a crinkle to her brow. "A laird usually entertains his warriors in the Great Hall. Is that where you will meet with them, separately from your Northmen warriors? How well will it serve you to keep a divide between them?"

"My tribe have their ways as do the clan warriors, but they are one."

"How can they be when you divide them?" she asked.

"They will grow together soon enough," he argued.

"How can they when you have yet to fully embrace the MacShane part of your heritage?"

He grabbed the pillow beneath his head, gave it a

punch as he turned on his side, and slammed it down on the bed before dropping his head on it. That her question had been a curious one and held not a trace of blame in it annoyed him all the more. Mostly, because it reminded him of his promise to his grandfather.

"The Clan MacShane is a strong clan that has always been led by powerful men. Do it proud, Bhric, and guide with pride, wisdom, and strength so that all those who came before you and fought and sacrificed did not do so in vain. And make sure your son understands that so he may carry on the name and tradition of the great Clan MacShane. Promise me this, Bhric."

"Aye, Grandfather, I give you my word."

His grandfather had died peacefully later that night. Could his wife be right? Was he not doing enough to unite his tribe and clansmen? Had he been more devoted to one than the other?

A rapid knock on the door had his troubled thoughts fleeing.

"It is me, Sven. There is a problem."

Bhric hurried out of bed and with no thought to his nakedness opened the door.

"Fen is loose," Sven said. "It is a good thing it is deep at night, and no one is about."

"What does Harald say?" Bhric asked, turning to hurry and don his garments.

"He does not understand how he got loose. No one dares approach the hound, he is far too vicious. The other hounds do not even go near him, at least not since the last battle. It is almost as if he lost his soul in that battle. All in the tribe know not to approach him."

"Not so those in the clan," Bhric said, and it made him see the truth to his wife's words that there was a divide between the tribe and the clan. "You are notifying people to remain inside until otherwise told?"

Sven nodded. "I have two warriors going cottage to cottage."

"I will go tell my wife she is not to leave the keep, then join you in the Great Hall."

Sven nodded and left.

Bhric eased the door open to his wife's bedchamber not wanting to startle her. A chill greeted him, her fire nothing but embers. He went and added logs, the dry wood catching fast. He stood, hating to wake her but intent on seeing her kept safe.

His eyes shot wide when he saw the bed was empty. He hurried a glance around the room and his heart slammed in his chest when her cloak was nowhere to be seen. He raced from the room and down the stairs taking them three at a time.

"My wife is not in her room and her cloak is gone," Bhric said as he burst into the Great Hall.

Sven's mouth fell open, though no words fell out.

"There's only one place she can be," Bhric said.

"The wounded clansman," Sven said and rushed after Bhric already headed to the door.

***

Tavia stepped out of the cottage and raised her chin, the sting of the cold air feeling good on her heated face. She had woken with worry about Lath and knowing she would never get any sleep if she did not go see for herself that he was all right, she had dressed and left her bedchamber. She was glad she had. A fever had set in, and slight as it was, it was still a worry. She had helped Hertha bathe Lath's head while Hume mixed a concoction of elderflowers and thyme to keep the fever from turning worse.

For comfort's sake, Tavia had placed a wet cloth that had also been soaked in snow on Lath's heated brow. It calmed him instantly and eased his restlessness. The wound looked no better or worse than it had earlier so that was a relief. Good care and lots of prayers were the only things they could do for Lath. The rest was up to fate. At least now he was resting comfortably and Tavia was ready to seek her bed and sleep. She was feeling guilty for sneaking out of the keep without telling her husband. She had not wanted to wake him, though the truth of it was that she feared he would forbid her to leave the keep at such an hour.

The village had been silent, not a soul stirred as she had walked the empty paths, and she hoped it would be the same on her return. Of course, she told herself she should confess the truth to her husband, but she warned herself it might not be a good idea. She would have time to think about it on her walk back to the keep.

She heard the low growl after taking only a few short steps away from the cottage.

She turned toward the wooded area running behind the cottages. "Is that you, Bones?"

The growl came again and Tavia spotted two glowing eyes in the woods. She approached slowly, fearing Bones may have gotten hurt hunting an animal at night.

With a calm and soft voice, she asked, "Are you hurt, Bones?"

She thought she caught a whimper precede the growl that had lost some of its strength. Without any thought to danger, she kept walking and entered the woods. She saw too late it was not Bones. This hound was similar to Bones, but larger. He bared his teeth in a snarl, appearing ready to strike.

Fleeing was not an option, since the hound would certainly catch her. But she reasoned if he wished her harm he would have already attacked her. She let instinct rule and plopped down on the ground.

"I am here to help," she said and laid her hand out beside her. "I mean you no harm."

She sat there waiting, her bottom growing cold from the snow on the ground. The hound kept his glowing eyes on her and gradually his growl lessened, and he took cautious steps toward her. He stopped near her hand, hesitated, then slowly extended his snout out to sniff at it. He then stepped closer and sniffed her arm.

Tavia remained as she was, not moving, not wanting to startle or frighten the large animal. Though, when he brought his snout to sniff at her face, her stomach churned, and she lost a bit of her bravery. Some of it returned when he laid down and stretched out on his side in front of her.

"Something pains you," she said, seeing the hurt in his eyes.

He whimpered as if he understood her.

She raised her hand slowly. "I need to touch you to see what is amiss. I will do my best not to hurt you."

She assumed he had presented his injured side to her and began to examine him with the lightest of touches. It was not until she reached his neck that she felt it and he let loose with a slight growl.

"I am sorry. I did not mean to hurt you," she said softly. It would be difficult with only a fraction of light from the partial moon to see the wound clearly, but she had no choice. He trusted her at the moment, and no one was around to warn her away or worse harm the hound for being too close to her. She would have to do her best with what little light there was and rely on instinct and touch to help him.

She probed the area gently and realized that something had embedded itself in the hound's neck, a portion of it sticking out, and the skin had healed around it. Whatever it was, it was causing him pain and had to be removed. From what she could see and feel of it, it seemed a shard of sorts perhaps part of an arrowhead or some weapon that had struck him and broken off. With lack of care for the wound, the object had embedded itself in him and was causing him pain.

Tavia was glad she had wisely stuck a knife in her boot, a last-minute thought before leaving her bedchamber. It was one her da advised her to carry, and she rarely did except tonight. Perhaps it was being in a place that was still foreign to her and not fully knowing many people that had her grabbing the weapon. Whatever it had been, she was glad she had it.

"This is going to hurt," she cautioned, stroking the hound gently.

Again, he whimpered as if he understood.

Her heart went out to him, and she spoke softly to

him as she worked to strip away the crust around the shard as gently as she could.

"You are a brave one and so courageous to seek help," she said, and his whimper continued as she continued to talk. Finally with the crusted scab cleaned away, she gave him a tender pat. "Again, this is going to hurt, and I am sorry for causing you pain."

She gathered a mound of snow beside her, ripped a strip of cloth off the hem of her garment, and prayed that all would go well.

"All set," she whispered and laid one hand on his head as her other hand took hold of the edge of the shard protruding from the wound. She hoped it would be quick and was not embedded too deeply in his neck where she would have to dig to get it out. She doubted the hound would tolerate that.

She took a deep breath and gave it a little yank to see if it was going to be difficult to extract. The hound whimpered and she soothed him with encouraging words and hoped one good yank would free it. She was relieved that it did. She immediately worried about excessive bleeding but first she cleaned around the wound with some of the snow, then worried it might bleed too much, she folded the strip of cloth and placed it on the wound, then she ripped another strip from her garment and wrapped it around the hound's neck, splitting the cloth near the end to tie a knot and keep it in place.

Tavia took a needed deep breath before she cleansed her hands with snow and began to gently stroke the hound's side, talking soothingly to him once again.

"I will have to keep a watch on you to make sure the wound heals properly and that you rest."

How she would accomplish that she did not know. Her husband would be sure to object since no doubt the hound was one of his war hounds and he would not want her near the animal. But surely he would not object to her checking on him to make sure he healed, would he?

She devised a plan while continuing to stroke the hound who had dozed off to sleep. She would take him to Harald and tell him what happened and explain that she would check on the hound each day to make sure he was healing well. Surely, her husband would see the wisdom in that.

***

Bhric knew little fear. He never took it into battle with him, rage was his companion there. He had no use for fear and yet it struck him now not knowing where his wife was while his most vicious hound was on the loose.

"Maybe she can command Fen as she did Bones," Sven said.

Bhric turned such a ferocious glare on Sven that he took a hasty step back and hurried to say, "I did not mean it humorously. She commanded Bones easily enough perhaps she can do the same with Fen."

"He snarls and growls at anyone who goes near him, and you think my wee wife can command him?"

"Not if he lost his soul, and if he did, he needs to be put down," Sven said.

"I will tear him to pieces if he has hurt Tavia," Bhric said with a snarl of his own. "We go into the woods."

Sven stood staring past Bhric and fearing what had turned his friend wide-eyed and speechless, he swerved around, his own shock freezing him.

His wife stood at the edge of the woods her undergarment torn at the hem, blood coating her tunic and some on her hands while Fen walked calmly beside her, a bandage around his furry neck.

Tavia hurried to speak before her husband could issue a command. "He came looking for help. A shard was embedded in his neck, no doubt from a weapon of some kind. His flesh had closed around it leaving him in pain. I removed it, but he will need to rest and heal. I was going to take him to Harald."

"Step away from him," Bhric demanded.

Tavia did as he said but the hound followed her, keeping at her side. "Please let me take him to Harald and see that he rests. I helped him. He will not harm me." She was surprised by her husband's quick and agreeable response.

"We will follow you," Bhric said, seeing the hound remained calm beside his wife and wanting to get him in a pen safely away from her and others.

Bhric went to approach his wife and the hound growled, stepping protectively in front of Tavia.

Tavia hurried a soothing touch to the hound's head. "Lord Bhric means me no harm."

"She commands him with her magic touch," Sven whispered.

"His name?" Tavia asked, her hand remaining on

the hound.

"Fen," Bhric said, and the hound's eyes went to him.

"Fen, it is time to go home," Tavia said, and the hound kept to her side as they walked.

Warriors stopped and stared when they saw their leader's petite wife walking with the large hound close at her side, and whispers started.

"Pay no one mind, Fen," Tavia said softly. "They know not the power of a gentle touch."

Sven stepped close to Bhric as they followed a distance behind Tavia and Fen, and whispered jokingly, "I would be careful of her touch, or she will be commanding you."

Bhric's anger flared in his eyes when he turned to look at his friend, and Sven grinned.

"If the hound was suffering with pain it is no wonder he had turned vicious," Sven said. "He will be a good war dog again, once healed."

Bhric held his tongue. He did not think the hound would go into battle again, not with the memory of lingering pain caused by the last one. And now that he knew a loving and caring touch, he would not want to surrender it.

He certainly would not. He would want to feel it again and again, and he would never want to be far from it. He would want to keep it as close as possible, never let it go, cherish it.

"Go see that Harald is ready for our arrival," Bhric ordered Sven and he took off. He raised his voice enough for his wife to hear him. "Fen stays with Harald."

"As you say, my lord," Tavia said.

Why did he have his doubts?

Harald waited with shackle and chain, and Bhric mumbled an oath beneath his breath when he saw it, knowing his wife's reaction when she spotted it.

"You will not chain him," Tavia called out when she saw the chain. "His neck wound will not heal shackled. He needs rest and care."

"He is a hound," Harald said as if that explained it.

"An injured hound who trusted no one or believed no one cared enough to tend him," Tavia said.

"Hounds do not think that way," Harald said.

"You think you send only foolish hounds into battle?" Tavia argued.

"Obedient ones," Bhric said to Harald's relief.

"So, you have no loyal dogs only obedient ones?" Tavia asked.

"Obedient or loyal, there is no difference," Bhric argued.

"There is a tremendous difference," she corrected.

Anger tinged Bhric's command. "You will not argue with me, wife. Leave the animal now."

A low, warning growl came from Fen.

"Not to worry, Fen," Tavia said calmly, petting the hound's head. "Lord Bhric may sound brutish, but he has a good heart."

Bhric motioned to Harald and the man stepped forward with the chains once again.

Tavia stepped in front of Fen. "I told you his neck wound will not heal if he is chained."

"He cannot be trusted," Bhric cautioned.

"He was surly because he was in constant pain. He

will do well now that his pain is gone," she said.

"Until I am sure of that he stays confined," Bhric ordered.

"Aye, confined will do," Tavia said.

Bhric was relieved that his wife finally saw reason and was surprised that her face had lighted with a smile. His relief did not last long.

"Come, Fen, you can stay with me while you heal. It will make it easier for me to look after you."

"Nay! Nay!" Bhric shouted as his wife went to take a step and, of course, Fen growled. "The animal will not stay with you. He will be kept in one of the empty storage sheds."

Tavia gasped. "A cold, dark place will not help him heal."

"It's that or the chains," Bhric said.

Tavia's chin went up. "Then I stay with him."

Bhric laughed. "Not likely. And do not think to tell me I cannot stop you since we both know I can stop you easily enough."

She knew her threat was foolish as soon as she had issued it, but what recourse did she have? Her husband's word ruled, and she had no choice but to obey.

Tavia spoke out of frustration. "I was mistaken, Fen. Lord Bhric does not have a good heart. He actually seems to have no heart at all."

Though her remark stung, he did not let it show, saying, "You finally understand me."

"Aye, unfortunately and with much regret," she said.

Again, her words stung and again he refused to let

it show, especially with Sven and Harald there. "As long as you obey it matters not."

"As you say, my lord," Tavia said and turned her head away from him to look to Harald. "Show me where he will rest so I may continue to tend his wound."

Harald glanced to Bhric, and he nodded his consent.

Tavia's annoyance grew as she settled Fen in the chilled, damp shed. He would not heal well here, and she made a decision there and then.

She crouched down by Fen in the guise of checking the bandage and whispered, "I will return when everyone sleeps to get you."

The dog licked her face as if he understood.

"It is time for the morning meal," Bhric said and offered his arm to her when she stepped out of the shed.

"I am tired and need sleep. I will eat later," she said, barely glancing at him as she walked past him.

Bhric let her go, knowing his order had greatly upset her.

"She is angry at you," Sven said, joining Bhric as she walked away.

"She will learn my word rules here."

"I would not wager on that," Sven said with a laugh. "She may be a wee one, but Ingrid believes she has strength to her. Not that she had thought that on first meeting her, but of late, your wife has demonstrated a courage one would never expect of one her wee size. She may turn out to be more than you can handle."

Bhric grinned. "There is not a woman I haven't

been able to handle. Her size alone makes it easy."

"Again, I would not wager on that," Sven said though this time he did not laugh.

Chapter Thirteen

"Five nights you say?" Bhric asked, finding what Sven just told him difficult to believe.

"Aye," Sven said with a nod. "When the night sentinels reported it to me, I thought your wife did it out of frustration and anger and the one night would end it. But last night has been the fifth night that the village sentinels reported that Lady Tavia walked through the village late when all were asleep and took Fen out of the shed and returned to the keep with him. Then just before dawn, before anyone stirs, she returns him to the shed where she visits him at least three times a day, bringing him food. I waited to tell you because Ingrid told me to leave it be that Tavia's anger would settle, and she would forget Fen. But it is obvious your wife is as stubborn as she is courageous, and she does not plan to stop her nightly abduction of Fen."

"You mean foolish," Bhric corrected. "I will see to it… tomorrow morning."

He glanced at his wife, sitting at the dais alone. Ingrid was off talking to some women and he, himself, was taking a turn around the tables to speak with his men and the MacShane warriors who gathered at one table together.

That his wife had been able to hide her nightly deed from him annoyed him. He had thought they had been getting along well starting the day after he ordered

Fen kept in a shed. That day she had ignored him completely, the next he had made sure she had taken the morning meal with him, and he had spent a portion of the day with her. She had been congenial and talkative on the days to follow. But thinking on it now, what had he learned about her? Nothing. She had kept him talking more about himself with only a spattering of talk about her. Why hadn't he noticed?

She may be more than you can handle.

Sven's warning echoed in his head, and he was not laughing.

***

Tavia smiled when Fen licked her face. The hound was far more intelligent than anyone knew. It had taken only two days for him to realize that he had to return to the shed before sunrise. She had gotten little sleep the first two days, fearful of Fen being caught in her bedchamber. By the third day she had slipped into a deep sleep and Fen had woken her with generous licks to her face, sensing sunrise was drawing near.

Fen's wound was healing well from the warm nights before the hearth in her bedchamber and the loving care she was giving him. She had grown attached to the large dog as he had to her, probably because they both felt alone with no loving touch to soothe them and with no one who cared deeply for them.

"I wish you were free to stay with me all day. I believe I would feel less alone," she said, giving him a good rub behind his ears, something he favored.

She got out of bed and began to dress while Fen sat

by the hearth getting his last bit of heat before spending another day in the chilly shed. Her husband had purposely sought her out the last few days and she had wondered why. She had taken advantage of that time to learn more about him and thought perhaps he had meant to do the same and learn about her. She had been surprised how easy it had been to speak with him, but then she had asked him about himself, and she had learned that if you got a person talking about himself you need not worry about holding a conversation, talk flowed smoothly.

She had to admit though that she had enjoyed the time spent with him. She smiled. "I like the feel of his large hand wrapped around mine, Fen. It not only feels good, but it also makes me feel… her cheeks heated thinking of the sensations that had poked at her when her husband held her hand or slipped his arm around her or lifted her with ease, and she shook her head.

"You know, Fen, after talking to Lord Bhric, I do believe he does have a good heart. He simply makes unwise decisions sometimes, but to him, they are necessary decisions. Once we show him that there is no reason to fear you, then all should be good, and we can spend more time together. At least, I hope so. Now remember, quiet does it," Tavia said and pressed her finger to her lips as they approached the door. She had made the gesture each morning to remind him they had to remain silent so no one would discover them.

But this morning Fen backed away from the door and gave a low, steady growl.

Someone was on the other side, and she did not need to guess who it was.

"Sit and stay, Fen," she ordered, and the hound obeyed, though a growl rumbled in his throat.

Tavia opened the door and smiled at her husband standing there, his arms crossed over his broad chest. "Good morning, husband. You are up early."

"As are you, wife," he said.

"I have been caught. Haven't I?" Tavia said, finding no point in denying it.

"You have," Bhric confirmed.

"Please do not punish Fen for my disobedience. He simply did as I directed," Tavia said, fearful the hound would suffer for her defiance. "Though I must say his wound is healing well from the warm nights in front of the hearth."

"I hear Lath is healing nicely as well," Bhric said, not surprised his wife would continue to protect the hound.

Tavia's face lit with a smile, thinking how well Lath was doing and she shared his progress. "Aye, he does do well. His fever has not returned, the stitches heal, though pain still lingers but has subsided."

"Why, Tavia?"

She understood what he asked. Why did she disobey him? She stepped aside so he could enter. Fen did not look at all happy to see him.

"Go rest by the hearth, Fen," she said softly, and he obeyed without hesitation.

The room was warm and the scent of her strong, a scent he had become all too familiar with after spending time with her. It was a scent that enticed his nostrils and tempted his manhood. And he had been questioning the wisdom of waiting to bed her. Thankfully, he wisely remained committed to waiting, or was it foolishness that kept him waiting?

Bhric kept his arms crossed over his chest and his feet planted a bit apart, his imposing stance meant to intimidate as he waited for her to respond. Her soft smile and soft voice made him think she was anything but intimidated.

"Truthfully, I'm not sure," she said. "Maybe I felt as he did… helpless and unloved." She shook her head. "I know you think hounds are creatures who are meant to obey and nothing more… much like what you expect in a wife. I suppose I feel a kindred spirit with him."

"You are not a hound. I treat you well and I see that no harm comes to you, nor will I ever harm you," he said, not wanting her to live as his wife in fear.

"But you will never love me let alone care for me and without at least one, I believe the heart withers and dies, so forgive me if what you offer me is not enough."

"I care for you. You are my wife," he said without thinking about it. So, did he care for her?

"You care for me because I am your wife, but you do not care for ME," —Tavia planted her hand against her chest— "the person I am. But how could you when you do not truly know me."

"You talk in riddles, woman," he snapped, annoyed. "You are my wife and I care for you, and I will see you kept safe since you have a habit of making foolish decisions."

"Aye," she said and smiled. "I wed you."

Her playful, teasing retort had him smiling. "A lucky day for you for sure."

"That can be debated," she argued still smiling.

His eyes roamed over her. How had she become so appealing to him when she challenged him at almost every turn? Or was that it? Did he like the unexpected challenges? Or her unpredictable nature when he had thought her so docile? She was a bit of a mystery, soft and obedient at times and difficult and stubborn at other times.

But weren't they common traits among most women? And were they the reason why women could be mysterious creatures? His thought almost had him laughing, but he contained it.

"Have you always had a way with animals?" he asked.

"I never gave it thought, but it is not so much a way as it is kindness." She stepped close to her husband and rested her hand on his folded arms. "Please give me and Fen a chance. You waste his intelligence on being a war hound when he is so much more."

"You took a dangerous chance with him. He has tasted blood. It is in him now to kill."

"Perhaps he has grown tired of it, especially after suffering in pain for so long. Perhaps the taste of blood no longer appeals to him," she said, casting a gentle glance at the hound resting comfortably by the fire, though his eyes remained on Bhric.

"If you have succeeded in spoiling him, letting him sleep in the keep, he may be good for nothing now."

Tavia gave his arm a light squeeze. "He would be a good hound for you, obedient and more importantly loyal… if you but give him a chance."

"I have all the loyalty I need," Bhric said and wondered if she also asked for a chance for herself as well.

She shook her head. "Not like the loyalty Fen would give you. He is healing nicely. Let him spend the day with us, so you can see for yourself."

That she thought to spend the day with him without any nudging from him caught his attention more than the hound spending time with him. Did she wish to spend the day with him, or did she feel he expected her to?

"You have no other plans?" he asked to see what she would say.

"Besides seeing how Lath does, I planned to see how the old couple, Glenna and William, who still linger here, are doing. They are not capable of travel. I believe it would be wise of them to remain here for the winter or perhaps seek a home with the clan."

"Will you have them obeying you as you do the hounds?" Bhric asked and immediately regretted his words when she was taken aback, though it was too late to recall them. He was annoyed that she so easily trusted people and hounds. One day it could prove dangerous.

"Friendship is all I have to offer people and hounds," Tavia said, her hand slipping off his arm.

He grew more annoyed that she moved her hand off him. He favored her touch, simple as it was. Though, he wondered far too often how more of an intimate touch of hers would feel.

"We will see how Fen does with us today," he said, thinking Fen would prove himself one way or another and seal his fate.

The Great Hall was empty. It would be an hour or

more before anyone would stir.

“Fen needs to go out and I would like to see how Lath does before breakfast,” Tavia said.

Bhric grabbed a fur-lined cloak from the few kept by the door and draped it over her shoulders, then grabbed his that hung there. They stepped outside to see a ray of light peek on the horizon, dawn ready to break. Cold air stung their cheeks and before Bhric could take his wife’s hand to help her down the steps, fearful they could be icy and her limp would cause her to slip, Fen took a stance on the step below the one she was on so that she had no choice but to maneuver the steps slowly.

Perhaps the hound would prove useful to his wife, a thought he had not considered but he intended to consider now.

Bhric took her arm, to assist her and Fen moved away to drift off and see to his duties. He noticed the hound’s eyes never left Tavia. He kept a good watch over her.

“You can feel the snow that will fall,” Tavia said, keeping hold of her husband’s arm not that she needed his help to walk. She liked his warmth and the strength of his arm and wished more from their marriage. She would even take friendship, since at the moment she did not feel they shared even that.

“Aye, we will have snow sometime today,” he said and thought how pleasant it would be to pass the snowy day in bed with his wife.

The unexpected thought startled him. What was the matter with him thinking that way? It would get him into trouble and yet the thought lingered.

Fen suddenly stepped in front of them, preventing them from taking another step. Bhric immediately stepped in front of Tavia, shielding her with his big body as he shouted out, "WHO GOES THERE?"

"It is Glenna, my lord," the old woman said as she drifted out of the receding darkness.

"What has you about so early?" Bhric demanded.

Glenna lowered her head when she stopped not far from them. "My husband is feverish, and I sought Hertha's help." She held up a pouch. "She gave me this. My apologies that we linger here, but William is far too ill to travel."

"Stay as long as necessary," Tavia said.

"See that your husband rests, we will discuss your stay here later," Bhric said before his wife could say more.

"Why not invite them to stay with the clan? Do you fear they are too old and are not fit enough to contribute their fair share?" she asked after Glenna took hasty steps away from them.

"Until I know more about them, I will not offer them anything other than a temporary place to rest," he said and took hold of her arm once again.

"You do not trust easily." She welcomed the return of his arm, curling hers around his snugly.

"A necessary and beneficial skill for a wise leader," he said without apology. "Besides, trust is better off earned."

Her question came without restraint. "Will I earn your trust, husband?"

His response did the same. "That remains to be seen."

His remark did not give her hope.

Dawn had the sky partially lit when they reached the cottage where Lath lay. Hume was standing outside stretching his arms to the sky and kept them that way when he spotted Fen beside Tavia.

"Fen will not harm you," she said, thinking she would no doubt repeat those words often today.

Hume appeared to be skeptical of her claim and lowered his arms slowly and was surprised when Fen obeyed Tavia's command to sit and stay.

"He is a war hound, Lady Tavia, and will attack with the least provocation. He may seem docile, but trust me, he is far from it," Hume warned.

"Your friend speaks wisely," Bhric said, glad someone else cautioned her and thinking he himself should heed the reminder. The glare his wife set on him was not meant to make him smile but he could not help it, her scowl was more adorable than threatening. Though, his smile did not last long.

"You are a warrior who has fought many battles and has worn the blood of your enemies… will you attack me without provocation?" she asked.

"Humans and animals are far different creatures," Bhric said.

"Are they? It seems that both have an animalistic nature to them," Tavia debated. "Isn't it that distinct nature you take into battle?"

Bhric recalled the deafening roars and snarls of his men as they charged into battle. Rage blazed in their eyes ready to kill which was not much different than an animal who attacked.

"Battle holds its own distinct nature," Bhric said.

Seeing Hume's eyes round with concern at her made Tavia realize that it was not wise of her to question her husband in front of others, and she acquiesced. "That it does, my lord."

Bhric found himself disappointed when his wife did not continue the debate. He liked that she got him thinking, questioning things. It made for better understanding and possibly different decisions in the future.

"Is Hertha inside with Lath?" Tavia asked.

"Aye," Hume said with a nod. "She is seeing to his care before his mum arrives with his breakfast."

"I will only be a moment," Tavia said with a quick glance at her husband and repeated it with a quick glance to Fen before entering the cottage.

"Is Lady Tavia safe with the hound, my lord?' Hume asked with concern.

Bhric's unexpected laugh surprised him. "The better question would be… is anyone safe around my wife with Fen nearby?"

"He protects her?" Hume asked, amazed by what Lord Bhric suggested.

"It would seem that way, though we shall see since he spends the day with Lady Tavia and me."

"Many say Lady Tavia has not only a healing touch but a commanding one as well," Hume said.

Bhric was curious and asked, "Have you seen this with your own eyes before now?"

Hume hesitated, then shook his head. "I cannot say I have, my lord. Though I have known her to speak up for others."

"Who?"

"Flora, her cousin, and—" Hume stopped abruptly as if he had thought better of what he was about to say.

"Say what you will," Bhric ordered.

Hume hesitated but a scowl from Lord Bhric had him speaking up, though reluctantly. "The witch. Lady Tavia defended the witch."

"You thought it wrong of her?"

"The witch cut open a heart that had been torn out of a man to peer into it. Why? What did she want to see there? Or what strength did she wish to gain from it?" Hume shuddered at the thought.

Torin had sent a message about the incident and how the witch had been caught with the heart. He had no idea what evil magic the witch could do, and it had been the reason he told Newlin to give the witch to Lord Varrick, the legendary warrior. If anyone could command the witch Lord Varrick could.

However, if others heard of his wife's defense of the witch, gossip could start from it that might not bode well for her.

"Lady Tavia can be too kind at times, my lord, and suffers for it," Hume said.

Tavia stepped out of the cottage leaving Bhric to wonder what Hume meant. How had her kindness caused her suffering?

Chapter Fourteen

Fen remained by Tavia's side as they walked through the village, his massive body reaching to her hip, his head held high, and his eyes alert to all around him. Most everyone looked at her strangely and Fen fearfully. Few people approached her, and she did not blame them. Fen's size alone could intimidate, but so could her husband's.

"We go eat now," Bhric said, hungry with their morning meal having been delayed and he took hold of her hand as they walked.

"I am hungry," she admitted, her hand closing around his now out of habit.

"As am I," he said. "Once done we will talk in my solar."

Startled, she asked, "Have I done something wrong, my lord, that I am summoned to your solar?"

"Nay," Bhric hastened to say. "My solar is warm and a good place for us to talk on this cold day."

She wondered what he wished to discuss and thought to ask him, but Sven came upon them before she could.

"Something that needs your attention, and it cannot wait," Sven said.

"I will wait in the Great Hall for you," Tavia said.

"Keep Fen with you," Bhric said to his wife and Sven's surprise.

Tavia stared after her husband when he turned with Sven and walked away. She was pleased that he had allowed Fen to stay with her and unsettled that he had left her. She could not quite explain the unexpected feeling, it was odd… an emptiness of sorts as if something inside her was suddenly missing. Had she grown accustomed to spending time with him, talking, sharing a rare smile or two? Had she grown to care for him without realizing it?

"My lady."

The soft voice caught her attention and she turned to see Glenna.

"If I may trouble you, my lady," Glenna said.

"Is something wrong, Glenna?" Tavia asked, seeing the worry in the woman's eyes.

"William, my husband, he insists he must do his share for us to keep sheltered here. If you could speak to him and assure him he needs only to rest and that when he heals, he can then repay your kindness to us."

"Of course," Tavia said and walked along with the woman to the cottage where she and her husband were staying.

William was sitting on a bench at the small table when Tavia entered. He was pale and looked as if he would spill over at any moment.

"You must go back to bed," Glenna scolded, hurrying to place her hands on her husband's slumped shoulders to keep him from falling off.

"Your wife is right, William. You need to rest and grow strong. That is your only worry at the moment. Now come and get in bed." Tavia slipped her arm around William's and helped him to his feet to

Glenna's relief.

Once Glenna had him tucked in bed, two blankets keeping his frail body warm, Tavia pulled a small stool close to the bed and lowered herself down on it. She rested her hand on William's shoulder.

"You have nothing to worry about, William. You and your wife are welcome to shelter here as long as you wish. If by chance you come to like it here, we would be only too pleased for you to make your home with us," Tavia said, thinking her husband would surely agree with her once he realized the couple had no other recourse left to them.

"You would do that, accept strangers into your clan?" William asked perplexed.

"You will not be strangers by then. You will be part of the clan, part of our family," Tavia said and was surprised to see tears trickle from William's eyes. She patted his shoulder. "Rest is your only worry. All else can be dealt with later." She turned to Glenna and saw tears in her aged eyes as well. "You do not want for food and drink, do you?"

"Nay. Nay, my lady," Glenna rushed to assure her. "Lord Bhric has been most generous."

"Wonderful," Tavia said with a pleasant smile. "All will be well. I will see it done."

"We are grateful, my lady," William said, and Glenna nodded in agreement.

Glenna thanked her again as Tavia took her leave and Fen rose from where he sat next to the door when she stepped outside.

Her stomach rumbled. "Food, Fen. We both need food."

Together they walked to the keep all eyes following them.

***

"This is a sacrifice but not one of our *blóts,*" Sven said as he looked down at the wild boar whose stomach lay split open its innards spilled out on the ground. "The blood was not collected in bowls or spilled on stones like in our rituals, and the meat was left to rot. A Northman did not do this."

Bhric glanced around the immediate area and spotted what he searched for. He went and snatched up a stick, then he returned to the boar and squatted down to take a closer look, poking at the innards with it.

"The only reason to sacrifice a wild boar is to strengthen one's own fearlessness. At least that is the belief of us Northmen," Sven said.

Bhric poked deeper into the boar, tilting his head as he did, hoping to find what he looked for. Once done he stood tossing the stick to the ground. He did not want to think of what it would mean, and he even thought to keep his finding to himself until he could make sense of it, but that would be unwise. It would be found out, then what?

"The heart is missing," Bhric said.

Sven stooped down to get a look himself, then stood. "Didn't Torin send a message about a heart being cut out of a man and a witch who sliced it in two?"

"He did," Bhric admitted, "but it wasn't the witch who cut the heart out of him."

"Who is to say the heart wasn't taken afterward?" Sven asked. "And what that might mean."

"We must find out who did this," Bhric said worried, if Sven questioned it what then would wagging tongues make of it? "Send a group of warriors to search for anyone in the area and bury the boar so that the sacrifice will not be in vain."

Sven nodded, pleased. "A wise decision."

Bhric made his way through the woods his mind heavy with thought. It most certainly had to be a man who had hunted, killed, and gutted the boar since it took not only courage but strength for such a task. But why kill the boar and take nothing from it but the heart?

News about the heart that had been sliced open by the witch had spread quickly among his tribe, and not from the messenger who had delivered Torin's missives. It had been the members of Clan MacShane whose tongues had carried and spread the news having received word from people they knew at Clan Strathearn and worried over what evil may have befallen the clan.

His concern was that the misfortune of the Clan Strathearn was now visiting upon the Clan MacShane and the Thrubolt Tribe. And why would that be? He did not like what he feared most would think… the arrival of his wife.

Bhric shook his head not only at the disturbing thought but that he continued to think of his tribe and clan as separate. They needed to blend as one if he was to see Clan MacShane remain strong as he had promised his grandfather.

He smiled with the memory of his grandfather, Lord Donald. He had never once spoken badly of Bhric's father or the Thrubolt Tribe. Instead, he had spoken of their courage and skill as warriors and how lucky Bhric had been to be born of a tribe and a clan with such immense strength and power. He had wisely known that by bringing both together nothing could defeat the Clan MacShane. Bhric had yet to see and implement his grandfather's vision and it annoyed him that he had taken so long to realize it.

Hadn't it been his wee wife who had seen it herself and had spoken of what he had failed to see that the tribe and clan were at a divide and needed to be brought together as one?

His wife. It seemed like all went back to his wife. He could not deny that things had not gone as well as he would have liked since his arrival home. His sister Ingrid had yet to warm to Tavia as did many in the Thrubolt Tribe, they were pleasant to her, but none had gone out of their way to befriend her, not so the Clan MacShane. They were pleased with her arrival and had been more and more welcoming to her especially after she had defied him and pleaded for Lath's leg to be saved. Then there was Marta who had not taken kindly to her and Greta as well though something had changed in her after seeing Tavia stitch Lath's wound.

He stopped abruptly. How could he expect his people to accept his wife if he had not accepted her? Tavia might not be what he wanted in a wife, but she was his wife and that would not change. She was kind and caring. Even the war hounds trusted her, so why shouldn't he?

He continued walking, the answer to his question tumbling around in his head. She had been deceitful, trapping him in the marriage when she knew he had intended to negate the arrangement.

How, though, could she be kind and caring one moment and so deceitful the next?

The question continued to stir in him and by the time he reached the keep his anger had mounted. He stormed into the Great Hall with a vicious scowl on his handsome face that had servants scurrying to hide in the shadows.

Fen took a protective stance beside Tavia where she sat at a table by the large fireplace for warmth.

Tavia, however, did not cower, she stood, concern wide in her eyes. "What has happened? What has you so upset, my lord?"

"YOU!" he said, pointing at her and causing Fen to growl.

"Easy, Fen, my husband means me no harm. He would never hurt me," Tavia said, and the dog's growl turned to a low rumble as if he was not as sure as she was.

"My solar," Bhric ordered and walked off.

Tavia hurried to follow, though kept her steps measured not wanting to disturb her leg that she had kept careful watch on and was doing well. She ordered Fen to sit and wait outside the room and the large hound appeared reluctant. She squatted down to give him a generous rub behind his ears, while mindful of his wound, then planted a kiss on the top of his head.

"All is well, Fen. There is nothing to fear," she said and kissed him again. "You could use a rest. Lie down and wait for me."

The hound did so, his eyes following her as she entered the room, and he gave a low whine when the door closed behind her.

"Sit!" Bhric ordered, pointing to a chair near the hearth.

Tavia did as he commanded, his anger unnerving her. What had she done to cause such ire in him? She had thought they had been getting along well and she had been pleased that he had not sent Fen back to the shed.

"Why the grand scheme to make me believe our marriage was consummated?" Bhric demanded. Her eyes went wide with fright, giving him the answer he had been looking for. "So, our marriage was never consummated."

Defeat replaced fright in her eyes.

He crossed his arms over his wide chest and his chin went up as he continued to demand, "I have had enough. You will finally confess the truth to me."

Her shoulders slumped as if a weight had suddenly left them. "Wasn't it obvious, my lord? My clan would have never survived the winter without this marriage."

"Not good enough, Tavia," Bhric argued. "I do not like being deceived and though you and your father deceived me not making me aware of your limp, I would have seen your clan taken care of for the winter and longer if necessary. There must be more to your deception."

Lies would no longer serve her well. She had no choice but to tell him the truth. "Hertha, Hume, and the children. They needed a new home, a permanent one where they would be safe, where Lord Ivan could not harm them. Hertha, Hume, Doritt, and Edward were to go with me to my new home. If our marriage did not take place and the children remained at Clan Strathearn, there is no telling what Lord Ivan would have done to them and to Hertha and Hume for helping not only them but the other children as well." Tavia shuddered. "And when Lord Ivan so generously proposed to unburden you from our marriage, I must admit I was relieved that my plan worked for he would have made me suffer horribly for his defeat."

That got Bhric's anger boiling. "Has Lord Ivan ever tried to harm you?"

"Nay, my da kept me a distance from him and thankfully my da rejected his request for marriage to him. Lord Ivan claimed he changed his mind when he saw that I had a permanent limp. He would not have a damaged wife. His way of saving face when his proposal was rejected."

"Yet he proposed to take you off my hands."

"Aye, to make me suffer for his failure in keeping the children from him that he had worked to the bone. No doubt I would have never seen a year let alone a few months as his wife and the thought of what he would have done to me…" She shuddered again.

His wife had lied and plotted and sacrificed herself to help others, children she had not known, members of her clan, and her clan at large. If she protected those so unselfishly, what would she sacrifice to protect her husband, children, and clan? His wee wife was far more courageous than he had thought.

Bhric reached down to swipe his arm around his wife's waist and lift her out of the chair to plant her firmly against his chest. "What will you do to protect me, wife?"

"Whatever I must, husband, and on that you have my word," she said without hesitation and settled her lips over his to seal her promise with a kiss.

That she sealed her word with a kiss surprised him, but it also stirred an arousal in him which naturally had him commandeering the kiss. He took charge, an unexpected jolt of desire racing through him.

The unsure retreat of her tongue when his slipped into her mouth let him know she was unfamiliar with an intimate kiss, and he introduced her to it slowly until she began to respond., slow and hesitant. That of course only flamed his desires, and he ended the kiss when he grew far too aroused, especially when the thought of not waiting to bed his wife rushed into his head.

He rested his brow to hers and he thought to tell her that they would make this a good marriage perhaps because that was what he had hoped for with a wife. But it was too soon to tell, too much yet for him to learn about her. However, he would have something from her, something important to him.

"You will give me your word that from this day on you will speak only the truth to me and never be fearful of doing so," he said and was pleased by her quick response.

"Aye, you have my word, husband."

He set her on her feet. "Why did you not tell me who you were when I snatched you off the ground?"

"You frightened me, and your words were harsh," she said without hesitation, "and my limp was more pronounced from my walk in the woods. I feared that you would think like others that I was less valuable as a wife because of it." She bit at her bottom lip as if to stop herself from saying more.

"Say it," Bhric urged, knowing what she would say and knowing it was the truth.

"My fear proved true, but then I expected it to. My da had not been approached by any clan with offers of marriage… until your mum."

His mum had not mentioned Tavia's limp to him, which meant she had not seen it as a deterrent. She had seen something else in Tavia, something that she had inherited from her mother and that Bhric's mother knew would serve him well. He wondered what that was.

One thing was clear, his wife had remained strong through endless ridicule over her limp and that could not have been easy. It did not set well with him that he had condemned her as others had without any consideration for what she must have gone through or the courage it must have taken her to get through it. He was beginning to see his wife differently and thinking she just might make him a good wife after all.

She had been on his mind frequently of late. Actually, she would not leave his thoughts whether she was with him or not. He even found himself missing her when he was not with her. He was growing accustomed to her and perhaps that was not a bad thing. Why then delay consummating their marriage?

He asked the question without thought. "You have never been with another man?"

"Never," she said.

"What of the traveling merchant?"

"Kevin is like a brother to me. He took time to talk with me. Tell me of his adventures, encourage me when I needed it," she said. "You are the first man whose hand I ever felt in mine, whose lips ever touched mine…" Her cheeks blossomed red. "Whoever saw me naked."

"And that is the way it will always be," Bhric ordered, ready to kill anyone who dared to touch his wife improperly.

"It is the only way I want it, my lord, and on that you have my word," Tavia said with a firm lift of her chin.

He felt a strange jab to his heart, not a worrisome one but a pleasurable one. He liked that she wanted only him, but was it out of duty or was there more to her declaration?

"I am ravenous," he announced, which he was but they had also talked enough for now, leaving him much to consider.

"So am I," she said, feeling their talk had settled some things between them and hoping it opened a path to the start of a good marriage.

Fen was on his feet when the door opened and he followed them into the Great Hall, his eyes wandering to Bhric every now and then. They returned to the trestle table where Tavia had been sitting and servants soon brought more food to them. Fen went and laid by the hearth not disturbing them, though Tavia made sure he was fed, not that anyone would go near him. She placed the food in front of him herself.

"Was there troubling news from Sven?" she asked as they ate.

Bhric saw no reason not to tell her and it was better that he told her then for her to hear it through whispers and gossip. "A wild boar was killed and left in the woods."

Tavia tilted her head in question. "Why would a hunter kill a boar and not take the meat?"

"It may have been a ritualistic kill."

"How so?" she asked, her stomach suddenly churning.

"The heart was missing."

Chapter Fifteen

Tavia sat hunched over on a small stool before the burning hearth in her bedchamber, Fen at her side. For three days, the thought of the missing heart had not left her troubled thoughts and still had not. Tongues gossiped of what it might mean… evil had followed Tavia to Clan MacShane. But how could that be when the men who had been involved with the missing heart at Clan Strathearn could no longer cause harm. Who then could possibly have done such a heinous thing? And was it connected in any way to what had happened at Clan Strathearn?

"I know not what to think, Fen," she said and hugged the hound, needing the comfort he brought her.

She wished Fia was there to talk with, the woman having a deep insight that Tavia wished she possessed. Right now, confusion reigned within her, and she was not sure what to do. She thought to hide away again as she had done after her accident, but that would solve nothing or be of any help. Hiding from a problem only made it linger and could worsen the situation.

"Time to face the day, Fen," Tavia said with more conviction than she felt.

She stood with a stretch. She had hoped the talk in her husband's solar had solved some of their issues and that the kiss they had shared was an indication that their marriage had a chance of developing into a good one.

Unfortunately, she had seen little of him the last three days. She had thought it might be on purpose, until he informed her that he would be busy working with his men to find the culprit who killed the boar. It was all the talk in the village, people speculating over it and the possibility of a witch being involved.

The worrisome thought sent a chill through Tavia, and she stood, Fen stretching to a stand beside her. "I shall see you fed, Fen, then we will take a morning walk."

It was early, Tavia having been unable to sleep once she woke. She was not surprised to see the kitchen empty, and that dawn had yet to arrive. She gathered sufficient food for Fen and once he finished eating, she stepped outside. She hastily drew her hood up and tucked her cloak snug around her, the bitter cold quickly bit at her.

"Snow will fall again today, Fen, and more than the last few days," Tavia said as they headed toward the village.

The torches that lit the winding path through the village had nearly burned out, but it mattered not to Tavia, her interest only in a wander to ease her troubled thoughts. She had no specific destination in mind, it too early to trouble anyone with a visit. She simply needed to walk and think or better yet not think at all.

A sudden growl alerted Tavia that someone was nearby.

"The hound protects you well."

"Easy, Fen, Greta means us no harm," Tavia said as she turned and faced the elderly healer.

"You wake early," Tavia said.

"As do you. A troublesome sleep?"

"Somewhat," Tavia said.

"You do not trust me, do you, Tavia?" Greta asked.

She spoke honestly to the healer. "I do not know you well enough to make such a decision."

Greta took hold of Tavia's arm and continued to walk with her, Fen remaining close at Tavia's side.

"It is time I was truthful with you."

"That would be appreciated," Tavia said.

"I did not think you good for Lord Bhric when I first settled eyes on you. Too small, I thought, too weak, no strength to her, and fearful. I feared you would not survive a birth let alone being wife to such a powerful man. Then I watched you stand for a clansman, plead for a chance to save his leg and his life. I watched with amazement as you stitched his leg with steady hands while you told a tale of courage and a strength few possess. I knew then I had been too hasty in my opinion of you and that Lord Bhric's mother, Orianna, had wisdom in choosing you as his wife. You will serve him well and I will be honored to deliver your bairns."

"Yet I hear hesitation in your voice," Tavia said, pleased with the healer's words yet cautious.

"The killing of the boar in the woods brings rumblings of ritualistic practice and what it might mean. Is evil involved or is there a simpler explanation? You have come from a clan that evil has touched and there are those who may assume evil has touched you."

"Do you believe that?" Tavia asked alarmed by the healer's remark.

"I would not be warning you if I did. I saw in you

something I had not expected to see… a kindness that goes deep in the heart with a strength that encompasses it. You will make Lord Bhric a good wife, but I will not tell him that for he must see and learn it for himself." When Tavia remained silent, Greta said, "You still do not know if you should trust me."

"What do you expect when you have shown me no friendship since my arrival and yet suddenly claim you will be truthful with me and also believe I will make Lord Bhric a fine wife?" Tavia asked.

Greta smiled. "You are wise not to trust. Time will show differently."

"I will bide my time until then," Tavia said.

Greta nodded and smiled. "You are far wiser than I thought." Her expression grew serious, and she halted her steps and gripped Tavia's arm. "Know that if you are in need I am here, and you can trust me." She released her arm and walked away.

Tavia continued through the village, relishing the quiet, though mindful of Greta's words. She would very much like to trust, truly trust the healer, but she had yet to learn if she could. And now with rumblings of her bringing evil here to Clan MacShane she was not sure if she could trust anyone.

Fen growled again and Tavia turned to see Wilona, her eyes wide with fear. "All is well, Fen. Wilona is a friend." The hound calmed but remained close to Tavia's side.

"I saw you speak with the Northmen healer and waited to see if you would like a hot brew, the cold bitter today," Wilona said.

"That would be most welcome, Wilona, but I

would ask that Fen be allowed to rest by your fire."

Wilona appeared a bit fearful of the prospect of allowing the large hound in her cottage, but she agreed to Tavia's relief.

Fen settled quietly by the hearth, closing his eyes as soon as he curled in a ball.

Tavia closed her chilled hands around the tankard as soon as Wilona handed it to her and let the heat soak in.

"There is talk, my lady," Wilona whispered.

"What talk?" Tavia asked anxiously, Greta's warning already having disturbed her.

"Talk of a Northmen ritual and what it means."

"Tell me," Tavia urged.

"Whispers were heard that when a Northman kills a wild boar it is to give him fearlessness." Wilona shuddered. "The clan fears that the Northmen seek that fearlessness to be rid of the Clan MacShane so the Thrubolt Tribe can reign."

The thought sent a shiver through Tavia. She knew that was not Bhric's intention and she sought to ease the woman's worries. "The Northmen are fearless as it is, they need no ritual to make them more fearless. Lord Bhric is here to keep the Clan MacShane strong so it may survive unlike other clans who have been conquered and swallowed up by more powerful clans. Lord Bhric will not allow that to happen. He will defend Clan MacShane with his life."

"I pray that is true, my lady," Wilona said with little resolve.

"Have you been to see your nephew?" Tavia asked to divert attention from Wilona's worries.

It worked and the next half hour was spent in pleasant talk.

"You bring hope when I feared there was none," Wilona said when she walked to the door with Tavia.

"There is always hope, Wilona," she said, something she had once found difficult to believe, and Fen and she left the cottage to continue their walk.

Tavia thought to see how Lath fared as she did at least once a day, but it was still early, and she did not want to disrupt anyone's sleep. She headed back to the keep planning to return to the warmth of her bedchamber when Fen gave a low growl. She strained to see through the darkness that was beginning to fade and was surprised to spot her husband walking behind a few cottages. She hesitated a moment, though only a moment, then she pressed a finger to her lips to order Fen to remain silent and followed discreetly behind her husband.

She would be discovered easily with the darkness fading away if she were not careful, so she kept to the darkest shadows as she and Fen kept a distance behind her husband. She held back when she heard voices and tucked herself at the edge of a cottage to listen.

"Have you found anything?" Bhric asked.

"Nothing," Sven said, annoyed. "Which is even more disturbing since tongues already wag and will create something out of nothing."

"Was that the intention all along?" Bhric asked. "To make the clan worry?"

"I suppose, but what if it was one of ours?" Sven suggested.

Anger sparked in Bhric. "You think anyone from

our tribe would dare do such a powerful ritual without my consent?"

"I do not know what to think. This land is foreign to me, and I miss home," Sven admitted.

"I will not hold you here if this place has yet to feel like home to you. If you wish to return home, I will not stop you nor will I think any less of you. I understand, for there are times I miss home myself."

"Why not leave another in charge here and return home where our hearts and souls truly belong?"

"I gave my grandfather my word that I would rule Clan MacShane with honor and strength and see it kept safe as my ancestors did before me. And also see that it retained its strength and power. I will dishonor him and the Clan MacShane if I fail to keep my word."

Tavia listened intrigued. She had not given thought to the immense responsibility of what inheriting the title of the Clan MacShane would mean for Bhric. He had to unite a tribe and a clan, both far different from each other and bring them together as one, live as one, fight as one, survive as one without alienating the other.

"This killing will not set well with our people," Sven said.

"Nor Clan MacShane," Bhric said. "They will think the Northmen are up to something and be cautious around us, making it more difficult for all to get along."

"Your word is law. Use it as you must," Sven advised.

"Until I know more I will issue no commands, though I will demand that no rituals take place without my permission."

"A good start," Sven agreed. "And how about the

hound Fen? Does your wife keep him as a pet?"

Tavia did not have to see Sven to know he was smirking. It was evident in his tone.

"Fen will decide his fate," Bhric said.

Tavia did not like her husband's response. It made her think that he was waiting for Fen to make a mistake and that would determine his fate, a fate that would not be to her liking.

Tavia could tell Sven's smirk had vanished with how serious his voice turned.

"Maybe, but tongues wag wondering that if she can command a mighty war hound such as Fen will she be able to command the powerful, Northman warrior Bhric as well?"

"And who dares question that, the Clan MacShane?" Bhric asked with a snappish bark. "It best not be anyone in the tribe or else I…"

Tavia could not hear the rest since the two men walked off and their voices grew distant. She did not want to follow too closely for fear of being caught. It would not bode well for her to be found spying on her husband. But she did not think her husband would have welcomed her company when speaking with Sven, so what choice had she?

She remained where she was for a moment and decided it was best if she made herself known. Light was breaking through the darkness and her presence would be discovered. She followed after the two men and was surprised to find them nowhere in sight. She had not thought she had been that far behind them.

She stopped by the shed where Fen had been kept and cast a glance around, though there was yet enough light to see clearly. Still, she caught no movement. Then Fen growled.

A sharp command was issued in a language Tavia did not understand and the large hound sat obediently. She turned to see who issued the strange command when a strong arm suddenly snagged her around the waist, lifted her off the ground, and carted her off into the shed, shutting the door on Fen when he tried to enter.

Chapter Sixteen

Tavia's heart pounded with fear in her chest, and it took all the strength she had to try and calm it after realizing there would be only one person who would dare to carry her off into the shed… her husband.

"You frightened me, Bhric," she chastised, wiggling in his arm to free herself.

He liked the way his name slipped easily from her lips though a touch of annoyance accented it. He made sure his tone accused but not harshly when he said, "You followed me."

His strength was too much, she could not free herself and fear poked at her stomach. Knowing she was helpless against him left her feeling vulnerable and she did not want to feel that way about her husband. With no choice left to her, she settled against him, her feet still dangling above the ground.

She turned her face up to him. Light was beginning to filter in through the cracks in the wood wall and she was not surprised to see that his stern expression did not at all hamper his fine features.

She spoke as she had promised she would… truthfully. "I was curious and thought you would not welcome my presence."

"I would tell you if the conversation was meant to be private."

That told her much and it disturbed her. She would

be deprived of the knowledge of certain things that went on in her home. She should be used to it since her da had not discussed all things with her and learning some of those things after the fact, especially those things that pertained to her, had upset her.

Her response was instinctive. "And I will do the same."

His toned turned harsh. "You shall keep nothing from me and do not bother to tell me that if I can do so than you may do so as well. My word rules."

Tavia responded as expected. "Aye, my lord."

He liked it better when she said his name, just his name. It was more intimate. Besides, she said what was expected of her, but he wondered if she meant it.

He yanked her tight against him. "Can I trust your word on that, wife?"

His face was close to hers and she caught the hint of mint on his warm breath and the way his eyes held hers with a strong glare. She spoke how she felt. "I have little choice, husband."

"That you do," he said, glad she spoke the truth to him though it was not her words that had interested him as much as her lips that were far too close to his.

Tavia spotted the change in his eyes that went from a glare to a spark of passion when they fell on her lips. She wondered if it was what flared her own passion or if it was the way he held her so intimately against him. It truly did not matter since pure instinct or perhaps pure passion had her pressing her lips against his.

Bhric had felt the subtle change in her, her body no longer ridged against his and a spark of passion chasing away the hint of fright in her soft blue eyes. He had intended to kiss her then, but she reacted faster, and he was glad she had.

He took charge of the kiss, his lips demanding against her soft ones, and she responded with the same intensity, her arms going around his neck. He quickly walked them to the back wall, bracing her against it and keeping her there not only with the strength of his arm but with the strength of his body.

He never felt the overwhelming urge to kiss a woman as he did now with his wife. He had enjoyed kissing other women but never felt an intensity to do so as he did now. He wasted no time in urging her lips open with his tongue and slipping in for a more intimate taste. Hesitant at first, but with gentle insistence from him, she responded eagerly—and never had a kiss been more satisfying.

His body, however, wanted more, much more, and he found himself situating her against him so that his manhood—that had hardened quickly—fit perfectly between her legs. He pressed against her with a slight rub and when she responded in kind, seeking what he offered, he increased and quickened the rhythm of his movement.

Tavia was not sure what was happening to her, but whatever it was, she did not want it to stop. Never had she felt so alive, so excited, so ready for whatever it was that gripped her with such pleasurable intensity.

She tore her mouth away from his to drop her head back against the wall and take much needed breaths. She loosened her arms from around his neck and gripped the top of his shoulders as best she could, the muscles thick and hard there. And she could not stop a soft groan that slipped out as he rubbed against her.

"Bhric," she whispered with a soft breathlessness.

He saw the passionate plea in her eyes that she was close to climax and to his surprise so was he. But he would not have them couple here in the shed for their first time, though he would not deny her the pleasure of feeling what awaited her in their marriage bed.

"Bhric," she urged on a whisper.

His name spilling with such urgency inflamed his passion and he would not be able to stop from spilling his seed if he did not end this now, and he did end it with a hard thrust against her. He quickly captured her scream of pleasure with a kiss.

Tavia shuddered as the last of the most exquisite feeling began to fade away and her lips fell away from her husband's, glad he had caught her unexpected scream with a kiss. She would not want anyone hearing her or one of her husband's warriors rushing in worried she was in danger or worse Fen rushing in and attacking Bhric thinking he had harmed her.

She was disappointed when he eased her feet to the ground and took a step back, so their bodies were no longer touching, though his arm remained around her waist. It was then she realized his touch was rigid and that he looked away from her as he took deep breaths. He had not responded as she had to what had transpired between them. Had he gotten no pleasure from it as she had?

"You found no pleasure with me?" she asked, concerned, having hoped for a mutual compatibility when it came to the marriage bed and all it entailed. Otherwise coupling would be nothing but a chore for them and that would not make for a good marriage.

His eyes were on hers in an instant, his words harsh. "When I spill my seed it will be inside you where it can take root and produce an heir to carry on the Clan MacShane name. At least now you have a taste of what to expect in the marriage bed and it appears that you will enjoy it."

His blunt, cold response had her stepping away from him and going to the door where she stopped and turned to boldly say, "That, my lord, remains to be seen, for I know not if your manhood will be of an adequate size to please me."

***

"What has you so surly today?" Sven asked.

"It is nothing," Bhric snapped.

It had been hours since the incident in the shed with his wife and he was still fuming over it, though it was not his wife he was angry with, it was himself. He had not anticipated enjoying the unexpected intimate encounter with his wife as much as he had. And while he made sure to satisfy the women he had poked through the years, never had he felt the intense need to see a woman brought to pleasure as he had with his wife. His rambling thoughts had him questioning just what he felt for his wife. Had she sneaked inside him and somehow touched his heart? Could he actually care for the wee woman? Or did he more than care?

He had found himself looking forward to spending time with her, talking with her, and trying to ignore how much he wanted to kiss her. Then there had been the dreams of coupling with her, always waking before the final climax and too often having to please himself. A few times he had gone to the door that separated their bedchambers ready to end the foolish dictate he had declared for himself, but stopped, annoyed he was allowing his shaft instead of his head to rule.

When he had seen that Tavia followed him and Sven, he had set a quick plan to catch her. Sneaking her into the shed had not been part of it, that had been instinct. And he went and spoiled their enjoyable encounter with harsh words, though her parting remark definitely hit its mark and he almost stopped her from leaving to show her just how adequate his manhood was.

That he had taken his frustration out on her when she had been concerned enough to ask if he had enjoyed their encounter is what had been troubling him the most. Now he could not get her out of his mind nor could his manhood since he felt as if he were in a perpetual state of arousal.

"I have lost count as to how many times you snapped at me and others today. None of the warriors want to go near you and your sister avoids you since you snarled at her over the simplest thing. And I am tired of walking softly around you," Sven said, annoyed after his silence had lingered too long. "Go bed your wife and be done with it."

Bhric turned a growling snarl on his friend.

"You do not frighten me, but you are frightening everyone else especially the Clan MacShane. Mumbles spread that they fear you are about to kill a few of them," Sven warned.

Bhric snarled again.

"If you do not believe me go walk through the village and hear it for yourself."

Bhric grumbled to himself, Sven having walked away leaving him no choice but to walk through the village alone.

Snow had begun falling not long ago and chores were hurrying to completion in preparation of the snow turning worse. Everyone would seek shelter out of the cold and would spend the day settled before the heat of a blazing hearth. Bhric would not mind spending it in bed with his wife.

He scowled and grumbled as he walked, paying heed to no one and failing to notice how all who saw him scurried out of his way.

His sister Ingrid spotted him headed in her direction and though she was a distance from him, she did not hesitate to turn and take a different path that had her accidentally bumping into Tavia.

Fen growled and Ingrid froze.

"Easy, Fen, Ingrid means us no harm," Tavia said with a pat on the hound's head. Fen kept a watch on Ingrid and Tavia understood why. She had made no mention of Ingrid being a friend or else Fen would have sat or gone off a short distance to sniff around, knowing all was well.

Tavia would have liked to call Ingrid a friend, but the woman had showed no signs of wanting to be one.

"I am sorry, my lady. I was not watching where I was going," Ingrid said, casting a quick glance over her shoulder.

"Please call me, Tavia, after all we are family,"

Tavia said in an attempt to befriend the woman.

"That is not proper, and my brother would not like it." Again, Ingrid cast an anxious glance over her shoulder.

"When is your bairn due?" Tavia asked, hoping to see if Ingrid would at least converse with her, something her sister-in-law had avoided doing since they met.

"About two months." She scowled like her brother. "You should not make my brother angry. He can be a bear when he is angry, growling, threatening, and frightening as well."

"He inflicts pain on others when he is angry?" Tavia asked, thinking she had been unwise in what she had said last to him, and upset to hear she might be the cause of him behaving badly.

Though she questioned Ingrid's remark. Since arriving here, she had watched her husband deal with problems with authority and not once had she seen him use brute force. So, Ingrid's warning made no sense.

"Nay, unless someone is foolish enough to throw a punch at him. But his growling and threatening way is enough to frighten people away from him or be caught in his lashing tongue. You do not want his tongue to lash out at you. You would be wise to be a good wife."

She was trying to be a good wife, but her husband did not make it easy, and she spoke her mind, annoyed that Ingrid thought the fault all hers. "With little to no experience when it comes to men and a husband, nonetheless, I will accept some of the blame for his surliness, but surely, he bears some of the responsibility himself."

"Do not lay any blame on my brother he is a good man," Ingrid snapped.

Tavia wondered if all Northmen and women were prone to snappish natures. "I never said your brother was not a good man. But I will not take all the blame for his surliness."

"Bhric can be surly when something troubles or annoys him. He can dictate far too much as well. He is the oldest of my two brothers and thought to order me about when I was young, much like my father did."

Though Ingrid complained about her brother, she smiled as she did so, leaving Tavia to believe she cared very much for Bhric.

"I suppose if I were truthful, it was because I could be a bit of trouble on occasion," Ingrid said with a grin.

"Only on occasion?" Sven asked, causing both women to turn as he came up behind them. "You were a hellion. Wait let me rephrase that… you are still a hellion."

"The reason why you fell in love with me," Ingrid said, curling her arm around her husband's.

"I married you because I thought I could tame you… a big mistake," Sven said with a hardy laugh. "Now come home with me. It is cold out and I will keep you warm." He hugged her close and Ingrid melted into his arms eagerly.

Tavia watched them walk away, though after only a few steps, Ingrid hurried to return to her.

She kept her voice low as she said, "Keep my brother satisfied and he won't be a snarling bear."

Tavia stared after her, wondering over her advice.

She barely turned when Wilona was upon her, Fen

busy sniffing at the falling snow and not concerned with the woman since she was known as a friend to him.

"My lady, please, you must help us," Wilona pleaded.

"What is it? Tavia asked, worried with how upset the woman appeared.

Wilona gripped her hands, rubbing them nervously. "The clan fears Lord Bhric means us harm."

She glanced over her shoulder as Ingrid had done and looked in the distance and Tavia saw that she looked at Bhric's approach. Not that he watched his surroundings, his head bent, and he appeared, even at a distance, as if he grumbled to himself.

"His annoyance is not with the clan, Wilona," Tavia said, trying to calm her fear.

Wilona's hand went to her mouth to catch the gasp that rushed from it. "He is angry with you, my lady?"

"It is nothing, Wilona. We are newly wed and still learning about each other," Tavia said, keeping the explanation simple.

"Do what he says," Wilona advised with a whisper. "It is always better to do what your husband says so he does not raise his hand to you. It did not take me long, though I suffered enough bruises first, to find out that was the best way to deal with my husband." She glanced over her shoulder again. "God protect you, my lady," she said in a rush and hurried off.

Tavia saw the cause of Wilona's hasty departure. Bhric had gotten closer.

How sad that Wilona had had no choice but to obey her husband out of fear. She could only imagine the horror of being stuck wed to such a cruel man. Bhric might put fright in people, even in her at times, but he was not a cruel man. She had discovered, after spending time and talking with him of late, that she enjoyed his company. He had also occupied her mind a good portion of the day and he snuck into her dreams at night. She was surprised that she found herself caring for him more and more each day, though if she listened to her heart, she might admit that she could actually be falling in love with her husband. Why else would she enjoy his touch and his kisses or find such pleasure with him as she had done in the shed?

A thought rushed in her head. His angry remark had been unexpected, and it had hurt her, and had left him surly enough for people to avoid him. His sister's advice rang clear in her head.

Keep my brother satisfied and he won't be a snarling bear.

Tavia gathered her courage and Fen. "Come, Fen, it is time to calm another beast."

Chapter Seventeen

"Bhric."

Bhric stopped, hearing his wife say his name softly as she had done when in the shed and bloody hell if it did not add torment to his already aching shaft.

"Bhric."

This time he looked up, her voice sounding closer and was surprised to see his wife standing in front of him. Her cheeks had been bitten red by the cold and her hood was nearly covered with snow, and her lips were as lush and inviting as ever.

She smiled and reached out for his hand, and he instinctively took hold of it. She shivered when his icy cold hand closed around hers and he went to let go.

She grasped it tight, knowing she was not strong enough to keep hold if he chose to yank it away, but at least her firm grip signaled that she did not want to let him go.

"I will warm you," she said softly.

Her innocent suggestion shot right to his shaft, and he knew he could wait no longer, and he did not want to wait any longer. He wanted to know his wife more intimately.

"Come with me?" she asked a bit hesitantly, hoping he would not deny her.

"Aye, wife," he said, his hand claiming hers more firmly as he followed along willingly, letting her take the lead, not knowing her intention, but knowing what he intended.

And, of course, Fen followed along with them.

The servants in the Great Hall stared when they watched the mighty Northman being led through the room by his wee wife and tongues began to wag as soon as they left the room.

Tavia entered her bedchamber, ordered Fen to rest, then led her husband to the door that connected their bedchambers. Once inside, the door closed, she released his hand, and she removed her cloak.

"Why do you bring me here, wife?" he asked, tossing his cloak on a nearby chest.

"I spoke in haste and anger in the shed and did not mean what I said. The feel of your manhood against me made me believe just the opposite. You may be overly adequate in size." She kept her courage strong even though her stomach churned nervously, fearing she might lose the courage to carry out what had been a good thought when it had first entered her head but now a bit unsure. "I thought perhaps there was a way I could please you as you did me."

Her question shocked Bhric, though his manhood responded by growing painfully hard. But then it had never completely softened after the incident in the shed, something unusual for him. That had only served to make him realize how desirable his wife was to him. No woman had ever lingered in his mind as she did or caused him to remain aroused. She definitely had a significant power over him, and he wondered if it had something to do with the thought that he could very well have fallen in love with his wife.

He could stop it here and take charge, but he felt a bit devilish and could not help but wonder what she would do if he said… "Your hand will do."

If shocked, she hid it well and he began to strip off his garments.

Tavia remained where she was hoping her fluttering stomach would calm as she waited for further instructions.

"Take your garments off, Tavia. I will have you as naked as I am," he said, not only eager to see her naked but wanting her ready when the time came.

Tavia had grown bold with the solution that had hurried into her head. She had not known what to expect, she only knew she wanted to make love with her husband, not to seal their marriage vows, but because she wanted to feel for herself if her heart spoke the truth and she had unwittingly fallen in love with her husband. Her chance was now, and she would take it even though her stomach fluttered nervously.

She thought to turn her back to him as she undressed but thought better of it. It would only make it that more difficult to turn and face him. Besides, he had seen her naked. There was no reason to shy away from him. She shed her garments but with no great haste, hoping her worries would calm as she did.

Unfortunately, her worry increased when she watched him stretch out naked on the bed, pillowing his arms beneath his head on the pillows so that his head was raised some. His body was thick and hard with muscle. One particular muscle had her worrying she would falter in her resolve. His manhood stood tall and proud and was nestled in a bed of light-colored hair, and the size of the sacs beneath it were impressive but it was the thick hardness of his shaft that almost had her running from the room.

Her own muscles tightened, and she raised her hands high to draw back her shoulders and ease the tightness that had settled there.

Bhric thought he would come there and then, seeing his naked wife stretch like a lazy cat getting ready to pounce and he could almost feel her claws closing around his shaft, and he shuddered.

"Sit," he ordered a bit more abruptly than he intended, patting a spot beside him on the bed.

Tavia approached slowly, trying to ignore the way her husband's eyes roamed over her body as if inspecting every inch of her. But her eyes had done the same to his body, though her glance had gotten caught on his manhood, which was where it was now.

He intended to reach up and snatch her up to lay beside him and proceed to make love to her, but the devil in him or was it curiosity to see how she would react that had him saying, "Latch onto my shaft good and pump it up and down."

He was shocked when she looked as if she might just do as he instructed. He thought she might run off in fright or disgust. Of course, he had planned to stop her, but now that she sat next to him, a curious instead of frightening look in her eyes, he thought he would see what she would do.

Her hand hurried to grip his manhood and he almost rose off the bed. Her grip was firm and determined and she did not waste a minute in doing as he had instructed, pumping his shaft. Watching her nibble nervously on her bottom lip as she concentrated on pleasing him grew him even harder.

"Am I doing it correctly?" she asked, surprised that she actually enjoyed the feel of him in her hand, his coating silky but his shaft so very hard.

He struggled against the unexpected moan that rose in his throat and managed to say, "Aye, you are doing good." His aye came out with a sizeable moan.

She stopped. "I hurt you?"

"Nay! Nay! Do not stop!" he ordered, eager for her to continue.

She hurried to resume tugging him and found herself wanting to explore more of him, wondering how his sacs would feel cradled in her hand. But she did not dare remove her hand again after seeing how upset he had gotten. She did not want to disturb his pleasure. She dipped her head to get a closer look at his manhood and was quite impressed with it, though was concerned with the size, it being so big and she so small.

Bhric groaned when he saw her face dip toward his shaft. If she took it into her mouth he would explode right into it. He was relieved when she only looked at it, though the thought lingered and brought him closer to climax.

Tavia continued pumping him, her tempo increasing of its own accord and her own body responding to it. She was shocked to feel her passion suddenly take flight fast and hard and to feel the wetness that rapidly gathered between her legs. He had not touched her and yet her own enjoyment of pleasing him was causing her own pleasure to flare strong and a soft groan escaped her lips.

Bhric's eyes had drifted closed lost in pleasure when he heard his wife's soft moan. His eyes flew open. He had not intended for it to go this far, not that he did not enjoy it, but it was not for her to serve him like this, not when they had yet to seal their vows.

"Let go!" he ordered sternly.

Tavia released him in a flash worried she had hurt him or had done something wrong.

Bhric sat up, grabbed his wife at her small waist and lifted her from where she sat beside him to lie next to him. He moved his leg over her closed ones and nudged them apart and his hand got lost between them.

Tavia had no time to gasp at the jolt of pleasure that pierced her nether region since he caught her lips in a kiss. It was a demanding and hungry kiss, and she returned it in kind.

He tore his mouth away after a few moments to whisper breathlessly, "You are beautiful, wife, and I care more for you than I ever thought I would or was possible."

She had no time to respond, his head dipped down and his mouth captured one of her nipples, his tongue rolling over it and her body arched in response. She thought she had known pleasure in the shed earlier, but it was nothing compared to this.

"Bhric!" she cried out.

He loved hearing his name shouted urgently from her lips and the way her rosy nipple hardened against his tongue. It hardened even more when he teased it with his teeth.

"Bhric!" she cried out again.

But he was not finished yet. He wanted to enjoy

her other nipple, turn it hard, though it already was hard when he settled his mouth over it. He could not take as much time with this one. She was near to climax and wet enough he hoped he would not hurt her when he pierced her maidenhead.

"It is time our vows were formally sealed," he said as he rose over her, his leg nudging hers farther apart so he could kneel between them, worried if he hovered over her and collapsed after climax he would squash her.

She arched her body instinctively and he grabbed her bottom when she did and fit his shaft between her legs. He kept tight hold of it so he could temper his movements in case he caused her any pain.

"Please, Bhric, please," she pleaded. "I need you inside me."

That she wanted him that badly fired his passion even more and he slipped slowly inside her, fearful he might not fit, and was relieved when he slid easily into her. She was snug, but welcomed him with ease and he pushed farther in.

"Bhric!" she shouted, and her body shot up against his shaft taking him deeper into her. She cried out, not in pain but in pleasure.

He smiled, glad he had caused her no pain and hoped it would remain so as he began to move vigorously inside her. It was not long before he dropped down to hover over her, his strong arms keeping him from collapsing on her.

She gripped the bedding and moaned loudly as he drove in and out of her and found herself matching his tempo. Faster and faster until… she let out a scream and clamped herself tight around his shaft.

Bhric threw his head back with a roar when she squeezed him tight, forcing him to explode in a powerful climax so potent that he actually collapsed on top of her.

Tavia had been left breathless from the earth-shattering sensation that shot through her, the ripples still flowing along her body, add to that the weight of her husband on top of her and breathing was not easy.

"Bhric," she struggled to say and when he did not move, she gave him a gentle shove. "Bhric." When he failed to respond again, she grew worried and used what strength she had to push at his shoulders to try and roll him on his side.

He was suddenly off her, his hands braced close to the sides of her head and his arms muscles straining as he held himself above her. "Are you all right? I did not hurt you, did I."

"Nay. Nay. I am good. I had little breath left in me after our extraordinary coupling and with your heavy weight upon me, breathing was difficult. When you failed to respond, I worried something had happened to you. Are you all right?"

She had worried about him when she had been unable to breathe. He shook his head. "I tell you truth, wife. I have never released with such powerful fury as I just shared with you."

She smiled happily to know she gave him something no other woman had. "I have nothing to compare it to as you do, but I know it could never be as amazing as it was with you. And I look forward to sharing more pleasurable times with you."

He kissed her quick. "And I will definitely make sure we share many, many more," he said and rolled to the side to slip his arm beneath her back and scoop her up to rest her against his side.

Tavia snuggled there without protest, finding herself more than comfortable in his arms. Though a slight chill ran over her with her body beginning to lose the heat their coupling had generated.

Bhric felt her slight shiver and released her for a moment to reach down to pull the blanket up. That's when he saw the blood on his shaft. He dropped back on the bed, taking her in his arms and pulling the blanket over them.

"I hurt you," he said.

"Nay, not at all. I felt nothing. I was filled with far too much pleasure to feel any pain."

"Are you sure? I have blood on me," he said.

She gasped. "I am sorry. I did not know that would happen."

"Nor did I, though I am glad to see I was proved right to trust your word. It makes me trust you that much more."

His remark made her happy for it was start to a workable, good marriage, perhaps even a chance at love. "I can wash it off you," she offered ready to sit up.

Bhric stopped her. "Nay. I might spring to life if you touch me there again."

"You enjoyed how I touched you?" she asked.

"More than enjoyed, *elskan mín*," he said as he hugged her tight against him, then realized he had referred to her as my love. Could it be possible? Could he have found love with this woman? He hurried to add. "You can touch me like that as often as you like."

"I did enjoy it," she admitted.

Bhric realized his wife spoke truthfully without thinking about it and he wished he could have recognized that sooner. He also wished he had paid more heed to her predicament, instead of laying blame on her. Her father had placed a heavy burden on his daughter's shoulders and made it worse by making her fearful of speaking the truth. And he had only added to that burden, but no more. Their vows had been sealed, and nothing could separate them. He would make sure of it starting tonight.

"You sleep here with me in this bed from now on," he said.

She smiled at him. "That pleases me very much."

Bhric grinned. "And I will please you very often."

"I would like that very much as well," she said, her smile spreading. "I would not mind spending the rest of the day here with you."

"We think alike, wife," he said, pleased she said what he was about to suggest.

"Can we have food brought here? I am starving."

"Again, we think alike. We shall feast and couple until we stuff ourselves with both," he said.

"A perfect plan." She snuggled against him, thinking that there was no denying what she felt, in her heart and even deeper down to her soul. She had fallen in love with her husband, and she wondered, hoped, her love alone could sustain them.

Bhric lay there more content than he had been in a while, looking forward to the rest of the day with his wife and even looking forward to a future with her. Things were different now. He even had noticed that the unrest that had plagued him had dissipated since spending more time with his wife. She was good for him. His mother had been right in her choice. All would go well now. He would see that he planted many seeds inside his wife for one to take root and grow and fulfill the promise he had made to his grandfather.

Aye, things would go well, and life would be good.

Chapter Eighteen

Tavia walked beside her husband through the village, his hand solid around hers and a smile on her face. It had been a week since they had sealed their vows and she had never known such bliss. It was as if Bhric had become a different man, pleasant, thoughtful, and attentive to her. Each morning she woke, she looked at her husband sleeping beside her and touched him gently making sure it was not a dream that her life actually had turned pleasant. They spent much time together talking and surprisingly at times laughing.

She hugged his hand checking again that this moment was real and not a dream. He acknowledged with a squeeze of his own. It had become a habit between them as if they needed to confirm it was real and all was well.

People stared and whispered and Tavia wondered if the whispers were about her and Bhric or Fen, who had become her constant companion. But she did not linger on the thought, she was far too happy to let it worry her. Bhric's word was law and he had allowed Fen to remain with her and that was all that mattered.

"I will see you to the keep before I speak with Sven," Bhric said, feeling a tug in his chest at the thought of leaving her. He knew not what had taken hold of him, he only knew that he did not like time away from his wife. He had grown to enjoy her company. She was wiser than he had first thought and inquisitive as well, which in turn made him question himself. She had made him see that some decisions he had made had not worked well in bringing his tribe and clan together. He had changed that, assigning members of his tribe and clan to work on tasks together. Not everyone was pleased, but his word was obeyed.

"That is not necessary, my lord," she said. "I wish to visit with Lath and see Hertha if she is not busy.

"Greta has been keeping her busy, allowing her to tend the tribe," he said, pleased that the healer had shown her support of his decision to have the tribe and clan share tasks by trusting Hertha to treat the tribe.

"I would like to see how that goes for her, since I do not believe all are happy with it," Tavia said, having spoken briefly with Hertha yesterday and learning that some Northwomen would not allow her to tend them. It was the same with the clan, preferring Hertha to Greta.

"They will all learn," Bhric said confident with his decision. "I will walk you to the cottage."

"It is not necessary, my lord, and Sven appears impatient to talk with you," she said with a nod behind him.

Bhric turned to see Sven waiting a short distance away. He was about to ask his wife about her leg but held his tongue. Having seen the scar on her leg more closely, he knew she had to have suffered greatly, but he had seen for himself how she did not let her limp stop her. She rested when necessary and saw that she did not tax the leg too much. The limp was part of her, and she had learned to adapt to it as he was presently attempting to do.

He leaned down and kissed her rosy cheek. “I will see you later, wife.”

“I look forward to it, Bhric,” she whispered.

Her warm breath fanned his cheek, and the gentle whisper of his name sent a ripple of desire through him. He took a step away from her concerned that if he lingered beside her, he would snatch her up and carry her off to their bedchamber.

“Behave, wife,” he scolded with a scowl that more teased than warned.

Tavia stepped toward him, keeping her voice low. “You must tell me, Bhric, if I demand too much of you…” She glanced around to make certain no one was close and though no one lingered nearby she still lowered her voice even more. “In bed.”

He chuckled. “That, wife, will never happen.” He gave her cheek a quick kiss again and turned shaking his head and smiling. “Fen, guard Tavia.”

The hound hurried to her side and took a protective stance.

“Come, Fen, we visit Hertha,” Tavia said, and the hound gladly followed along with her.

Snow had fallen on and off over the last couple of days. Thankfully, it was not enough to hamper her from walking. She had made sure to pay heed to her leg and she was pleased that her efforts had kept her leg doing well.

“You will find Hertha at Greta’s cottage, my lady,” Hume said when she asked after greeting him.

“And how does Lath do?” Tavia asked.

“He presently sleeps, but he is doing surprisingly well. The wound is healing nicely, and he has managed to stand on the leg for brief periods without difficulty. He says the pain lessens each day and his mother asked if he could be moved to her cottage where she could look after him."

"What do you and Hertha think about that?" Tavia asked.

Hertha believes his mother will tend him well and that we both can visit him daily to make sure all continues to go well."

"I am glad for him, and I am grateful for the care you have given Lath," Tavia said.

"You gave him far more than we did, my lady. You saved his leg."

"We all did, Hume. None of us could have done it alone," she said and after exchanging a few more words, Tavia went to take her leave.

"Be careful, my lady," Hume warned. "Tongues wag with no thought to what peril they may cause."

Tavia stared at the closed door, Hume disappearing in haste behind it and leaving her to wonder why he had cautioned her.

It was a short distance to Greta's cottage, her mind troubled the whole way, thinking over what Hume may have meant. She was glad to see Hertha outside talking with a Northwoman, her smile wide and the woman appearing pleased with their conversation.

Hertha waved, her smile growing when she spotted Tavia and the Northwoman turned, her smile fading when her glance fell on Tavia, and she hurried away.

Hertha took hasty steps to reach Tavia, turning her away from the healer's cottage. "I have only a few moments since I must go with Greta to visit the ill. You look happy, my lady."

"I am, Hertha. I do not know how it quite happened, but Lord Bhric and I are getting along nicely, and he has been treating me well. I have hope of a good marriage with him."

Hertha's smile faulted. "Be watchful, my lady, word spreads that you have bewitched Lord Bhric as you did Bones and Fen and that you now command him to do your bidding. That you keep him to yourself away from others. They believe you are responsible for the tribe and clan members being forced to work together. And they worry if anyone says a word against you that you will cause them ill will."

Tavia could not hide her shock at the ridiculous notion. "That is nonsense."

"I agree, but others do not, and such talk and belief could prove dangerous for you," Hertha cautioned.

Greta emerged from the cottage and summoned Hertha with a wave.

"Send for me, my lady," Hertha said before she hurried off.

Tavia understood what Hertha meant. If she sent for her, they would have time to talk. She would do so later today and see what more Hertha had to say.

Greta handed Hertha a basket covered with a cloth, then reached for her staff she had left leaning against the closed cottage door and with a wave to Tavia the two women turned and walked off.

Upset with what Hertha had told her, Tavia decided to return to the keep. She noticed then how women whispered when she passed by, and men turned their heads away. Why had she not noticed this before now?

She had paid heed only to her husband this last week, spending endless time with him. She recalled how Marta had reprimanded her over it when she caught her alone in the Great Hall, only servants left to hear.

"Are you a fearful child that you will not let your husband leave your side?" Marta had asked. "He is a Northman of great power and greater duty, leave him to do what he must."

Tavia had thought that she and Marta had been getting along better of late, though perhaps it had been because they did not see much of each other and when they did, Marta was her surly self but since she had last reprimanded her, the woman had held her tongue. Until today.

Tavia had wanted to lash out at the woman for chiding her like a child, but she tempered her response. "What goes on between my husband and I is none of your concern, Marta, and I warned you once about admonishing me. Do it again and I will see you permanently removed from the keep."

Marta sneered. "Your word has no such power and while I know your kind, Lord Bhric will learn soon enough of your true nature and be rid of you."

Tavia had stared after her speechless when she turned and left the room, thinking the woman was impossible to contend with and something needed to be done about her.

Once in the Great Hall, Fen stretched his long body out in front of the hearth and Tavia pulled a small stool close to stretch her cold hands out to the heat to warm them. She watched the flames dance excitedly and wondered if she had been in a dream this last week and she was finally emerging from it.

***

Bhric stood with his arms crossed staring at Sven in disbelief. "Bewitched? The tribe believes my wee wife has bewitched me?"

Sven nodded, looking around to see they had walked far enough away from the village for no one to hear them. "Aye, how else would you explain neglecting your duties for the last week to spend endless time with your wife?"

Bhric vehemently disagreed. "I have not neglected my duties."

"You fail to walk through the village alone so the people may approach you with any issues or problems or set aside a day for them to come to you with them. Your wife is always on your arm. You mix the tribe and clan for various tasks and our warriors are not pleased that you force them to share sentinel duties with clan members. You have taken more meals in your bedchamber than with others. And you have not joined the men in practice."

"That does not mean she bewitched me. It means I have gone without a woman too long and with my wife enjoyable in bed, I find I cannot get enough of her."

"Bewitched," Sven said and not with a smile.

Bhric's brow shot up as he reminded, "What was it… five or six days that I did not see you after you wed my sister?"

"Aye, but Ingrid did not command two war hounds

with ease or save a warrior's leg that our healer claimed could not be saved or lead me by the hand through the village to our bedchamber, especially when you made it clear you were unsatisfied with your wife. And then there is the boar's missing heart. Was it a witch who took it and for what reason? Could it be to command a powerful Northman warrior?"

"This is pure nonsense," Bhric argued. "Tavia does not have the strength to kill a wild boar."

"She commands a vicious war hound. Who is to say she did not command the boar?"

"You cannot believe that. Her limp alone would make it difficult for her," Bhric continued to argue.

"Her limp? Have you not noticed that it has not been as pronounced since not long after the boar's death? Did she gain strength from the animal's death… from his heart?"

"She tends her affliction well since arriving here," Bhric said, defending her.

Sven shook his head. "True or not, if the people believe it, then it is a problem and will only grow worse if you do not do something about it."

"On that we agree," Bhric said, suddenly fearful what danger such lies could cause his wife.

"As a longtime friend, Bhric, I advise you to consider all that is being said. Your wife spoke with a witch while we were there and from what others had said, it had not been the first time. How do you know what the witch may have done to her or to you when you went to retrieve her from the dungeon that day?"

"Why would a witch want anything to do with me or my wife?" Bhric asked, realizing this problem would need his immediate attention or it could prove impossible to contain.

"What if it was not the witch who wanted something from your wife but your wife who wanted something from the witch?"

"What could she possibly—" Bhric suddenly turned silent.

"You realize for yourself what others might think. Your wife's limp grows less and a husband who did not think she would make him a good wife all of a sudden… acts as if he has fallen foolishly in love with her? Do you not see why tongues wag?"

Bhric felt himself a wise and strong leader and as such he could not ignore what Sven had told him. He did not have to think that he was falling in love with his wee wife… he knew he had. Why else would he feel an emptiness when he was not with her or enjoy her company or find a pleasure with her he had never known?

Bewitched.

"I advise not only as your friend but also a member of the tribe. Do not let this go, Bhric, or it may grow beyond your ability to stop it," Sven warned.

A scowl scrunched Bhric's face and anger erupted in his dark blue eyes. "I will do what is best for my tribe, but if anyone harms my wife they will pay with their life. Now go gather some men and meet me at the practice field. It is time they are reminded of their leader's strength."

***

Tavia grew worried when time passed, and her husband had yet to return. He had sent no message as to what may have kept him which surprised her since he had been thoughtful of late. Had he heard the gossip? Did he believe it?

Voices caught her attention and she saw Ingrid enter the room with Marta. They stopped where they were and talked, glancing her way. Marta then took her leave and Ingrid approached Tavia.

Fen rose from his sleep to sit in front of Tavia when Ingrid drew near.

She stopped a distance from the hound, resting her hand on her rounded stomach. "You command him well."

"I do not command him, instinct does, as does yours with your hand resting with caution on your stomach to protect the bairn inside," Tavia said, her cautious stance and the way she kept her distance made it obvious that Ingrid did not trust her. The gossip must have infested itself in the whole village or had it only infested the Thrubolt Tribe?

"You waste your breath and time with my brother if you think he would remove Marta from the keep," Ingrid said as if it was some sort of victory.

Tavia had no desire to argue with the woman. "As you say."

Ingrid's face scrunched with annoyance as if she had hoped Tavia would argue with her. "Senseless threats are useless and make you appear a fool."

"As you say," Tavia said again, realizing the woman did seem to want to argue with her and she sensed that somehow she would suffer the blame if she engaged in an altercation with Ingrid.

"Northmen and women are strong, and we do not frighten easily."

Tavia stood, Fen stepping forward to give her room and Ingrid took several quick steps back and stumbled. Tavia hurried to reach out and help her so she would not fall.

"DO NOT HARM HER!" Marta cried out and ran to Ingrid who had tumbled to the floor.

"Sit, Fen," Tavia ordered, fearful the hound would think Marta charged her.

"Lord Bhric will hear that you lashed out at his sister," Marta threatened as she struggled to help Ingrid to her feet.

Tavia hurried to correct her. "I did not shove Ingrid. I reached out to try and stop her from falling." She stepped forward. "Let me help you get her to her feet."

"Stay back, WITCH!" Marta screamed as footfalls were heard entering the room. "I will not let you rob the breath of the child inside her."

Sven ran to his wife and scooped her up off the floor while Bhric came to a stop next to Tavia.

Marta pointed an accusing finger at Tavia. "She pushed her. I saw it."

Tavia was not surprised that Ingrid did not correct the woman, but she was surprised when her husband turned an accusing glare on her.

At that moment, she felt her heart break and her dream shatter.

Chapter Nineteen

Accusations and shouts were thrown around, orders for Tavia to stay away from Ingrid, Marta demanding something be done, and Fen in front of Tavia, shielding her, ready to attack anyone who dared to come near her.

"ENOUGH!" Bhric shouted and silence suddenly descended on the room. He glared at each one of them. "You all shout yet my wife has yet to say a word. He turned to her.

"What is there for me to say, my lord? You have all already judged and condemned me." It hurt to see the doubt in his eyes. Only a short time ago he was smiling at her, and he had been reluctant to leave her. They had unexpectedly found something the night they had made love for the first time, something that had brought them close together or so she had thought. If he could believe what they said about her, then the last few days had been nothing but a dream, and she had woken to a nightmare.

"I saw her," Marta accused.

"Not another word, Marta," Bhric ordered and looked at his sister. "I will have the truth from you, Ingrid."

Ingrid's chin went up and her hand once again went to rest on her stomach. "I approached her about her threatening to have Marta removed from the keep."

That caused Bhric to turn a suspicious glare on his

wife.

Ingrid continued. "We exchanged words, and she took a hasty step toward me. With all that is being said about her, I thought she meant me harm and I stumbled back."

"That was when I saw her reach out to push her," Marta added.

Sven turned his anger on Bhric, demanding, "What are you going to do about this?"

Tavia saw now that there were those who did not want her there and even if she and her husband got along, there would be those ready to cause her trouble.

"I will speak with you in my solar, Tavia," Bhric said. "The rest of you will take your leave."

Sven stepped forward. "If she has caused my bairn harm, Bhric, so help me I will see her suffer."

"I will let your threat pass this time, Sven. But threaten my wife again and you will not like the consequences," Bhric warned with a sharp tongue.

Anger marked Sven's words. "I think it best if Ingrid and I return home for the birth of our child. I want him born on the soil of our homeland."

"If that is what you wish, I will not stop you," Bhric said.

"Do not be hasty, Sven. My brother needs us," Ingrid said. "Besides, Bhric always does what is right for the tribe."

Tavia knew she was doomed. She was not part of the tribe, nor would she ever be, so she spoke up thinking she had nothing to lose since she had lost already. "Lord Bhric rules Clan MacShane here. Will he do what is right by them?"

"My solar," Bhric ordered before anyone could say a word.

"Come, Fen," Tavia said.

"The hound remains here," Bhric ordered.

Tavia's temper shot up with her chin. "I think not, my lord, for I do not trust those who find it so easily to lie not to harm Fen. He comes with me." She walked off, Fen at her side.

"You let her command you?" Sven asked annoyed.

"Watch what you say to me, Sven," Bhric warned.

"I say what must be said," Sven said, defending his remark.

"You trust a woman you barely know over a man who has been friends with you since you were young?" Ingrid asked. "Or pay no heed to the concerns of your tribe?"

"I came here to keep my word to our grandfather, to rule the Clan MacShane. I welcome you and your husband here, Ingrid, but know that here you are part of the Clan MacShane. If it is the tribe you prefer than return home with your husband."

Bhric turned and walked away, a knot in the pit of his stomach, twisting ever tighter. How was it that only a few hours earlier he felt joy, the future full of promise and now all that was lost? He found it difficult to believe his wee wife would cause his sister harm. He had only seen kindness from her. It made no sense. But he had two women who swore to it and their word would spread and only add to the gossip already spreading about his wife.

Tavia stood by the hearth when he entered his solar, Fen by her side, instinct telling him she needed protection.

"You disobeyed me," he said.

"You left me no choice. Fen protects me and I protect him, and I will not leave him with liars who wish me harm," she said, showing strength when she felt anything but it.

"You think they mean to harm you?" he asked, her suggestion disturbing him for that would mean she was not safe in her own home.

"Why else would they lie? And why do they wish for people to doubt my word, to think badly of me?" Sorrow filled her eyes. "They had you believing it."

The hurt in her eyes stabbed at his heart since she was right. There was an ounce of doubt in him.

"I gave you my word that I would speak only the truth to you, and I have. Yet you gave no thought to that promise when faced with this problem. You did not stand by me and claim me innocent without a shred of doubt. You wavered unsure which means my word means nothing to you. What does that tell me?"

"Tell me what happened?" he ordered, not knowing what to say to her since he hated to admit she was right.

"Why would you believe my word against your sister and those you have known far longer than me?"

"Why would they lie?" he snapped.

She shook her head. "I do not know. That you would have to ask them? But you should also ask why would I lie? Why would I have any ill will toward your sister? Or is it that you have heard the gossip that runs through the village and wonder what others do… that I have bewitched you."

"Have you?" he asked without thinking.

Her hand went to her chest as if he had stabbed her with a dagger so painful were his words. "Say it, husband, say I tricked you into my bed and now I tricked you to seal our vows and bind me to you forever. Say that nothing we shared these last few weeks has been real that it has meant nothing, that I felt nothing, that I tricked you—nay—bewitched you into believing it so."

Tavia fought hard not to cry but she was sure her heart was breaking, the pain hurt so badly.

Bhric felt as if he was losing her almost seeing her fade away in front of him and his heart felt like it was splitting in two.

"Tell me what happened so I may get to the truth," he urged.

"The truth is you do not trust me and that is all the truth you need," she said and ran out the door choking back tears, Fen close on her heels.

Bhric let her go when he warned himself to stop her, take her in his arms, hug her tight, and never let her go, but the leader in him cautioned he had to get to the truth. It was the only way he could truly protect her.

He lingered in his solar, his thoughts heavy.

***

Bhric was not surprised to see the Great Hall empty for the evening meal.

"Where is my wife?" he asked the servant lass.

"In her bedchamber. Hertha is with her, she sent for her."

"Lady Tavia is not feeling well?" he asked concerned.

"My lady did not say. She simply asked that Hertha be sent to her."

"Has Lady Tavia eaten?"

"Nay, my lord, and she refused the offer of food brought to her bedchamber."

"See that food and drink are brought to my bedchamber, enough for two," Bhric ordered.

The servant bobbed her head and took her leave.

"My lord."

The soft, hesitant voice had him turning to see another servant lass.

"I am Shea, my lord. May I speak with you in private?"

Bhric was not in the mood to settle any disputes in the keep. That was Marta's chore.

"It concerns what happened here today, my lord," Shea said when she saw that he was hesitant, then she quickly gave a quick glance around before lowering her voice. "I saw everything that happened here."

***

"Wagging tongues are worse after what happened today," Hertha said, sitting at the small table with Tavia in her bedchamber. "And the divide grows worse between the tribe and the clan. I do not know how Lord Bhric will ever bring the two together. Some of the Northmen and women talk about returning to their homeland. Those in the clan are eager to see them go."

"I cannot believe people think I have bewitched

Lord Bhric," Tavia said, growing more upset over the news.

Hertha chuckled. "Well, he was bewitched but not by you… by love."

Tavia chuckled as well. "That is nonsense. He does not love me."

"He may not know it yet, but he is in love with you just as you are with him. The last week or more has confirmed that. All you had to do was look at you both and see it for what it was… love." Hertha chuckled again. "I denied it up and down when Auda told me that I loved Hume. But she insisted she was right, and it was there for all to see. She was happy for me and Hume, so it was easy for her to spot it. Not so for people—"

"Who think me a witch," Tavia said.

"I have been thinking on that and it is why I wanted to speak with you. I believe someone in particular is purposely planting the suggestion to all that you are a witch. It makes me fear for your safety."

"But who would do such a thing?"

"Marta, Ingrid, anyone who believes you are not a fit wife for Lord Bhric. Anyone who wants to see you gone," Hertha said. "And with news of you visiting the witch in your da's dungeon, it is a perfect tale to weave. You must tell Lord Bhric so he can protect you."

"He does not trust me or believe anything I say."

"I do not believe that, my lady," Hertha said. "Someone wants him confused, wants him to make a mistake so there is more blame to lay on you. Tell him and see what he says and if he thinks it is foolish, then you and I will need to find the culprit ourselves."

"You are a brave one, Hertha," Tavia praised.

"I found my courage and there is no stopping me now," Hertha said with a broad smile. "You found your courage a long time ago, my lady, but you have only just begun to use it. Do not stop now."

***

"Tell me, Shea," Bhric said once settled in his solar.

Shea nodded. "It started with words Marta had with Lady Tavia while she sat by the hearth, Fen sleeping beside her."

"What words?" She appeared hesitant to say, and Bhric eased her concern. "There will be no reprisal from anyone for what you tell me here. You have my word."

Shea nodded and continued. "Marta accused Lady Tavia of being a fearful child who clung to her husband. She said you were a Northman of great power and greater duty, and she should leave you to do what you must. Lady Tavia responded calmly, telling Marta that what went on between you and her was none of her concern. She also reminded Marta that she had warned her once before about admonishing her and if she did it again, she would see her permanently removed from the keep." Shea paused a moment, then quickly continued. "Marta sneered at her and told her that her word had no such power and that while she was familiar with Lady Tavia's kind, you would learn soon enough of her true nature and be rid of her.

Marta then complained to Ingrid when she saw her, though the story she told Ingrid was far different from what had taken place."

Anger rumbled in Bhric, not only at the lies spewed but at his failure to believe his wife. "What happened then, Shea?"

"Ingrid approached Lady Tavia and they exchanged words. Ingrid sounded as if she wished Lady Tavia to argue with her, but Lady Tavia remained calm and responded with 'as you say' when Ingrid told her that senseless threats are useless and made her appear a fool. She said 'as you say' again when Ingrid told her that Northmen and women were strong, and they do not frighten easily. That was when Lady Tavia stood, and Fen stepped forward to give her room and Ingrid hurried several quick steps back and stumbled of her own accord. Lady Tavia hurried to reach out and help her so she would not fall, and Marta yelled out not to harm her as she ran to Ingrid. Lady Tavia quickly ordered Fen to sit so he would not think Marta rushed to attack. Marta then threatened that you would hear about what happened and Lady Tavia tried to explain she was reaching out to help Ingrid and offered to help her get Ingrid to her feet. That was when Marta called Lady Tavia a witch and suggested Lady Tavia intended to harm the unborn bairn."

"I heard that part. Why did you not come forward there and then?" Bhric asked.

"I hurried out before anyone saw me for fear of what Marta might do to me if I challenged her words. She is unfair to the MacShane servants when they displease her, which is often. She leaves some to work endless hours and get little sleep, so they often fall asleep while working. But after I heard what was being said about Lady Tavia, I could not hold my tongue. My lady has been kind to me. She calls me by my name, asks how I am doing when she sees me. She is a good woman and I do not believe she is a witch."

"How long have you worked in this keep, Shea?" Bhric asked.

"Since I was little. My mother worked here, she is gone two years now, and she would bring me with her. This was my home, and Lord Donald treated all of us well."

"But now my arrival here changed that?"

"Marta's arrival changed that, my lord," Shea said, her voice turning low without realizing it.

"I am grateful that you had the courage to come forward and tell me the truth," Bhric said. "You will be rewarded for it."

"That is not necessary, my lord, I just want Lady Tavia to be safe."

Bhric thought on her words after she left. His wife was not safe with all the lies being told about her, but who was telling them and why?

He made his way to his bedchamber. He had much to discuss with his wife. He only hoped she would talk with him, though it did not matter for he had much to say to her.

Chapter Twenty

Bhric should not have been surprised or annoyed not to find his wife in his bedchamber. She was angry with him and rightfully so, but he would not have her anger fester and grow a wedge between them. He did not want that, not ever.

He opened the door that connected their bedchambers and found her sitting by the hearth, Fen sleeping beside her, though his head shot up. When he saw it was Bhric, he dropped his head down but kept his eyes open.

"A servant told me you sent for Hertha. Are you not feeling well?" he asked as he approached her.

"I feel fine. I but wished to speak with her," Tavia said, keeping her word to speak the truth to him. She waited assuming he would want to know what they discussed and was surprised by his response.

Bhric stretched his hand out to her. "Come and sup with me. There is much for us to discuss."

She knew she was being petulant, but she was angry at him and with herself for believing they could have a good marriage but mostly because she allowed herself to fall in love with him when there was no chance of him feeling anything for her at all.

"I am not hungry. I am tired and shall sleep here in my bedchamber tonight."

"That is not going to happen, wife," he said and

reached down and scooped her up off the bench and into his arms. "Stay!" he ordered Fen abruptly when the hound hurried to his feet.

"I am safe, Fen." Tavia was quick to tell the hound, fearful he might attack Bhric if she did not alert him that she was not in danger. She slipped her arms around her husband's wide neck as he carried her to his bedchamber and whispered, "You do not mean me harm, do you, my lord?"

"That would depend, wife," he said, kicking his bedchamber door closed behind him, "if you consider a good pounding from me harm."

He had planned on supping with her and talking, telling her what Shea told him, but when he snatched her up in his arms his only thought had been to give her a good pounding, to make her realize she belonged to him and always would and that nothing, no one would ever come between them.

He dropped her on the bed, and he was not surprised to see passion flare in her eyes. There was something that connected them, and it had nothing to do with her bewitching him. It was something he had not expected but he welcomed.

Love. He loved his wee wife, her limp and all, and he wanted her to love him.

"Listen well, wife, for you will rarely hear me say… I was wrong. And you have my word that never will I fail to come to your defense again."

Tavia felt as if all the pieces to her heart miraculously rushed back together, and she was once again filled with joy… and love. Though as angry as she was with him, that she loved him could not be denied. That would be impossible for he had somehow worked his way into her heart, always to remain there.

Her joy was too much to contain, and she stretched her arms out to him. “I do so love you, husband.”

Joy struck Bhric like an arrow to his heart and he reached down and scooped his wife up in his arms again and planted a powerful kiss on her lips that she quickly responded to.

When he finally tore his lips away from hers, he whispered in her ear,” “I love you more.”

Tavia drew her head back to look in his eyes as if the truth of his words would be revealed there. “You love me?”

He smiled. “I know it is difficult for you to believe since you are a wee bit of a thing and have a limp, and you are not a wife who obeys her husband well—” His smile faded as his dark blue eyes settled intensely on her soft blue ones. “But those are only some of the things I wrongly assumed would make you a poor wife when they are the very things that gives you the courage and the strength it takes to be my wife.”

Naturally, happy tears had to rush in her eyes, but she ignored them and grabbed his face to hold firmly as she kissed him as if sealing those words forever within her.

“I cannot wait,” she said breathlessly when the kiss ended.

“Either can I,” Bhric said, understanding what she meant.

He placed her on her feet, and they shed their clothes with haste. Once naked he lifted her with one arm around her waist so he could kiss her as he walked them to the bed.

"Inside me. I will have you inside me and you will waste no time giving me a good pounding," she ordered.

"Is that a command, wife?" he asked with a chuckle.

"If need be," she said, a light laughter interfering with her serious tone.

He stopped by the edge of the bed. "A command is not needed, but I will obey it."

That he would obey a command from her gave her a sense of power, a sense of being equal to him, and it spiked her passion.

Bhric dropped her crossways on the bed. "On your knees, wife, so I can obey your command."

Tavia scrambled to position herself eager and ready to feel him inside her. She gasped when his large hands gripped her bottom tight and his shaft drove into her with a hard thrust. She let out a gasp that turned to a moan that increased as he slammed harder and harder into her.

Bhric kept a good grip on her backside, holding her in place as he used his shaft like a mighty weapon but for pleasure rather than pain. Pleasure that overwhelmed and sped through him wishing he could linger but knowing he was far too close to the edge and from his wife's increasing moans she was just as close.

Tavia gripped the bedding beneath her and dropped her head to bury a loud moan in the mattress. Lord, but she did not think anything could feel so good and she wanted to linger. Unfortunately, she was not going to last, her passion soaring rapidly.

She lifted her head and groaned loudly. "I—I—"

"Let go!" Bhric commanded and shoved into her with an intensity that he knew would take not only her but himself over the edge, and it did.

Not able to contain the explosion of sensations that rocked her body, she let loose with a scream that was sure to be heard throughout the keep and when she felt more sensations building behind the first, she cried out, "Do not stop, Bhric. Please do not stop."

Bhric was in the middle of his own explosions, and he quickened his thrusts that had slowed, intensifying his own pleasure and when his wife cried out for a second time, he found his own climax exploding harder than ever.

He stood with his hands still on her backside, his shaft still inside her lingering a while after the last shudder had long ended. He had pounded her hard, enjoying every moment of it and from the strength of her moans she had as well, but he worried he may have hurt her.

He stroked her bottom, "Are you all right, Tavia?"

"Hmmm," she mumbled, her face partially buried in the bedding.

He could not help but smile, her soft mumble sounding like a satisfied purr. He eased himself out of her and she purred again and dropped onto her back to smile up at him.

"Now I know why you enjoy pounding so much."

He lifted her quick and moved her to lay lengthwise on the bed, then dropped down beside her and hurried her into a hug. "A good pounding is enjoyable, but other times I want to feel you in my arms."

"I never knew there were different ways for a husband and wife to enjoy each other," she said, resting her head in the crook of his arm.

"There are plenty and we can explore them all if you'd like," he said.

"I would like," she said eagerly.

At that moment, he blessed his mother for choosing Tavia as his wife. She had been right all along… Tavia was perfect for him.

Her hand went to her stomach when it rumbled.

"You are hungry and so am I. Let us eat and talk, for I have much to tell you."

Tavia sat in her nightdress at the table, enjoying the bounty of food there.

"I like you better naked," Bhric said.

"But you do not want me cold, do you?" she asked.

Bhric got up and walked around Fen, enjoying food from a bowl Tavia had given him after bringing him in from her bedchamber, and fetched her shawl to drape around her shoulders.

"You are not cold naked?" she asked with a slight shiver.

"I am a Northmen. I am used to the cold."

"You are a Scotsman as well," she reminded.

"Something I am glad you continue to remind me of and something I should have been more vigilant about when considering today's incident."

"You told me you were wrong," she said. "What made you realize that?"

Bhric reached across the table to give her hand a squeeze. "I would like to admit that I recalled your promise to me about always speaking the truth, though I will say I did think of that but too late. It was a servant lass, Shea. She saw the whole thing. She even heard the words that were exchanged between you and Marta before the incident with Ingrid. Words that were repeated differently to Ingrid."

"I am relieved that Shea saw it all and spoke up, but what if she had not? Would you have continued to believe the others over me?" Tavia asked, a bit disheartened.

"I would have come to my senses after we both had calmed down and talked with each other and would have realized that my wife would never lie to me. It is something I will not forget again. Forgive me, wife, for doubting you."

"You are forgiven," she said, feeling good to squeeze his hand reassuringly and lovingly once again. "I realize it cannot be easy for you to unite your tribe and clan, Like us, I believe that until trust exists between them lies can easily keep them divided. You are wise in forcing them to work together for there are things that they will need to do that will require trust. I do believe it has already begun, Hertha telling me that some Northwomen are trusting her healing skills. Though, Hertha wears a constant smile so I do not know how anyone would not trust her, she is so pleasant to be around."

"I am glad to hear that. What else did you and Hertha discuss?"

Tavia was eager to share with him, happy trust truly did exist between them. "She warned me of what was being said about me that I bewitched you and she suggested that someone might be spreading such gossip on purpose and that I might be in danger."

"The thought did cross my mind as did the thought that you command thc hound, and he stays by your side. At least it is a deterrent for anyone to approach you. I will make sure my warriors keep watch on you," he said, worried for his wife's safety.

"But we know not who wishes me harm, so how do we know who to trust?"

"You are right, though Marta tops the list," Bhric said annoyed that it was more than likely one of his own who threatened his wife.

"Has she served you long?" Tavia asked curious about the woman.

"She has served my family since I was very young without a problem and when she asked to come with me here to oversee the keep, I saw no reason to deny her."

"I do not understand why she dislikes me so much," Tavia said puzzled.

"Marta was once wife to a powerful tribe leader whose tribe was attacked by the fierce Sturlung Tribe after a bitter dispute between them. She lost her husband and daughter in the attack, and she, herself, was sold to another tribe. She finally settled with my tribe and as I said she has served my family well, though she truly has been more like family, much like a grandmother to me and my brothers and sisters. I tell you this because she knows the courage it takes to survive being wed to a tribe leader and I believe she does not think you have the strength to make me a good wife."

Tavia felt bad for the woman, losing her husband

and daughter and being forced to serve others. "I have no wont to hurt Marta, she obviously has suffered enough, but I can no longer tolerate her in the keep."

"I agree," Bhric said with a nod, "especially with what Shea told me how unfairly Marta treats the MacShane servants when they displease her and works them endlessly with little sleep. It is obvious she is having trouble adapting here."

"What will you do?" Tavia asked, hoping he had a good solution to their problem.

"I have a plan," he said with a smile.

"Tell me," Tavia said eager to hear.

***

Bhric and Tavia stood side by side in front of the dais in the Great Hall, their hands clasped in a firm grip, the next morning after the meal was complete. Both had been surprised to see two clan and tribe warriors talking while sharing food, then leaving together. It was a start and Bhric was pleased.

Fen sat next to Tavia, staring at those summoned to the Great Hall after the morning meal was finished and the room empty.

Sven did not look too pleased and kept a protective arm around his wife. Marta's face was pinched in annoyance and Shea stood off to the side as expected from a servant.

Bhric addressed them with authority. "I have gathered you all here since I have reached a decision regarding yesterday's incident. I will ask again if anyone wishes to speak differently than they did yesterday?"

"I stand with my wife," Sven said.

"As you should," Bhric agreed and got a perplexed look from Sven which quickly turned angry when Bhric continued. "As I stand by my wife."

"How can you believe her over us?" Ingrid asked upset.

"I was right. She bewitched him," Marta said.

"Ingrid and I will leave for our homeland," Sven said, and Ingrid gasped, shaking her head.

"I will not stop you, but I will have you hear me out," Bhric ordered and summoned Shea forward with a wave of his hand. "Shea heard and saw all that happened here yesterday, starting with what Marta said to my wife."

"She lies!" Marta snapped. "Begone with you to your chores."

"Shea stays where she is and why do you say she lies when you have not heard what she has to say?" Bhric asked.

"Because I know she has a lying tongue and is lazy never doing enough," Marta complained.

"I wondered if you might say that, so I asked some of the other servants about her," Bhric said.

"They will lie for her," Marta said.

"Even the ones from our tribe? They had nothing but praise for Shea. Not one servant had a bad word to say about her, just the opposite actually. They could not praise her kindness and hard work enough." Bhric pointed at Marta when she went to interrupt. "You will hold your tongue until I give you permission to speak."

Marta clamped her lips shut as her eyes narrowed

in anger.

"Shea, you will tell them just what you told me yesterday," Bhric ordered the servant who stepped forward nervously.

Tavia remained silent at her husband's side, watching everyone's faces as Shea repeated what she had told Lord Bhric. She watched Ingrid's face pale and her mouth fall open and Sven's eyes widen, while Marta refused to look at anyone.

Ingrid spoke when Shea finished. "You lied to me, Marta. You told me that Lady Tavia, spoke harshly to you, accusing you of being lazy and not doing your job properly, and threatening you that she would see you removed from the keep no matter what it took. You never once said you reprimanded her and had done so on another occasions."

"She deserved it," Marta spat. "She is not fit to be Lord Bhric's wife."

"That is not for you to say, Marta," Sven said, then looked to Bhric. "My apologizes to you and Lady Tavia. I was wrong in how I spoke to you both."

"I am so sorry, Bhric," Ingrid said and stepped toward her brother. "Lady Tavia did not lunge at me. The stumble was of my own doing."

Bhric let go of his wife's hand and went to his sister to take her in a hug.

"I believed everything Marta was telling me about your wife," Ingrid said through tears. "I suppose it did not help that I agreed that Tavia was not strong enough to be your wife, between her small size and her limp but I was wrong. What appears weakness to others is what actually gives her strength. She has proven that with the many challenges she has faced since arriving here and has managed to remain strong through them all."

"The largest challenge of all being me," Bhric said with a smile.

Ingrid smiled as well and gave him a jab in the chest as she stepped away from him. "You are right about that, brother. I do not know how she puts up with your stubborn, demanding ways."

Bhric was glad to see his sister smile and tease him like she usually did.

"Sven and I will not be going anywhere. Clan MacShane is our home now. Besides, you could never do without Sven, you need him," Ingrid said as she joined her husband, his arm going around her.

"You are right, Ingrid," Bhric said after returning to his wife's side. "I could never do without Sven's loyalty and never-ending friendship."

"Thank you, my lord," Sven said knowing Bhric's remark was his way of forgiving him.

"As for you, Marta," Bhric said.

"I am sorry, my lord. I will hold my tongue and do what is expected of me," Marta said.

"That is not enough, Marta," Bhric said his voice harsh with authority. "You lied about my wife and there is no excuse for that. You also have been treating the MacShane servants unfairly."

"They are a lazy bunch," Marta snapped.

"Not from what I learned speaking to our people," Bhric said. "Did you think I would not speak to all involved to learn the truth before making a wise and fair decision? You have shown me that you cannot be trusted when after all these years of not just serving my family but being part of it, I never doubted your trust."

"I want only what is best for you, my lord," Marta said tearfully and pointed at Tavia. "She is not to be trusted, and she is weak and will never serve you well let alone be able to bear you many bairns."

"That is not for you to judge or decide. Your duty is to serve me not decide for me. You will be sent home and it will be my father's chore to decide what is to be done with you."

"Please, my lord, do not send me away. I have looked after you since you have been young, you are like a son I never had. Please, my lord," Marta begged.

"If that is so, then you should have done all you could have to help my wife adjust to her new life here, not condemn her. And you should know, Marta, that I love my wife very much and I look forward to the life I will spend with her and the bairns she will give me, for she truly is a strong and loving woman."

Tavia was not the only one to stare at Bhric shocked. He may have claimed his love to her privately, but never did she think he would claim it publicly.

"Shea will be in charge of the keep's servants and my wife will run the keep as is her duty," Bhric announced.

Marta turned and fled the keep in tears.

"See that she does not spread more lies, Sven, and we need to talk. I do not like what is being said about my wife and I fear someone may be spreading lies about her on purpose," Bhric said.

"Lady Tavia and I can share a brew while you two talk," Ingrid suggested and looked to Tavia. "It will give me a chance to apologize and to truly get to know her."

"I would like that," Tavia said, hoping for a fresh start with her sister-in-law.

Bhric hugged his wife and kissed her cheek. "My mother was right about you. You will make me a good wife and I will make you a good husband."

Tavia was afraid to feel blissful once again, fearing something would challenge it, and it did.

A warrior rushed into the keep, snow covering his cloak. "Another animal has been found dead in the woods, my lord, and his heart is missing."

Chapter Twenty-one

Tavia walked through the village, a light snow falling. Fen sniffed the snow-covered ground not far from her, his glance never long away from her. It had been several days since a wolf had been found gutted and the heart removed. People did not waste time speculating on what it might mean. To the Northmen, a wolf indicated power and strength but also savagery. Was it a sign that a savage was among them? Would he grow tired of killing animals and kill a human next? Or was this the work of an evil witch who sought more power to do her evil deeds?

Some villagers turned their backs on Tavia as she walked and while it troubled her, she was not surprised by it. Some were upset with what happened to Marta, blaming Tavia, believing she bewitched people, fearing what she might do to those who would speak against her. She had no idea how to change their perception of her. Also, she did not think it had helped that Bhric had proclaimed his love for her. That news had spread rapidly and only added to the belief that she had bewitched him. How had he gone from displeasure with his wife to love so swiftly? She had to have done something to him, a potion or spell of some sort the wagging tongues insisted.

The gossip did not have her questioning how she and Bhric felt about each other, their love was undeniable. It was love that gave her pause. How was it that love could claim a heart so suddenly? She could not explain it just as she could not explain how she missed him terribly when he was not with her or how happy she felt every time she saw him or how her passion soared for him with the simple touch of his hand, and how she loved to fall asleep in his arms at night and wake wrapped in them in the morning. How had he become such an essential part of her life?

Love! Love had struck them without either of them realizing it until they had no choice but to accept the truth. Now neither of them would ever deny it.

"Good day, my lady."

Tavia turned with a smile. "Good day, Glenna. How is William doing?"

The older woman sighed. "One day he is good, the next not so much. I fear he will never be as strong as he once was." A smile suddenly lit her face. "I remember when I first saw him. He was strong and handsome, but he did not like me much since the chieftain at the time insisted he wed me or his da would be put off the farm. The chieftain had heard that William was going to leave the clan and seek his own fortune. He was a good farmer and warrior when needed and the chieftain did not want to lose him. We fell in love along the way, buried two bairns before their time and made sure our son, Terence, got to do what William was unable to… leave the clan and seek his own fortune." Tears trickled down her cheeks. "A new chieftain changed things, demanded more than William could give and we were forced off the farm." She shook her head fighting her tears.

Tavia rested a gentle hand on the woman's back. "You have a new and safe home here with the Clan MacShane. You need not worry any longer."

"You are far too kind, my lady," Glenna said.

"Nonsense. It is what family does and Clan MacShane is your family now. Let me walk with you back to your cottage and visit with William."

"He would enjoy seeing you," Glenna said.

Tavia caught Marta watching them, her sneer obvious.

"Marta does not speak well of you, my lady," Glenna said. "Every time she brought food to us, I would ask her to please thank you for your generosity. She would snap at me and tell me it was Lord Bhric who was generous not you."

"Marta is protective of Lord Bhric and accustomed to her ways. She is having difficulty adapting here," Tavia said, seeing no reason to disparage the woman. Hurtful words helped no one and would only make matters worse.

"Again, you are too kind, my lady," Glenna said as they continued to the cottage.

Bhric watched his wife walk with Glenna and he also saw the way Marta's eyes followed her.

"Does she watch her tongue?" Bhric asked Sven, his glance staying on Marta.

Sven laughed. "What woman watches her tongue?"

Bhric turned a scowl on him. "That one since I told you to make sure of it."

Sven's laughter vanished. "Ingrid has been keeping a watch on Marta and making certain her tongue tells no tales. Though there are plenty of tales circulating."

"Someone is behind the animals' deaths and the gossip about my wife that is purposely being spread. To what end, is what worries me. At least we have determined that whoever slaughters the animals waits to do so until the snow falls so their tracks will be covered leaving us unable to follow any trail."

"The culprit is also wise enough to go beyond our sentinels' reach. If we did not send out patrols we would not have found the animals. That tells us it is someone who knows our ways, someone most likely among us."

"Or it could be someone who reports to another what goes on here," Bhric said.

"It cannot be one of ours," Sven said.

"We cannot rule out anyone. Who would have thought Marta would have lied about my wife, she having been like family to us? You and Ingrid did not even give it a thought."

Sven hung his head. "You are right, neither of us did. But what of Clan MacShane?"

"As I said no one can be ruled out, everyone is suspect," Bhric said, his glance taking in the whole area where he and Sven stood and talked.

"There are many who still believe your wife has bewitched you as she did Fen and Bones."

"Finding those responsible for the animal killings and seeing them suffer for it will help, but I fear time is the only thing that will help the other problem. It was my lack of not accepting Tavia as my wife that has caused this problem. The tribe would have accepted her if I had," Bhric said, realizing much of the blame for his wife's sufferings was on him.

"That is true. You did not treat her as well as you should have." Sven grinned. "You should have trusted your mother's choice in a wife."

Bhric cringed. "I do not need to be reminded of that."

Sven laughed. "I think you are reminded of that every day."

"I should have sent you home," Bhric snapped.

"I am home and glad for it," Sven said proudly.

"So am I, my friend, so am I," Bhric said with a hardy slap to Sven's back as they walked, continuing to talk.

***

Tavia thought on William after visiting with him. She had spied in him the strong man he once had been, and she also saw the love in his eyes he had for his wife. But she also spotted worry in his eyes and the way his wrinkles creased when he spoke about earning his keep. No amount of reassuring seemed to help. He was truly more worried about the course of his wife's future than his own.

Frantic barking drew Tavia's attention as well as others. Bones came racing up to Tavia, Fen quick to stand in front of her growling and snapping, warning him away.

"Easy, Fen, Bones means me no harm," Tavia said, and the hound calmed though remained alert. Bones had not stopped barking and turning away from her. "Is Uta hurt?" Tavia asked. The hound barked, ran, and stopped, then looked back at her and ran again. Tavia called out as she and Fen ran after Bones, "Someone fetch Uta's father and Lord Bhric."

Tavia paid no heed to her leg, she rushed as fast as she could, Fen running up ahead of her. They had gone only a short distance in the woods when Bones stopped beneath a large pine tree barking.

"Bones! Bones!" came a shout from within the tree branches.

"Uta!" Tavia shouted, Uta's plight causing a rush of painful memories to surface.

"I hurt my arm, my lady, and cannot get down," Uta called out.

"Help is coming, Uta," Tavia yelled.

"I am cold, my lady," Uta shouted back.

Tavia turned to Bones and pointed toward the village. "Go hurry them along."

Bones took off barking.

"Bones left?" Uta called out with worry.

"I sent him to hurry the others along," Tavia said, her voice raised strong enough for the lass to hear her. "Someone will be here soon to get you down."

"Please do not leave me alone, my lady," Uta cried out.

"I am staying right here, Uta, as is Fen," Tavia assured her.

"Thank you, my lady," Uta called out, then a crack of a branch was heard and Uta screamed.

Bhric heard the scream along with Uta's father and several other men and he ran. The others ran as well but were not as fast as he was. He arrived to see his wee wife reaching her arms up to catch Uta, and as she did she turned swiftly to shield her with her body as a large branch came tumbling down on top of both of them.

Bhric's fierce roar sounded as if it would split the earth in two.

Fen had dodged the falling branch and had worked his body halfway under it to try and reach Tavia by the time Bhric reached him.

With a roar of a Northman charging into battle, Bhric grabbed the thick branch, lifted it, his muscles tightening from the weight of it, and flung it away with another roar. The other men reached them by then and were staring down at Tavia's lifeless body.

Bhric squatted down and turned his wife over gently to find Uta beneath, her eyes wide with fright, not so his wife. He moved Tavia completely off Uta and her da hurried and scooped her up. He rested his wife in his arms. She was far too pale and there was no movement to her.

Fen stood at Bhric's shoulder and whined as he pushed his wife's cloak aside and laid a hand to her chest.

"Does she breathe?" Sven asked anxiously.

"Aye," Bhric said and tapped his wife's face gently. "Tavia, wake up. Wake up." He scooped up a handful of snow and rubbed it over her face and her eyes fluttered slightly.

"Oh, good Lord, not again!" Hertha cried out and ran to Tavia, dropping down beside her. "Did she fall from the tree?"

"Nay," Bhric said, "she caught Uta as she fell and protected her with her wee body as a tree branch collapsed on them. She breathes but she does not wake, though her eyes fluttered when I brushed her face with snow."

Hertha scooped up more snow and laid it on Tavia's brow and neck and slapped her face with a bit of strength. "Wake up, Tavia. Wake up. You are safe." She sent an apologetic look to Bhric for her actions.

"Do what you must to wake her," Bhric said.

Hertha piled more snow on her and continued to repeatedly slap her cheek with a degree of strength that would wake her.

Fen protested with a growl and Bhric was quick to warn him. "Silence! Hertha helps Tavia."

The hound quieted but kept cautious eyes on Hertha.

"Wake up, Tavia. You are all right. There is nothing to fear. Wake up," Hertha kept prodding.

Tavia's eyes finally fluttered open to Bhric's relief and Fen stepped around him to lick Tavia's face.

Bhric went to stop him.

"Nay, my lord. It is good for her to feel a familiar, comforting touch," Hertha cautioned.

Jealousy was not often known to Bhric, though he had learned that when it came to his wife it was. He felt it now, his wife fighting to open her eyes as the hound licked her face.

"Fen," Tavia said. "Bhric. Get Bhric."

His heart swelled with relief and was glad her first thought was to fetch him. "I am here, my love." He took hold of her hand and squeezed it, and he was pleased and further relieved when she returned his squeeze.

"Uta?" she cried out worried for the lass.

"She is fine. You kept her safe," Bhric said, looking to the lass still in her father's arms to see tears running down her cheeks. “Do you feel any pain anywhere?”

“Nay,” she said, shaking her head. “I recall turning to avoid the thick portion of the branch, knowing the smaller branches would not harm us and could very well protect us.”

“A quick and wise decision. I am going to sit you up,” Bhric cautioned. “Tell me if you feel pain anywhere.” He eased her up after she nodded.

“No pain,” she said with a smile.

Hertha moved aside as did Fen when Bhric announced he would get her to her feet.

“Aye,” Tavia agreed. “The cold feels as if it has seeped into my bones.”

Bhric stood, leaving his wife sitting, then reached down and slowly brought her to her feet.

Tavia smiled until she went to stand on her own and a pain shot through her leg that had her gasping and gripping her husband’s arm before she dropped in a dead faint.

***

“You are never to do that again. Do you understand me, wife?” Bhric ordered, his pounding heart calming now that his wife was tucked safely in their bed, her scarred leg resting on a pillow and warm wet cloths covering it.

“Will you please stop pacing, you are making my stomach churn,” she said and patted a spot on the bed beside her. “Come sit by me.”

Bhric shook his head as he went to her and sat. “I have known a fright I have never known when I took what I thought was your lifeless body in my arms. I have grown accustomed to having you close. I would feel like a part of me is missing if I lost you. So, you will not place yourself in such a dangerous position again."

"I will do my best," she said, not wanting to cause him worry, but happy to hear he felt her such a strong part of him.

He leaned over to rest his brow to hers. "I cannot lose you. We need time to love each other."

"Lots of time," Tavia said and pressed her cheek to his before kissing his lips gently.

"Endless time, wife, endless time," he whispered in her ear after the kiss ended. He reached down to feel the cloths on her leg. "They have chilled." He stood and began removing them. "Hertha and Greta both agree the cloths must be heated to help ease the pain."

"You do not need to tend my leg, Bhric. Hertha would gladly do it," Tavia said.

"Nay, I will do it, so that I can make certain you stay put in that bed," he said with a scowl at his wife. "And you will not leave that bed until your leg heals."

"I cannot stay abed too long, or my leg will worsen. The rest of the day will do, then I must walk, though with caution, and my leg will heal fine." She was glad he wished to tend her. She felt safe with him especially since old memories were creeping up to haunt her after today's incident and with him there he would keep her busy with talk and later when she slept she hoped his strong arms would keep her nightmares at bay.

Bhric trusted she told him the truth about her leg,

but that would not stop him from seeking Hertha's advice just to be certain.

"How is Uta?" she asked as he dropped the cool cloths in a bucket by the hearth and brought the other bucket that sat there over by the bed.

"She is being punished," Bhric said and continued before his wife could protest. "Her father's choice and I agree. Uta must learn to listen when she is told. All have been forbidden to go into the woods alone, since the incidents with the animals, not even a short distance as she did. And her father has repeatedly warned her not to climb trees, especially in the winter. She could have suffered serious injuries if it had not been for your help. Or worse, the both of you could have died. She must learn to obey my edicts and her father's word."

Bhric's hand roamed gently over the wide scar on the front of her leg. He had avoided it before now and had made no mention of it to her, thinking she would tell him about it in her own good time. However, he did not want to wait any longer.

"Tell me how you got this, wife," he ordered, leaving no doubt that this time he would have an answer.

Tavia dropped her head back on the pillows braced behind her back. She knew this day would come and while she thought she was prepared for it, the incident today proved she was not at all prepared to revisit it.

"You do not have to go into detail," Bhric said and laid the first heated cloth on her leg, pressing his hand against it so her leg could soak up the heat.

Tavia sighed with the relief it brought her. "I climbed a tree."

"I know that, but why did you climb the tree?"

Tavia closed her eyes as she said, "To save a bairn stuck there."

Chapter Twenty-two

Bhric was pleased to see his wife walking with his sister Ingrid through the village, talking and laughing. His sister had made an effort to get to know Tavia in the last few days and he was glad and grateful. If she accepted Tavia, others in the tribe would be more likely to follow suit. Maybe then healing could start for all.

Since the incident with Uta, his wife's leg had healed well though she remained cautious. And now that she had told him how she had gotten the limp, he found that what he had once thought of as weakness, he now thought of as a mark of great courage.

"She told you."

Bhric kept his eyes on his wife as Greta stopped beside him. "She did."

"It took courage to do what she did," Greta said.

"Who and what courage?" Sven asked, joining Bhric and Greta.

"You should tell Sven," Greta said. "All here should know of her bravery. They may think differently of her then." She walked away, leaning on her staff as she went.

"Tavia told me what caused her limp," Bhric said, recalling the strength it had taken for her to relive her ordeal as she had told him the story. Her words came back to him, and he felt her pain all over again.

"There was a young lad, Shep, six years, in the clan

who loved climbing trees and he was a good climber. The problem was that he began to climb higher and higher in the tallest of trees. His da feared he would fall and injure himself badly or worse die. But Shep paid no heed to his da's worries or commands not to climb too high. One day after a snowfall Shep climbed higher than he ever had. Unfortunately, his climb down did not go well. A branch broke and he fell and got stuck amongst the branches. Rescue became difficult since the men who tried to reach him, including his da, found the branches at a certain point not thick enough to hold their weight. Someone of light weight and height was needed to rescue him.

A cold fear had chilled Bhric when he heard his wife say, "I volunteered."

"I had climbed trees when young, so I had no fear of doing so. I reached Shep without a problem only to discover his arm had been pierced by a branch in his fall. He was crying and frightened. I tore a piece of my shift off to bandage his wound, then after talking a bit with him we began our descent. The lad clung to me with every step we took, his small body trembling against me. All was going well when I stepped on a branch and heard a crack. I had not considered that the men who had tried to rescue Shep had caused some of the branches to splinter and even a light weight would be enough for the damaged branch to completely break away.

"His small arms hurried around my neck as I wrapped my arms firmly around him and just in time. The branch gave way, and we went tumbling down through endless tree branches. I had wrapped my legs around Shep to protect him and so a branch would not catch him and pull him out of my arms. A splintered branch caught my leg, slicing through it and hooking on, suspending me and Shep upside down near the bottom of the tree. The men were able to easily get Shep from my arms. I on the other hand was not so easy to free. The flesh had been torn wide, the bone exposed, and the splintered branch sticking off a larger branch was embedded like a hook in my leg. The only way they could get me down was to take the branch down with me. Thank God I passed out and I would have preferred to remain so until the healer finished tending my leg. The healer thought the same as Greta did about Lath, either way, cut it off or stitch it, I would not survive. My da demanded she stitch it as best she could, and she did. No one knows how I survived the ordeal or the pain that I never thought would end, but I did, and my limp is a reminder of it."

Sven stared at Bhric after he provided a summary of what his wife had told him and Bhric looked away thinking how he had stared wordless at his wife when she had finished, realizing the immense pain she must have suffered. He thought to tell her how brave she was, how proud he was to have such a courageous wife, but instead he remained silent as he wrapped his arms around her and held her tight and said what came instinctively to him, "I love you, Tavia, always."

Her arms had gone around his neck, and he felt her tears when she pressed her wet cheek against his, and tears choked her words when she spoke. "I had prayed to die, the pain was so horrendous, but now I know why my prayers went unanswered. Fate had something wonderful in store for me… you."

"She truly is a brave soul," Sven said, interrupting Bhric's thoughts, though the joy his wife's words had brought him still lingered in his heart.

"Aye, that she is, and just the woman I need as a wife," Bhric said proudly.

"The men are near ready," Sven said, glancing to where the warriors gathered.

"Both tribe and clan warriors?" Bhric asked.

"Aye, along with mumblings of discontent."

"And you?" Bhric asked.

"I see your wisdom. If we do not fight together we both lose," Sven said. "And what better way to start than to have the tribe and clan search for anything that may lead us to whoever is killing the animals and stealing their hearts."

***

"I believe three more workers are needed in the kitchen and two more in the keep," Tavia said to Shea as they entered the Great Hall.

Even before Tavia was back on her feet, she had begun to discuss the workings of the keep with Shea. After talking with her, Tavia had more servants added in the kitchen and keep itself.

"That would be of great help, my lady," Shea said, a bright smile lighting her pretty face.

"You will bring all complaints and problems to me immediately. Leave something to fester and it will be difficult to heal well, so do not feel any issue is too small to discuss with me."

"As you say, my lady," Shea said, and her smile

faded as she seemed to hesitate for a moment. "There is a small issue."

"Tell me," Tavia urged eager to see to it.

"I worry that you have remained on your leg too long, having walked in the village earlier and then through part of the keep with me. I believe it would be wise of you to sit and rest while you enjoy a hot brew."

A smile hurried over Tavia. "A very wise suggestion indeed, Shea."

Shea's smile returned, relieved Tavia took no offense to her remark. "I will fetch you a hot brew, my lady."

Tavia went and sat near the hearth where Fen had gone as soon as she and Shea had entered the room. The hound was right. They both needed a rest. A slight pain remained in her leg, but then she had walked without rest this day. She had enjoyed her walk with Ingrid. It had been nice to talk and laugh with her and see that she was truly trying to befriend her.

Ingrid had caused Tavia's cheeks to heat when she claimed that her brother was a virile man and Tavia would surely carry many bairns for him and she was also happy that her brother's bairns and hers would grow together like brothers and sisters. It was a thought that had pleased Tavia, never having had siblings and wishing she had. She was glad her bairns would not face the same loneliness.

Shea returned with the brew and Tavia sat alone with her thoughts as she enjoyed it. She smiled softly when her thoughts drifted to the moment she had told Bhric about the accident. She had seen the pain in his eyes for her and also a spark of anger that she had suffered such an ordeal. But mostly, she had been pleased when he did not praise her for her bravery but told her that he loved her. That had said more to her and meant more to her than anything.

Tavia lingered at the table over her hot brew and when her head began to grow heavy with fatigue, she decided to seek her bed for a brief rest. Fen stretched reluctantly to his feet until she said, "We go take a rest, Fen."

He shot past her to the stairs.

Once in the room, Tavia removed all but her shift and slipped into bed, cuddling the covers around her. "A short nap, Fen."

The hound paid her no heed since he was already sound asleep by the hearth.

***

Bhric looked down at his sleeping wife and smiled. She was just where he wanted her and though she was not naked, he would remedy that soon enough. He went to disrobe when his glance fell on her face. She appeared in a peaceful sleep. She had to have been tired to seek their bed during the day, unless… had her leg pained her? Had she done too much? He had noticed of late the time she had spent with Shea seeing that changes were not only implemented in the kitchen but in the keep as well. Should he disturb her when what she needed was rest?

"Are you going to continue to stand there or join me?" Tavia asked without opening her eyes.

"You tricked me to think you were sleeping when

you heard me enter the room," he accused though not harshly.

She smiled as she opened her eyes. "Nay, the heavy scent of the woods entered the room with you and invaded my dream, which you must now make sure to finish for me."

"And what dream is that, wife?"

"The part where I could feel your hard shaft slipping into me after you found me in bed sleeping and joined me." Her arms stretched out to him and went around his neck as soon as he leaned down.

He gave her a gentle, lingering kiss. "Was I naked?"

"Aye, as was I."

"Did I tempt you with kisses?" he asked and kissed along her neck.

"All over," she said on a pleasurable sigh.

"I like your dream."

"Then join me in it," she urged with a whisper.

Bhric stood to hurry and oblige her when a horn sounded, and he stopped to listen and heard footfalls racing up the stairs.

A knock at the door came before a voice called out, "An urgent message from Birger, my lord. Sven says to come at once."

Tavia was out of the bed with haste and slipping into her garments just as quickly.

Worry for her da and clan was easy to see in the tight lines of her face, so he waited for her and hoped the news would not prove disastrous.

Fen followed them down the stairs and into the Great Hall where the messenger waited. It was one of

Bhric's warriors and he was gulping down ale like a man dying of thirst.

"Bernard, what word have you from Birger?" Bhric asked and he felt his wife's hand close tightly around his.

"Things do not go well, my lord," Bernard said, clinging to his tankard. "An illness plagues the people."

"And you bring it here?" Bhric accused with a sharp tongue.

"We need help, my lord, and I am the only one who the illness has not touched," Bernard explained.

Tavia could not wait to ask. "Is my da ill?"

"Aye, my lady, bedridden these last two days," Bernard said.

"I must go to him," Tavia said, releasing her husband's hand, ready to rush off.

Bhric grabbed her hand before it completely left his. "Nay! You will not go there. I will not chance you getting the sickness."

"My da needs me," she pleaded.

"Nay, my lady," Bernard said. "Your da insisted you not return home. He will not have the sickness strike you or anyone else. He and Birger hope that Lord Bhric will know what to do to help them."

"Birger is ill?" Bhric asked.

"Aye, but not as ill as some. He still sees to his duties," Bernard said.

"Auda, the clan healer, how is she?" Tavia asked.

"The illness had her abed for two days, but she is on her feet now though a bit weak," Bernard said.

"How many deaths?" Bhric asked and felt his wife squeeze his hand.

"Three, my lord. Two from the clan and one of ours," Bernard said. "We beg of you, my lord, please help us."

Bhric was skilled when it came to battle, fighting an enemy, but an enemy that could be seen and that a weapon can destroy. He had no such skills when it came to fighting a foe that could not be seen.

"Hertha and Greta, my lord," Tavia said.

Bhric shook his head, thinking his wife foolish. "I will not send either one and chance losing them."

"I agree, but if Bernard explains the illness to both healers they may know how to treat it. Bernard can then return with their advice and Auda can see if it will help," Tavia suggested.

"A wise suggestion, wife," Bhric said proud that his wife thought so quickly of a possible solution. She was proving more and more to be much of what he had hoped for in a wife and proving more and more that he had judged her too quickly and harshly, something he continued to regret.

"Aye, my lady, that might prove beneficial," Bernard said.

Bhric turned to Sven. "Bring Greta and Hertha here."

"I will go with him," Tavia said.

"No need for you to go," Bhric said.

Tavia tugged at her husband's hand. "A word, my lord."

Bhric signaled Sven to wait and stepped a distance away. "Why the urgency to go?"

Tavia was glad he did not threaten her with that no matter what she had to say, he would not let her go. It meant he was willing to listen and that pleased her.

"No doubt all know by now that a messenger has arrived from Clan Strathearn. Doritt and Edward have a terrible fear that they will be returned to Lord Ivan. I want to assure the children that all is well, and they are safe."

He could not fault her for thinking of the children and making sure they did not suffer needlessly in worry.

"You will take Fen with you," he said, and his wife beamed with a smile of happiness that poked at his heart. Bloody hell, but he loved his wife.

"You are the best husband," Tavia said and went up on her toes to kiss him.

Bhric grabbed her around her waist and lifted her so that she could reach his lips easily.

"Later," she whispered in his ear when the kiss finished.

"Sooner," he whispered back and was pleased when he felt her shudder against him. He placed her on her feet. "Sven, my wife and Fen go with you, be watchful of her."

Sven laughed. "That war hound will not let anyone near her."

"And either will you," Bhric ordered.

"Aye, my lord," Sven said and grabbed a cloak from the ones that hung on pegs near the door to drape over Tavia before they left the Great Hall.

"My solar, Bernard," Bhric ordered, taking advantage of time alone with the man.

Bernard followed apprehensively behind him.

Bhric filled a goblet with wine and handed it to

Bernard once in his solar. "What haven't you told me, Bernard?"

Bernard gulped down a good portion of wine before he spoke. "Many in the clan and even among our own people believe the witch cursed the clan to suffer before Lord Varrick took her away."

"Did anyone hear her curse the clan?" Bhric asked.

Bernard shook his head. "None can say they did."

"What else do you keep from me?" Bhric asked, easy to see the man was reluctant to say more.

Bernard fortified himself with more wine before responding. "I have been warned to hold my tongue."

"Who warned you?" Bhric demanded, angry that someone had had the audacity to warn one of his warriors to keep something from him.

"Auda, the clan healer. She warned me not to speak of it or—"

"Or what?" Bhric demanded again when Bernard suddenly stopped speaking.

"Forgive me, my lord, but I do not know if I should say."

"I will make it easy for you, Bernard. You will tell me or suffer for it," Bhric ordered.

"I will not be the one who suffers, my lord."

Bhric was ready to threaten the man when he gave it thought. "Auda attempts to protect someone."

"Aye, my lord," Bernard said relieved.

Bhric did not have to guess who. He knew. "My wife."

Bernard nodded, holding his tongue as if fearful something might slip out.

"It is just you and me, Bernard. You will tell me,"

Bhric said in a commanding tone that brooked no opposition.

Bernard did not hesitate to obey. "There is talk that the witch allowed herself to be caught to carry out her evil plan. She cast a spell on your wife so that you and others will fall to her command. She will then cast a spell on Lord Varrick, and he will fall to her command. Once done, she will rule both clans and more if given the chance."

"This is dangerous talk," Bhric said, fear rising up within him for his wife.

"It is, my lord," Bernard hastily agreed and lifted his goblet to his lips as if to stop himself from saying any more.

"You downed the last of your wine only moments ago, what do you fear saying?"

Bernard kept his voice low though there was only himself and Bhric in the room. "How is it that your wife has the skill or power to command a war hound, my lord? I only ask because it is what others will ask and believe when those in Clan Strathearn learn of it. Not that I would say a word, but eventually it will be heard. And news will also be heard of how well you and your wife get along, from what I can see, when you were not at all pleased with her when you left Clan Strathearn."

Bhric could see how it could be misconstrued, especially with an illness having hit the clan and he was quick to order, "You will repeat none of this to anyone."

"Aye, my lord, but—"

"But what?" Bhric urged when Bernard hesitated.

"But what by chance if it is true?"

Chapter Twenty-three

Bhric kept his eyes on his wife as she talked with Hertha, Greta, and Bernard in the Great hall. They were deep in discussion asking Bernard endless questions while Greta and Hertha exchanged opinions. Had the witch placed a spell on his wife or as Sven had once suggested… had Tavia asked the witch for… what? Had she requested a spell to have him fall in love with her? He did not want to believe that, but would he be a fool not to consider it? But what were the consequences of him doubting their love for each other?

"You do not look pleased," Sven said when he stopped next to Bhric. "More troubling news?"

"Something I will need to keep watch on."

"Should I be aware of it?" Sven asked.

"Not yet. I want to see what comes of it without anyone knowing," Bhric said. "Though you will keep me aware of any rumors concerning my wife."

"The clan favors her, some of our people warm to her and then there are those who distrust her. They wonder how she commands the war hounds so easily and how their leader went from disappointment in his chosen bride to declaring his love for her. Then there is what happened with Marta. She has been good to many, and they are upset that she lost her position in the keep. Clan MacShane on the other hand loves Lady Tavia and finds no fault with her. All of that is according to your sister."

"And how does my sister truly feel about my wife?"

Sven laughed. "You know your sister."

"She will find out for herself."

Sven nodded. "Should I watch out for anything in particular?"

"You seem to have it all in hand just keep me apprised."

"Should we be concerned?" Sven asked.

Bhric said what he did not like to think. "It is a possibility."

"Lord Bhric," Tavia called out, waving him over.

"None of us gave it thought, my lord," Bernard said in way of an apology when Bhric reached the table where they all sat.

Bhric slipped in beside his wife on the bench. He rested his hand on her thigh and gave it a squeeze while looking at Bernard. "Tell me."

Greta responded. "From what Bernard tells us there are various possibilities that can be causing the illness… poison being one of them and a distinct possibility."

That Bhric had not expected to hear. "What makes you suspect poison?"

"Bernard is not ill while the whole clan suffers," Greta said. "The question is why?"

"Birger sent me to scout deeper into the woods to see what might be afoot," Bernard explained. "I was gone several days and returned to find the clan struck with sickness."

Hertha continued to explain. "He had not eaten any

of the food the others had and once home he ate what food he had with him."

"All ate the food from the storage shed," Bernard said. "I am eager to return and dispose of all the food there. If it proves the food is poisoned, the clan will heal and get well."

"They are only poisoned enough to make them ill?" Bhric asked. "What of the ones who have died?"

"It would seem so," Greta said, "and as for those who died? They either consumed more than others or they were weak to begin with and not strong enough to fight the poison. Or they could have gotten a portion of food that was more heavily poisoned."

Bhric did not like what he was hearing.

Sven felt the same. "Someone tries to weaken the clan, make them unable to defend themselves."

"Aye," Bhric agreed. "I will have a cart prepared with food for you to take with you. See that Birger has guards posted on the food shed once you restock it and ask about who was seen coming and going from it. A troop of warriors will go with you, but they will camp a distance from Clan Strathearn. They will scout the area and see if they can find anything and keep you all safe until the sickness passes. You will keep them apprised of how things go, and they will pass it on to me. You will rest tonight and leave in the morning."

"Aye, my lord, I will see to it, though I would prefer to leave as soon as the cart is ready," Bernard said. "The faster I return, the faster many may heal. Besides, I have come to care for a woman in Clan Strathearn and she has taken ill. I would like to return to her as soon as possible."

"You are a good and brave warrior, Bernard. I will not forget it," Bhric said.

"Thank you, my lord, but I do nothing more than my duty."

"You will rest while the cart is prepared with food for you," Bhric ordered.

"I am grateful, my lord, and look forward to reporting good news to you."

"Come and rest at my cottage," Greta offered. "Hertha and I will prepare a mixture that will prove helpful to those more ill than others."

"Bernard," Tavia said as he stood to go with Greta and Hertha. "Please tell my da to get better soon so he may come and visit with us and see how happy I am with my husband and new home."

"I will tell him, my lady, and I am sure he will be pleased to hear how well you do for he has worried over you as do others in your clan," Bernard said and walked off with Greta and Hertha talking.

"I will see all is made ready for Bernard," Sven said and left as well.

Bhric's hand left his wife's leg to slip his arm around her slim waist and tuck her close, pleased by her remark. "So, you have come to realize what a wonderful husband I am?"

Tavia kissed his lips lightly. "There are some things I favor more about you than other things—" She scrunched her face.

Bhric did not like hearing there were things about him she disliked. "What are those other things?"

She ran a gentle finger over his lips. "When you fail to kiss me throughout the day. When you are gone too long from me, and my heart begins to ache. When you leave our bed before I wake in the morning. When it has been too long that I have felt your hand in mine. When I look upon you and fear that this is all a dream, and I will wake one day to find it all gone."

His hand went to the back of her neck, taking tight hold. "Do you feel my grip on you?"

Tavia nodded, his hand strong there that all but boasted, *I will never let you go*, and that brought her not only relief but a spark of pleasure.

"It is no dream. It is all real between you and me, and it will always be that way. Somehow I fell not just in love with you but deeply in love with you. A depth of love that can never be broken, never wane, never end. I cannot say when I realized I loved you or if the prelude to my disfavor with you was actually that I favored you, since I did find you appealing, and refused to admit just how much I did." That thought had him pausing a moment. He had not known she was his wife when he had nearly run her down with his horse and yet he had felt a stir in him for her. That was before she had visited with the witch. That meant his feelings for her had begun with a first look when he had had no knowledge of who she was. He rested his brow to hers relieved. "The love we found was relentless and refused to be denied no matter how stubborn each of us were and still are. I only wish I had been as quick to see what my mother knew and saw… that you would make me a perfect and loving wife."

They kissed again, lightly and tenderly then Tavia rested her head on his chest, his hand drifting off her neck and his arm going firm around her. She wondered over the fact that she had found love with a man she had thought would find nothing but disappointment with her for their entire married life.

Love surely was strange, absent from your life one minute then suddenly appearing the next and wondering where it had come from. How had it snuck up on her? Or how had she been so blind not to see it in the first place? And now knowing it, feeling it, relishing it, she never ever wanted to let it go. The thought had Tavia hugging her husband's arm as if somehow her meek hold could keep him with her forever.

"Any idea who might want to poison your clan?" Bhric asked.

Tavia was glad for the distraction from her thoughts, or she feared she might get teary-eyed. "Lord Ivan would be the first to come to mind, but what would he gain from it? The clan would revert to you upon my da's death. There would be no benefit in it for him. Could it possibly be someone who wishes ill will to you?"

"I imagine there are those who do not want to see a man who has Northmen blood in him inherit a title, a clan, and all its land, though I cannot say anyone displayed displeasure with it. My grandfather had made a point of gathering neighboring clan lords and chieftains alike and introducing them to me. He talked of my knowledge and skill as a warrior and how it could benefit each of them. That was how I met Torin. He attended in his father's stead, and we became instant friends."

"What of Lord Bennett, the previous lord of Clan MacVannan and Ivan's uncle?"

"He had been ill at the time and unable to attend the gathering.

When his wife grew quiet for several minutes, Bhric asked, "What troubles you, Tavia?"

She gave a quick glance around, seeing servants busy with scrubbing the tables and replacing candles. "Can we talk in your solar?"

"We can," he said, sliding off the bench and taking her with him. He took her hand as they walked to his solar, Fen quick to follow them.

Tavia went to the hearth, staring down at the flames appearing as if she questioned the wisdom of being there.

Fen sensed her unease and kept a watchful eye on her from where he lay curled up near the hearth.

Bhric came up behind her, his arms going around her to turn her gently to face him. "You will tell me what weighs so heavily on your mind."

"I did not think it would ever be necessary to ask you this question, but I find I must," she said, sounding reluctant to her own ears. "I hear the whispers and chatty tongues and now with news of illness at Clan Strathearn those tongues may grow out of control. What I need to know is that you do not doubt my love for you. That I requested no spell from Fia to cast on you nor did she offer one and how could she when she has no such power? She is simply a healer with a thirst for knowledge that would enable her to tend the sick and needy. If anyone cast a spell on either of us, it was fate since I believe we were destined for each other and perhaps, as strange as it may seem, both of our mothers knew that."

Bhric did not need to think on her words since he felt them in his heart. Their love was not conjured by a witch or touched by evil. It had been born of them both through trial and error and with much courage.

"I will be truthful, wife, as you have been with me."

That he believed her truthful touched her heart. She had feared it would take far longer for him to believe that of her and it made her love him even more.

"I questioned it briefly, thinking myself foolish if I did not consider it. But it was difficult to imagine, especially since I found you appealing when I saved you from being trampled on and sat you upon my horse." He frowned briefly. "Giving it thought, I got angry with you after that for not revealing who you were to me and what I presumed as weakness without even getting to know you. Besides, you had yet to visit the witch, yet to gather any spells, and that means I found you appealing of my own accord."

Truth slipped from her lips as well. "I visited with Fia many times before you arrived and never once did she speak ill of you. She told me you respected strength and courage, and I should show you the same."

"And you have, far more than I expected or thought possible," Bhric said and went to kiss her.

She rested her fingers to his lips. "Others might think differently, what then? Will they condemn me and call for me to be burned at the stake as so many did for Fia?"

Bhric took hold of her hand and kissed it, seeing worry swirling in her soft blue eyes. "I will not let that happen to you."

"Fear, especially fear rooted in lies, can cause frenzy among the people and provoke them to make demands."

Bhric took hold of her chin. "Listen well, wife. My tribe knows to obey me since they fear more of what I will do to them than they fear the witch. You are safe with me never doubt that. Now I will have what I presently desire most… a kiss from you."

Tavia reached her arms up and her husband lifted her around the waist, so she could easily slip them around his neck, and he could easily reach her lips.

His kiss never failed to send a thrill through her, never failed to light her passion, never failed to make her realize how much she loved him and never failed, at this precise moment, to let her know how much he loved her.

Bhric rested his brow to hers when the kiss ended and let a moment pass for his breathing to ease before he said, "I would bend you over the table, toss your garments up and take you here, but having been interrupted too often of late, I will not chance being deprived of you again. Tonight, wife, nothing will stop me from making love to you."

"You peak my passion with such words and the image it sets in my mind, so I hold you to your word that you will make love to me tonight, husband."

"You have my word," he said and went to kiss her again when a knock sounded at the door.

"The messenger is ready to leave and wishes to speak with you, my lord," a servant called out.

They both grinned, her husband's concern having proved true.

"I will be right there," Bhric called out.

"Tonight, husband," Tavia said with a smile before kissing his cheek.

Bhric set her on her feet and took her hand mumbling all the way to the door and beyond.

***

After seeing Bernard off Bhric and Tavia made their way through the village to Lath's mother's cottage so she could see how the young man was faring. They had almost reached it when Sven suddenly appeared and rushed at them.

"Looks like more bad news," Tavia whispered to her husband when she saw Sven's face puckered with concern.

"Tell me," Bhric said when Sven reached him.

"Another dead animal in the forest," Sven said.

"You will return to the keep while I see to this, Tavia," Bhric ordered.

"Nay," Tavia said. "I will not run and hide as if I have done something wrong. I will visit with Lath then return to the keep."

"As a Northman I admire your bravery but as your husband I worry over your foolishness," Bhric said and kissed her quick then turned to Sven. "Have a warrior keep watch on her."

"She has Fen," Sven said as if a warrior was useless. The scowl Bhric set on him had him saying, "I will assign a warrior to watch over her, my lord."

Whispers started as soon as her husband left her side and Tavia did her best to ignore them. It was foolish to believe that she had anything to do with the dead animals since the only time she had been in the woods and barely a few short steps in, was when she had found Fen. She was beginning to understand how Fia must have felt hearing what people assumed about her and fear began to poke at her as she made her way along the path.

"He sleeps peacefully right now, my lady, and he is doing well, walking a bit each day. He truly is improving," Lath's mum said, having stepped outside her cottage to talk with Tavia. "I will wake him if you wish."

"Nay. Nay, sleep helps heal him. I will visit tomorrow," Tavia said.

Lath's mum got teary-eyed. "I am forever grateful to you for saving my son's life, my lady, and seeing him well-tended. You are a blessing to this clan."

"Thank you, that means much to me," Tavia said, the woman's kind words touching her heart.

With a promise to her husband that she would return to the keep once done with Lath, she turned to go there now.

After walking only a short distance, Marta stepped in Tavia's path so abruptly that she stumbled and Fen rushed in front of her growling, sending Marta hurrying several steps back from the hound and Tavia.

"The witch brought evil on your clan, and she also sent it here with you," Marta accused. "You claim to love Lord Bhric. If you truly did, you would leave here so he and all others would be safe."

"I brought no evil with me, Marta, and you know more well than I do that Lord Bhric is a powerful and fearless warrior who would never run from evil. He would destroy it." Tavia saw heads bob in agreement of those who stopped to watch her and Marta, the warrior who followed Tavia being one of them.

"You will get what you deserve," Marta spat.

"Do not threaten me, Marta," Tavia warned, knowing she had to show strength not only to Marta but to those watching.

"Or what?" Marta challenged.

"Or you will answer to Lord Bhric," Tavia said.

"He is not blind. He will see you for what you truly are… evil," Marta accused again.

"Enough, Marta, begone with you," Tavia said with a dismissive wave of her hand, having seen more people gathering to listen and not wanting the confrontation to get out of hand.

"You cannot get rid of me that easily. I will be proven right," Marta said.

"You will not be here to see whether you are or not," Tavia said and hearing several gasps realized many thought her remark a threat and hurried to correct it. "You will be leaving for your homeland soon."

"We will see who will be leaving here," Marta said.

"Have you not gotten yourself into enough trouble, Marta?"

Tavia was relieved to hear Ingrid's warning.

"I have cared and tended you, your sisters, and all your brothers since you were all young. I know what is best for each of you. I knew you loved Sven before your mother and father did and I spoke in favor of him for you, for I knew he was good for you. This one,"

Marta said with a dismissive wave at Tavia, "is no good for your brother."

"I appreciate the care and love you gave me, my sisters, and my brothers, and I thank you for speaking up in favor of Sven. But my mother chose Tavia as wife to my brother and I believe it is time we all respected her choice whether we agree with it or not," Ingrid said. "And while some refuse to see it, it is obvious my brother loves his wife."

Marta went to argue.

"Enough, Marta," Ingrid said, "or you chance falling out of favor with my whole family."

That threat had Marta gasping and it actually brought tears to her eyes. With a lift of her chin, she turned and rushed off.

Ingrid took hold of Tavia's arm to walk along with her. "Marta has been a part of our family for as long as I can remember, and it truly hurts me to speak that way to her. I cannot understand why she has taken such a dislike to you or why she lied as she did about what went on between you and me. She has always been protective of me and my sisters and brothers, but I have never known her to be as unfair as she has been with you."

It made Tavia wonder as well. Why was Marta so vehemently opposed to her?

Ingrid stopped a moment, her hand going to rest on her large-rounded stomach.

"You are feeling well?" Tavia asked, concerned something might be wrong.

"I am and I will be glad when the little devil is born, he is forever kicking me," Ingrid said with a soft laugh and began walking again. “No doubt we will hear good news from you and Bhric soon.”

“It is possible,” Tavia said glad she could speak the truth and glad it might be possible that she could be with child.

Let’s sit and have a hot brew and talk,” Ingrid said and Tavia was only too happy to agree.

Bhric and Sven found their wives in the Great Hall a couple of hours later.

“Is all well?” Ingrid asked anxiously as both men approached the table.

“Aye,” Sven said. “It was nothing more than a dead animal mauled by another animal. His heart still intact.”

Tavia breathed a sigh of relief at the good news for a change.

Bhric joined his wife on the bench beside her. “We will eat and seek an early bed.” His arm hooked her around her waist, and he yanked her close to nibble teasingly at her neck.

“I agree,” Sven said and went to do the same to his wife.

“Whoa!” Ingrid said, her hand pressed to his chest, stopping him from getting close. “Do you see the size of me? I do not need anything else that is big inside of me right now.”

Bhric shook his head and Tavia chuckled.

Sven stuck his chest out. “At least she admits I am a good size.”

Tavia’s cheeks blushed and Bhric kept shaking his head.

“You two really are made for each other,” Bhric said.

"As are you and Tavia," Ingrid said. "I simply did not want to admit that Mum was right."

"As she usually is," Bhric said and called out, "food and drink!"

Talk went on as warriors from the tribe and clan entered the Great Hall for supper. Laughter filled the air, food was enjoyed, and much ale and wine drunk.

"Time to keep that promise, wife," Bhric whispered in her ear and rubbed his face in her soft dark hair, the scent of mint pleasing his nostrils.

Tavia smiled and responded by slipping her hand beneath the table to rest it between his legs and give his aroused manhood a squeeze.

Eager to have his wife to himself, Bhric went to announce their departure when a warrior burst through the doors.

"A FIGHT, MY LORD!" the warrior shouted.

Tribe warriors stood as did Clan MacShane warriors, anger on all their faces and their hands going to their weapons at their sides.

The warrior seeing what his shout had caused hurried to say, "Between tribe warriors."

"Stay here, wife," Bhric ordered annoyed his plans had been disrupted.

"Absolutely not," Ingrid said. "Tavia comes with me. I have been eager to watch a good fight."

Tavia did not have much choice. Ingrid grabbed her by the arm and propelled her out of the keep behind Sven and Bhric, both men shaking their heads, Fen keeping pace with them.

Two large men stood surrounded by Northmen who cheered them on as they threw endless punches.

The crowd parted to allow Bhric to enter, and the two men stopped abruptly when they caught sight of him.

The one man, blood running from his nose and mouth into his blond beard, said, "He said my wife was ugly. He deserves a beating."

The other man, whose one eye was nearly swelled shut, laughed. "She is ugly, but then so are you."

Punches were thrown again, and everyone cheered them on.

Tavia suddenly felt people closing in around her. No one had ever gotten that close to her with Fen by her side. That was when she realized the hound was not there. She made her way through the crowd and found him a distance away staring into the darkness growling.

She approached him cautiously. "What is wrong, Fen?"

He turned, growled, took a step forward, then whined.

"Someone is hurt?" she asked, and he hurried forward, the darkness swallowing him up. She did not hesitate she followed after him.

No torches lit this area, and she took cautious steps calling out to the hound. When she heard him whine, she headed toward the sound quickly. Her feet caught on something, and she tumbled forward landing heavily on the ground. Fen was quickly at her side. She turned, sat up and braced her hands on the ground to push herself to her feet.

Her hands were wet and sticky, and she brought them up close to her face to see what she had touched. That's when she spotted the flickering flame of a torch light rushing toward her, and not soon after two screams suddenly pierced the night air.

"SHE KILLED HER. SHE KILLED MARTA!"

Chapter Twenty-four

Tavia stared down at Marta, blood pooled beneath her head. Her eyes were closed and her body lifeless. She dropped down beside the woman and leaned her face close to Marta's lips to see if she could feel a breath. She also pressed her hand to her chest to see if she could feel it rise and fall.

"Get away from her! Get away from her! You will not steal what breath may linger in her," one woman accused.

"Get Greta. Marta is still alive," Tavia ordered her tongue sharp as she bundled what she could of Marta's cloak and pressed it to the back of her head.

"She killed her!" came another accusing voice that was echoed repeatedly by others.

"Good Lord, what happened?" Ingrid said, rushing toward a kneeling Tavia and stopping beside her, her eyes wide with shock.

Sven was not far behind his wife and stood next to her, a look of complete disbelief on his face as he stared down at Marta.

"Get up, wife," Bhric ordered when he appeared beside her.

"I cannot," Tavia said. "I keep the wound from bleeding."

"I saw her. I saw her," the woman with the torch accused. "I saw her trying to steal what breath is left in

Marta."

Fen kept a protective stance near Tavia, growling threateningly at the woman and she stumbled as she hurried to step back.

Hertha arrived and several people attacked her verbally.

"Do not let her help. She is a cohort of evil."

"She protects the witch."

"She will see Marta dead."

Hertha was stricken by the vile accusations but refused to remain silent. "I am a healer. I do no harm. Lady Tavia is not evil nor is she a witch. It is all of you who are evil speaking such vicious lies."

Tavia whispered a thank you to Hertha when she squatted down to look at Marta.

"A wound to the back of the head and lots of blood as you can see," Tavia said and felt a strong hand grip her arm and lift her to her feet.

"Hertha and Greta will see to her, wife," Bhric said.

Tavia saw that Greta had arrived and she leaned heavily on her staff as she peered down at Marta and spoke quietly with Hertha.

"I did not harm her," Tavia said, fearful her husband would think otherwise.

"I never thought you did, but you cannot stay here. The blood on your hands and garments do not bode well for you," he said and sent an anxious glance to Sven. "See to things here and send everyone to their cottages. Find me when it is done."

He went to hurry his wife to the keep and stopped when she gasped.

"My leg," she said. "I must have twisted it when I stumbled over Marta. Her husband went to pick her up. "Nay, I will not appear weak in front of everyone."

Bhric admired her for that but refused to allow her to suffer in pain. He coiled his arm around his wife's waist and lifted her feet slightly off the ground. She looked as if she walked along of her own accord when he actually carried her with one arm, her garments long enough and the dark night enough to conceal the truth.

"Who would do this and why?" Tavia asked as they neared the keep, Fen turning his head back now and then to keep watch.

"Let us hope that Marta wakes and tells us," Bhric said.

"Or I will continue to be blamed," she said with a shiver of the consequences that that would bring.

"Only fools who refuse to see what is in front of them would believe you hurt Marta," Bhric said and when they entered the keep he called out, "A bucket of warm water and cloths in my solar now."

"They believe what they will," Tavia argued and turned a glance on herself since there was finally sufficient light to see. Her eyes went wide at the amount of blood stained on her cloak and tunic and her hands were nearly covered with it.

Bhric removed her cloak and tossed it into the hearth's flames as if somehow removing the stain from her would see her innocent. As soon as the bucket of water and cloth were delivered, Bhric got busy cleaning her face first before he started on her hands.

"I have blood on my face?" Tavia asked and instinct had her raising her hands to touch it, and stopped, as if she could feel it when her hands were already covered in it.

"A few spots nothing more," Bhric assured her since it was the truth, and he gently rubbed the offending specks of blood off her cheek.

When he finished, he pushed up her sleeves before plunging her bloody hands into the bucket of warm water.

"What is in front of them that they do not see?" Tavia asked, his remark returning to her.

"You are a wee one and Marta is not. There is no way you could have hit her in the back of the head with enough strength to cause such a damaging wound."

"Witch's power," she whispered.

"Hush!" he ordered, her feather-light whisper sending a fright through him.

"It is what they will say," Tavia said. "There is too much speculation being whispered about me, and this incident only ignites the flames more."

Bhric took her hands out of the bucket and began to dry them, rubbing them vigorously with a cloth. He would not admit she was right, and he worried over the danger it would bring.

Sven announced himself with a shout and knock at the door that rushed opened before Bhric called out for him to enter.

"Marta remains unconscious, but the bleeding from the gash to her head has stopped. She rests comfortably in Greta's cottage. Greta says time will be Marta's fate."

Bhric understood. The more one lay unconscious from a wound the less likely they were to survive it. He had seen it numerous times after a battle and most times it did not turn out well.

"Arguments are breaking out between our tribe and the clan, the tribe condemning Tavia and the clan defending her," Sven said.

"Gather everyone outside the keep. I will speak to them," Bhric ordered.

Sven nodded and rushed off.

Bhric felt his wife tremble and saw that she had paled considerably. "I will see you to our bedchamber where you can rid yourself of those blood-stained garments and rest your leg."

"Nay," she said shaking her head vehemently. "I will not appear the coward."

"And what will they think if you stand beside me? That you control me with your evil ways?" he asked, angry that anyone could think that his kind wife was evil or that he, a mighty warrior, would fall prey to such nonsense.

Tavia felt helpless. It reminded her of the time after her accident and how she had allowed herself to wallow in self-pity far too long which made it even more difficult to climb out of it. It was a wasted time, and she would waste no more time.

"I would always stand beside you no matter what is said or thought of you since I know you are a good, honorable man and warrior and because my love for you would allow me to do no less. Wi—"

Bhric pressed his fingers to her lips preventing her from saying any more. "You made your point, wife. I would do no less for you though I question if such action will keep you safe."

She smiled softly. "I worry not for my safety since I have you and Fen."

Bhric glanced at the hound who remained alert not far from Tavia and at that moment he could not be more pleased that the war hound had become her constant companion.

"Your leg?" he questioned, this one time hoping she had no choice but to rest it.

"I will manage," she said with a defiance that made it clear she would not be dissuaded from her decision.

Bhric felt he should deny her for her own safety, but could not deny her, her courage. "You will obey my every word, wife, which means if I order you to retreat to the keep you will do so without question." When he watched his wife's face scrunch in thought, he was quick to say, "That has no need for thought. You obey or you remain in the keep."

"As you say, husband," Tavia said compliantly.

Bhric cringed. "Why when you sound so obedient do I think the complete opposite?" He shook his head not expecting or wanting her to answer.

Tavia had Shea get her clean garments from her bedchamber and Bhric insisted on helping her to change into fresh ones.

"I thought this night would be far different," he said as he helped his wife strip off her soiled garments.

"The night has many more hours left to it, husband, and a huge need for it to end with a touch of love," she said softly.

Bhric drew her against him to steal a kiss. "On that we agree, wife."

Once dressed, Bhric gathered up the blood-stained

garments and tossed them into the fireplace, the flames greedily swallowing them up.

"We will have no reminders of this dreadful night," he said.

"You cannot dispose of harsh memories so easily. I found the best thing to do is make new ones." She stretched her hand out to him. "Let us start making new ones tonight."

He took firm hold of her hand. "Besides being courageous, you are also wise."

"It is good you finally realize that," she said with a playful smile.

He hooked her around the waist with his arm. "There is a lot I am realizing about my wife like…" His whispered words were for her ears alone and they sent a blush rushing over her face.

"And they say I am evil," she said, her cheeks flushed red and a tremble of passion rocking her body.

"The people are gathered," came Sven's shout after a strong tap at the door.

"As are we," Bhric said, after yanking open the door.

Sven looked from Bhric to Tavia and back again. "You think it wise to bring her with you?"

"Tavia has done nothing wrong, and all must see that I stand by my wife," Bhric said.

Sven gave no response. He stepped aside and followed behind the couple and Fen.

Bhric kept his arm around his wife as they walked to ease any discomfort to her leg.

"The brief rest helped," she whispered to him so he would not worry and glad the pain was barely felt so she could keep her concentration on what mattered.

She found concentration more difficult than she had expected, seeing the large crowd that had gathered and spread out from the bottom of the keep's stairs. Several torches flickered throughout the crowd and cast light on the sea of faces, all waiting anxiously to hear their leader speak.

Tavia held tight to her husband's hand where they remained at the top of the stairs and had to stop herself from reacting to her husband's booming and authoritative voice as he began to speak.

"Tonight, one of our own, Marta, a beloved member of our tribe and my family, was brutally attacked. Greta presently sees to her care and when Marta wakes she will be able to tell us who did this heinous thing to her. In the meantime, a search will be conducted for the person. Whoever did this will be punished… severely." Bhric's voice grew stronger and more powerful. "Listen well for I am aware what many say, and I refuse to hear such lies! MY WIFE is not the culprit! She did not attack Marta."

"How do you know for sure!" someone yelled out.

Bhric's voice grew more powerful. "IT IS OBVIOUS. A woman my wife's size does not have the height to bash Marta's head with a rock nor does she possess the strength to throw a rock and cause such damage. This evil deed took strength and height to accomplish."

"A witch has such strength," another person called out.

"MY WIFE IS NO WITCH!" Bhric's voice carried with such strength over the crowd that some actually drew back. "She has done nothing but good since arriving here even when I treated her poorly because I judged her wrongly."

"She mystifies you!" another called out.

"What woman does not do that to a man?" one of Bhric's warriors yelled and the men in the crowd laughed. Not so the women.

"She cast a spell on you," a woman shouted.

"THAT IS UTTER NONSENSE!"

A hush settled over the crowd and a path was cleared for Greta to step forward and be heard.

"Lord Bhric is no fool. He would not let himself be snagged by a spell. But like all men he cannot ignore if lucky enough to be struck by love. He can fight it as he tried to do, but love has its own strength and try as you might, it will eventually claim victory over you." Greta spun slowly in a circle. "What man here will deny it or a woman as well?"

Not a voice spoke up.

Bhric realized then what was happening and spoke with authority. "Someone tries to divide us, tries to weaken us, tries to conquer us."

Angry shouts filled the air.

"We stand together, or we fall apart. What shall it be?" Bhric commanded with authority.

"TOGETHER," the crowd shouted without hesitation and cheers rang through the crowd.

"WE FIGHT!" Bhric yelled like a courageous leader, leading his warriors into battle, and the crowd erupted in cheers.

The crowd drifted apart, a sense of unity filling the air and Bhric turned to Tavia. "Stay here while I go speak with Greta."

"The day has worn me out. I will seek the comfort of our bedchamber," Tavia said.

"The stairs will be too much for you to climb. Wait in the Great Hall for me," he ordered.

She smiled and turned and entered the keep.

Bhric shook his head. His wife would not heed his command but if he hurried he would catch her on her way up the stairs to their bedchamber.

He took the steps two at a time down to hurry to Greta. "Tell me the truth about Marta."

"Time will tell the truth about Marta," Greta said. "Though I will tell you what Hertha surmises and I tend to agree with the young woman. She has an intuitive sense about her that will make her a fine healer and a good one for your clan when I am gone."

"Many years away," Bhric said, not ready to lose Greta.

"Hertha believes that with the blow to the back of Marta's head that she did not see her attacker."

"The culprit came up behind her so she could not see who it was which could possibly mean she would have known the person. Someone is purposely trying to turn the tribe against my wife but for what reason?" The troubling thought deeply disturbed Bhric and made him even more anxious to return to his wife.

"Dig deeply," Greta advised. "I believe more goes on here than you suspect."

Bhric nodded and could not help but ask, "You have seen much in your many years as a healer. What is your opinion on how Marta will fare?"

"She will wake, or she will die. It is up to fate,"

Greta said. “Now go to your wife. She is in need of you.”

Bhric rushed back to the keep glad for the late hour, glad that he and Tavia could be alone together, glad they had each other.

He found her halfway up the stairs, leaning against the wall, giving her leg time to rest. He scooped her up in his arms and carried her the remainder of the way.

Tavia’s arms instinctively went around his neck, and he was not surprised by what she asked, “What did Greta say?”

“That you are not responsible for Marta’s attack, and she doubted Marta herself would know since she was struck from behind.”

“I wondered over that when you mentioned that Marta would be able to identify her attacker. With having been struck in the back of the head that would be unlikely.”

“I purposely said that in hopes that the culprit would reveal himself,” Bhric explained, though had not expected any satisfying results. He did not believe the true culprit was that foolish.

“It was worth a try,” Tavia said, “and still might prove successful.”

Bhric hurried out of his own garments before helping his wife with hers once in their bedchamber. “Greta advises that there is more going on here and I agree with her. Something is not right about this. Someone drives a wedge between my tribe and clan while making you appear the culprit. But why?”

“If we discover that, then most likely it will be easier to discover the culprit,” Tavia said, snuggling against her husband after they both slipped beneath the blankets.

They exchanged opinions and possibilities until sleep could not be avoided and they drifted off, Tavia a bit disappointed her husband had not kept his promise to make love to her since she yearned to feel his love tonight more than ever. But she understood that he must have a lot on his mind and let it be.

Sometime in the night she woke, her husband's hands roaming intimately over her, stoking her passion and she easily responded to the pleasure. He was familiar with every inch of her now, knowing exactly where to touch that would have her respond eagerly. But she knew the same of him, knowing those special spots to touch, to kiss, to hug with tender care.

They shared, his hands going where she enjoyed them the most and her touches that elicited moans of pleasure. Their touches were slow and lazy, enjoying every intimate touch, kiss, or nip of a sensitive spot.

"I love you, wife," he whispered in her ear as he slipped over and into her.

"And I you," she said on a pleasurable sigh and wrapped her legs around him to tuck him deeper inside her.

He moaned and it was not long before they both exploded together more satisfied than ever then wrapped themselves around each other to drop into sleep once again.

***

Two days later a woman was heard running through the village, "She wakes! She wakes! Marta wakes!"

Bhric was quick to go see her, his wife having settled into a nap after they had made love, his need for her overwhelming him at times. That she never denied him made him think that she felt the same and how much they enjoyed each other only seemed to prove that. He was growing more and more comfortable with her and far more comfortable with the intimacy they shared than he had ever expected. They had a chance of having a good life together and he did not want to lose that chance.

He entered Greta's cottage to see Marta sitting up in bed, her face pale and a bit gaunt.

"My lord," she said with a bob of her head.

"I am relieved you have woken," Bhric said. "It would upset me to lose you."

Marta got teary-eyed. "I hope to serve your children as I served you."

Bhric did not respond to that since he knew Tavia would not want her tending their bairns. "Do you recall what happened, Marta?"

She shook her head and winced, remaining silent for a moment. "I recall hearing about a fight and hurried to see for myself what it was all about. I do not recall anything after that except waking here. Though I wonder if Lady Tavia practices her evil against me."

Bhric scowled. "I will not have you spreading lies about my wife, especially when she was the one who found you and called for the healer' help. You could have laid there and died if it had not been for Tavia."

"I was told Lady Tavia was found bending over me, stealing the last of my breath," Marta said, defending her remark.

"She listened for a breath and finding one called out for help. You owe her your life," Bhric said, making sure his annoyance was heard. "Rest and heal, Marta, so you will be well enough to return home."

Marta's eyes turned wide. "Ingrid will need my help with the baby coming soon."

"Perhaps, but my wife does not need to suffer your disparaging tongue," Bhric warned.

"I only want what is best for you, my lord," Marta said, a tear falling from her eye.

"Tavia is best for me, Marta, even though I was too foolish to see that for myself at first. Thankfully my mother knew better as she always does. She also knew better for you when she chose to take you, more welcomed you, into our family. She saved you from a life of suffering."

"She did and I am forever grateful to her," Marta admitted.

"Then do not repay her with unkindliness to the woman she chose as my wife."

"Aye, my lord," Marta said with a bob of her head.

"Show me you can accept my wife and treat her with respect, and I will reconsider sending you home."

"Thank you, my lord," Marta said.

Bhric had no doubts that Marta would do whatever was necessary to stay and help Ingrid, but what troubled him even more was why the woman who was much like a grandmother to him hated his wife so much. And if whoever attacked Marta had used that hatred against her to see his wife blamed for the attack.

Something insidious had worked its way into the

clan, but for what reason? That was what he needed to find out.

Chapter Twenty-five

An ill stomach woke Tavia at dawn a couple of weeks later and she rushed out of her husband's warm arms to grab the bucket by the hearth and retch, though she more gagged since her stomach was empty.

"Easy," her husband said as he pulled back her hair draped around the bucket then eased her down to sit on a bench.

When she stopped retching, he took the bucket from her, rinsed a clean cloth in the bucket of water kept fresh by the hearth then squatted down to wipe her face gently.

Tavia sighed with the simple pleasure his tender touch brought her. It not only showed how much he cared for her but how much he loved her.

"This is the third morning you have retched," he said.

It had not been that long since she missed her monthly bleed. She suspected she might be with child but with such a short time span she was not certain.

She raised her head. "I suspect, but I cannot be sure that I am with child."

"While I hate seeing you suffer, the prospect of our bairn growing inside you fills me with great joy," he said, his broad smile proving that joy.

"I would prefer we keep this between you and me until I am certain," Tavia said.

"I agree, but you will be cautious knowing it is possible."

"Aye, Bhric, I will take no chances should our bairn be nestled inside me."

He lifted her in his arms and carried her to the bed, slipping in beside her once he tucked her beneath the blanket. "It is early. You should sleep more."

"I cannot since now I am famished," she said, snuggling against his warmth.

He loved how easily she fit herself against him as if they had been carved perfectly for each other, two pieces—never thought to fit—brought together as one, together for always.

"Give yourself a moment to rest and then we will go eat," he said, and she yawned before fitting her head comfortably in the crook of his arm.

They were woken an hour later with a knock at the door.

"A troop of warriors approach, my lord."

"I will be right there," Bhric called then turned to his wife. "Get dressed and wait in the Great Hall." He hurried into his garments.

"You expect a problem?" Tavia asked anxiously.

"When a troop approaches without sending word ahead, it warns me to be cautious," he said. "Now hurry and dress." He gave her cheek a quick kiss, then raced out of the room.

Tavia slipped her garments on with haste and was out the door not soon after her husband, Fen rushing in front of her on the stairs. He sensed an urgent worry and was ready to protect her.

Her husband was not in the Great Hall when she

entered, but Hertha came rushing in, fighting back tears.

"My lady, you must help us," Hertha pleaded when she reached Tavia. "Lord Ivan approaches, and the children fear he has come to take them away.

A chill ran through Tavia. She strongly disliked the man and did not trust him, but she trusted that her husband would let nothing happen to the children.

"Tell Doritt and Edward not to worry. They are safe here and no one will take them away," Tavia said with confidence.

"I will keep them out of sight just to be cautious," Hertha said.

"If that helps them feel safe, then by all means keep them tucked away. However, I strongly believe he is not here for the children."

"I pray you are right, my lady. Doritt and Edward are so happy as are Hume and me. We have come to look at them as our own and it would break my heart to have them snatched away from us."

"Worry not, Hertha. Lord Bhric would never allow that," Tavia said and grabbed her cloak to step outside as soon as Hertha fled the room.

"Bhric," Tavia said when she stepped outside to see him standing at the top of the stairs with Sven while a short distance away two men on horses rode through the village toward the keep.

"I told you to stay in the Great Hall," Bhric said, turning to his wife.

Tavia went to his side, Fen sticking close to her. "I will hear what is said."

"This is for me to see to," Bhric insisted.

"With me by your side," Tavia said and latched onto his hand.

Habit had him clasping her hand firmly and keeping her tucked at his side. "You will hold your tongue."

Sven started laughing. "You forget what all men agreed to the other night… there is no woman alive who holds her tongue."

Tavia had to smile thinking of her cousin, Flora and how well she proved Sven right.

Lord Ivan and the man who accompanied him dismounted, the man remaining behind Lord Ivan as he stopped at the bottom of the stairs.

"We will talk and not in your wife's presence," Lord Ivan demanded.

Lord Bhric's powerful voice carried out toward the village and a strong winter wind scooped it up and carried even farther. "You do not come to my home and rudely make demands, nor do you arrive here without forewarning."

"It is a matter of urgency," Lord Ivan argued annoyed at being reprimanded.

Bhric did not trust the man nor whatever he came here to tell him. But it was wiser for him to hear what he had to say in private than to remain where many could hear.

"You will speak your piece and take your leave," Bhric ordered.

"It is a three-day journey back home. I would appreciate shelter for at least the night," Lord Ivan argued.

"You and your men may camp on the outskirts of

the village," Lord Bhric informed him. "And I will see that you are provided with food. Now come inside and have your say."

Lord Ivan's glance kept going to Fen once inside the Great Hall, Fen not having taken his eyes off the man.

"The hound follows her faithfully… she command's it?" Lord Ivan asked, keeping a distance from the animal.

"He is faithful to her and," —Bhric sent a hasty glance to his wife— "obeys her without question."

Tavia smiled softly, understanding her husband was reminding her that the hound was more obedient than she was.

"So, it is true," Lord Ivan said, shaking his head.

"What is?" Lord Bhric snapped.

"I thought it nothing but gossip, uncontrollable wagging tongues who want you gone from here and returned to your homeland."

"This is my homeland. I was born on this soil in the bedchamber where my mother was once born. I am a MacShane, and I will let no one take that from me."

"Then you need to beware for there are those who whisper that evil resides within your clan," Lord Ivan warned.

"You spew nonsense and lies," Bhric accused harshly.

"Not I," Lord Ivan defended. "It reached my ears by way of others. Talk of war hounds that became docile and now obey a new master. How a MacShane warrior avoided a death that should have claimed him and now obeys a new master. How truth tries to surface and is punished for it." His eyes turned accusingly on Tavia. "And how a mighty warrior suddenly claims to love a wife he thought not fit for him and had had second thoughts of honoring the marriage agreement."

Bhric lunged forward and grabbed Ivan by the throat with such a strong grip that the man started choking. "Are you accusing my wife of being evil?"

Lord Ivan clamped his hand on Bhric's wrist, struggling to get his hand off him.

"Let him at least answer you," Sven advised.

Bhric let go of the man with a shove that sent Ivan stumbling back. "Be cautious of what you say about my wife."

Ivan rubbed at his throat and coughed a few times. "I say what I hear and what many fear."

"And what do many fear?" Bhric demanded.

"That evil followed you home," Lord Ivan said.

"Again, I tell you that is nonsense," Bhric argued.

"Then what say you about the animals that have been killed and their hearts removed?" Lord Ivan asked.

Bhric wondered how the man could know so much of what had gone on here. Gossip could spread quickly, but mostly in pieces that always ended up being a mixture of truth and tale. It was as if someone here, from tribe or clan, had whispered in Ivan's ear.

"Who told you about the two dead animals?" Bhric demanded.

Ivan scrunched his brow as if not quite understanding. "Two? There were four dead animals and all on a direct path to your home, dead weeks now, their hearts missing, killed or sacrificed for some evil purpose. Evil followed you home, Lord Bhric, perhaps unknowingly to you, but it followed you home."

Bhric had no doubt that Lord Ivan's claims would spread soon enough, the man would make certain of it. Though, it would not take much since Bhric saw that the servants were already huddled in whispers.

"It was the witch," Lord Ivan said and guzzled down half the tankard of ale a servant had handed him before he continued. "You know not what spell the witch could have cast on your wife each time she went to visit the witch in the dungeon. What better way to have her evil deeds carried out?"

Tavia was not able to hold her tongue. "Fia is not evil. She is a wise woman."

"A wise and powerful woman when it comes to evil," Lord Ivan corrected.

"You are angry that my da refused your proposal of marriage to me," Tavia challenged.

"I am relieved beyond belief," Lord Ivan said with a dramatic hand to his chest. "If I had had the misfortune to wed you, evil would have invaded my clan. And if your da had accepted my offer to take the witch from him, I have no doubt my life would have been short-lived. Thankfully, I have no worry of that now, but Lord Varrick does."

"You are bitter over your defeat, and bring lies here to seek revenge," Tavia accused, worried his lies would take root, grow, and spread, strangling the truth in its path.

"I came here with no malice, only to help. The witch has already brought evil to Clan Strathearn, striking the lot of them ill. But you know that since one brave soul ventured here for help."

Bhric continued to wonder over how well-informed Ivan was. He could understand him hearing of the illness at Clan Strathearn but to know a man was sent here to ask for help was not something he would be privy to.

Glad he had only recently received good news from Newlin, he was pleased to say, "Clan Strathearn heals well. They have all recovered."

"Could it be because evil had its fill there and followed you here?" Lord Ivan questioned, looking to Bhric. "What danger could your people be in when it decides to strike?"

"There is no danger my warriors fear or cannot handle," Bhric said.

"They do not question how your wife can command war hounds and turn them docile unless she wishes otherwise?"

"I owe you no explanation and if you think to stir unrest in my people, I warn you that you will learn how faithful and obedient they are to me," Bhric cautioned, wondering the true reason for Ivan's arrival here. The man was by no means magnanimous, so why was he here?

Shea rushed forward to whisper something in Sven's ear and the fear that struck his face had Bhric asking, "What is it?"

"Ingrid is ill," Sven said and rushed from the room.

"And so it begins," Ivan said with a sad shake of his head.

Tavia did not fail to see what others missed, the glee of pleasure in Ivan's eyes.

Tavia could not keep pace with her husband and

waved him off. When he moved toward her for them to remain together, she shooed him away, knowing he was anxious over his sister. "Go, your sister needs you. I will catch up." Fen remained with her as she kept a tempered gait so her leg would not betray her.

She stopped suddenly when turning a curve along the path to see a commotion in front of Sven and Ingrid's cottage.

"It is her fault. She is evil!" a woman yelled, pointing a finger at Hertha.

"She does the witch's bidding," another called out.

Tavia rushed forward with no regard to her leg. "LEAVE HERTHA BE!"

The accusing women hurried to get out of Tavia's way, fearful of her and Fen, his vicious snarl displaying his sharp teeth.

Hertha latched onto Tavia's arm when she reached the worried woman. "I did nothing wrong, my lady."

"I know that, and I will see you kept safe," Tavia assured her. "Now tell me what happened."

"I was talking with Ingrid, asking her how she felt when she doubled over in pain. I got her into her cottage, and she insisted I get Greta and I did. I gave her nothing and did only what she asked of me." Hertha glanced cautiously around. "I saw a pouch on the table when I helped her inside and into bed. It was not there when I returned with Greta."

"We must tell Bhric," Tavia said.

"HERTHA! In here now!" Bhric demanded from the open doorway.

Tavia kept firm hold of Hertha's arm as they entered the cottage together.

"What did you give her?" Bhric demanded.

"Nothing, my lord," Hertha said and went to step forward to help Ingrid who was retching.

Bhric blocked her path. "My sister says she asked if there was something you could give her since her morning ills had returned."

"Aye, but I warned her she should not take anything now with her time so close and suggested a chamomile brew to help soothe her. But I had yet to give it to her."

Ingrid was shaking her head and when she stopped retching said, "You left the pouch on the table and now it is gone."

"I left no pouch for you, but if you let me I can help ease your retching," Hertha offered.

Greta waved Hertha forward. "Fix the brew."

Sven went to protest.

"I will watch her, though it is not necessary," Greta said. "I have come to know Hertha and she has a good and caring heart. I am pleased and relieved that she will be here to tend me when my time comes."

Hertha brushed away a tear. "I will see you stay well for a long time to come." She took the healing pouch from her waist and began to prepare a brew.

"Someone wishes ill will on this clan," Greta said.

"Aye," Bhric agreed. "And I intend to find out who and why."

***

Tavia walked with Hume through the village, her husband walking with Sven not far behind her. The brew Hertha had fixed helped almost as soon as Ingrid drank it. She now slept peacefully, the bairn still active in her stomach to Sven's relief.

Bhric had refused to allow her to speak with Hume alone, not that his concern was with Hume, it was with talk that was growing that Ingrid's illness was Tavia's doing. There was talk that Ingrid did not want Marta sent home that she wanted the woman's help with the bairn once he was born. Many believed Tavia thought otherwise and was angry with Ingrid for even thinking of it.

She did her best to ignore the stares and whispers, but it was difficult. She was glad not only for her husband's presence but for Fen's as well, including his snarl that warned people away.

"You say there are various herbs or plants that can purge the stomach," Tavia asked to make sure she heard him correctly, her mind far too troubled by the accusing faces that followed her through the village.

"Aye, but the person would need to be familiar with such properties and how to use them," Hume said. "And it would be difficult to acquire them with winter upon us unless, of course, a person already possessed them."

"You and Hertha are in possession of such plants?" Tavia asked.

"Of course," Hume said with a nod. "Sometimes purging is necessary. Greta has her share of purging mixtures as well. Though after examining some of them, I believe ours are more potent."

"The mixture used on Ingrid?"

"Potent," Hume said, shaking his head. "They will blame Hertha. She will not be safe. None of us from

Clan Strathearn are safe here."

Tavia wanted to deny that, but she feared Hume might be right and she blamed herself for that.

Bhric was by her side, his arm hooking with hers as soon as Hume stepped away eager to return to Hertha.

"Lord Ivan is right evil is here among us, husband," Tavia said as they headed to the keep.

"Most hearing that would believe you agreed with him about the witch and her evil ways," Bhric said. "But since I know you do not believe Fia evil, then it is another evil you speak of, is it not?"

"Aye, it is, and I would not be surprised if you thought the same."

"You make a good counsel, wife, since we think alike," Bhric said and hugged her against him.

"Evil arrived with Lord Ivan," Tavia said, keeping her voice low.

"I do not think it has to do with revenge, and the witch, Fia, is simply a pawn in his plan. There is more to it than we can see, and we need to find out what it is before he does damage that cannot be repaired."

Chapter Twenty-six

Tavia laid in bed the next morning willing her stomach to remain calm, then her husband's arm found its way over her, and she cringed. "Do not touch me!"

Bhric pulled his arm away worried, his wife never having denied his touch. "What's wrong?"

"My stomach is calm, and I am giving it no reason to do otherwise, so I am remaining still," she cautioned.

He rose to lean his head on his bended arm and look down at her stretched out stiff beside him. "I do not like that the bairn prevents me from touching you when we wake. It is something I look forward to and enjoy. But I also do not want to see you suffer each morning."

"You are more certain than I am that I am with child," Tavia said, stroking her stomach gently.

"I am the oldest of my siblings, so I recall seeing my mother ill some mornings and my father hugging her and declaring that his seed took root quickly. My seed seems to be as potent as my father's," Bhric said with pride and saw his wife pale.

He was off the bed in a flash, grabbed the bucket, and was back to sit her up before she began to retch.

"This is not pleasant," Tavia said when it finally passed, and she lay with a cool cloth on her brow.

"My mother's morning illness did not last long, hopefully yours won't either," he said, hoping he offered encouraging words.

A thought crossed Tavia's mind, but she said nothing to her husband, not knowing if it would prove helpful or perhaps worried what may come of it. It was something she would have to do on her own.

"One can only pray," she said. "I am glad Ingrid retched for only a short time and she now does well and that no one else has turned ill."

Bhric had taken precautions after poison was suspected at Clan Strathearn. He placed guards at the food sheds and instructed Shea to let only those she trusted prepare the meals. He believed his immediate response to the threat had prevented the culprit from doing more damage.

"Aye, we are all relieved no illness or poison spread, though Sven is concerned since Ingrid is determined and eager to find the culprit who did this to her." He turned silent for a minute before addressing an issue he worried might upset her. "Ingrid asked me not to send Marta home just yet. She has engaged her help in finding the culprit believing whoever hurt her is also responsible for what happened to Marta." When his wife surprisingly remained silent, he continued. "Ingrid believes that if Marta helps her discover who truly is responsible, then she will see that you had nothing to do with it and perhaps change her mind about you. I should also tell you that Ingrid wishes her help when the bairn arrives. Marta is wonderful when it comes to caring for bairns."

"Why then did you put her in charge of the keep?"

"She requested it."

"Didn't you find that odd?" Tavia asked, since it

seemed so to her.

"I never gave it thought. Marta has proven herself capable of handling most any task given to her. I had no doubt the keep would run well under her direction. Besides, running the keep would include seeing to the care of the bairns that came along."

Tavia would not allow that, but she had her own reasons to see Marta remain here, so she held her tongue, for now.

With no objection from his wife, Bhric said, "I am going to let Marta remain here for now so that she may help my sister."

"Aye, a good decision," she said.

That his wife agreed surprised Bhric, though he wondered if she had truly paid heed to what he had said since she appeared more lost in thought. Glad she posed no argument, he let it be.

"Lord Ivan finally takes his leave today," Bhric reminded.

"He has finally run out of excuses to further delay his departure."

"Or whatever reason brought him here has been settled," Bhric suggested. "He has given no indication to what that might be in all the various discussions I or Sven have had with him. He has not approached me about having Doritt and Edward returned to him or has even made mention of the incident that brought the two here. He rarely speaks with my tribe but talks often with those of Clan MacShane."

Tavia removed the wet cloth from her head to drop in the water bucket beside the bed before turning to slip in the crook of her husband's arm.

"He came here for a purpose, and I wish we knew what it was," she said.

"I would say to spread lies and fear about evil residing here."

"But why? For what purpose?" Tavia questioned. "Every time he visited with my da it was for a specific reason: a request, a demand, a warning. He is a man who wants and demands and does whatever it takes to get it."

"He came here to warn of evil," Bhric reminded.

Tavia looked up at her husband. "But to what conclusion? To see me blamed, then why so? To instill fear, then why so?"

"I see your reasoning. Why bother to come warn us if it did not benefit him in some way?"

"Aye," she confirmed eagerly, glad he saw what she did. "Everything he demanded of my da, in the end, would benefit Ivan." Her stomach grumbled then.

"You need to eat," Bhric said, "and Ivan leaves and troubles us no more. But I will see that my warriors escort him off MacShane land."

Tavia had her doubts. "He may take his leave, but what does he leave behind?"

***

With her husband busy seeing Ivan off and addressing some issues in the clan, Tavia was left free to do as she pleased as long as her leg was not troubling her or the bairn was not playing havoc with her stomach, according to her husband.

She smiled thinking how he had shaken his head

when she had responded with, "As you say, husband."

He had learned that response truly meant she would do as she pleased, and he had learned since to conquer it by replying, "Within reason, wife, or else."

The exchange always ended with a tender kiss as it had a short time ago, far different from when she had first responded with those words. She could not be more pleased for it. That was why she needed to see a few things settled for herself.

Not knowing how long she would have to herself, she chose to tackle the one thing that was most important to her—the bairn she still questioned she carried. There should not be a doubt in her mind, but she believed fear that her mum's fate might be hers as well kept her from accepting she was with child. A thought had entered her head that she believed might offer some help.

Bhric's mum had been close friends with Tavia's mum, and she hoped there was a chance she would know how her mum fared when she carried and delivered Tavia. Also, why she lost her life in the process. But with Bhric's mum not being here, there was one other person who might know, who served Bhric's mum… Marta.

Tavia made her way to Ingrid's cottage, thinking it was the best place to find the woman. After only two days of rest, Marta refused to remain abed and when she heard of Ingrid possibly being poisoned, she let no one stop her from seeing to the woman's care.

"Wait out here, Fen," she ordered when they reached the cottage, and he made no protest too busy sniffing the ground.

She entered after a brief knock.

"I will not let you harm her or the bairn," Marta said, taking a protective stance in front of Ingrid, tucked comfortably in bed.

"Lady Tavia means me no harm, Marta," Ingrid said. "And if you treat her badly my brother will send you home and then who will I have to help me?"

Marta grumbled and stepped aside. "A brief visit."

"Actually, Marta, it is you I came to talk with," Tavia said and while Marta's eyes turned suspicious, Ingrid's eyes widened in surprise. "Perhaps a brief walk outside."

"Where I hear nothing? Absolutely not," Ingrid said, sitting straight up in bed ready to hear every word.

"I prefer whatever you have to say to me, my lady, be said in front of Ingrid, so my words are not misconstrued," Marta said with a lift of her chin.

"As long as what we discuss is kept private between us three," Tavia said.

"I will not keep anything from Lord Bhric," Marta said curtly.

"Aye, you will," Ingrid demanded, "for I am curious as to what Lady Tavia wants to speak to you about."

"Your tongue does not always keep counsel as it should, something I have reminded you about many times," Marta reprimanded.

"True, but I give my word on this one. I will hold my tongue," Ingrid said. "As will you." When Marta did not respond, Ingrid said, "Be sent home or remain here, which will it be, Marta?"

Marta scowled. "I will hold my tongue as long as it

brings no harm to Lord Bhric."

"I have no desire to harm my husband, I love him," Tavia said.

"Good, now that we have that all settled speak up," Ingrid said eagerly.

"You served Lord Bhric's mum, did you not?" Tavia asked.

"I did," Marta said proudly.

"By any chance were you with her when she visited with my mum?"

Marta hesitated briefly. "On a few occasions."

"You never mentioned that," Ingrid said surprised.

"It was of no importance," Marta said, easily dismissing it.

"It is important to me, "Tavia said. "Please tell me what you thought of my mum."

"I did not know her well enough to say, though I did see that your father loved her very much," Marta said.

Tavia could see her words were forced. "What are you not telling me, Marta?"

"There is nothing more to say," Marta said, stubbornly.

Tavia was not done yet. "Did you attend my delivery?"

"I was sent from the room," Marta admitted.

"Did you learn what happened that caused my mum to lose her life?" Tavia asked.

Marta turned her head away for a moment as if lost in memories. "I was told that once you were delivered your mum bled profusely. No one could stop it. She knew she would not survive, and it was said that she pleaded with Bhric's mother to look after you and keep you safe. Lady Orianna swore she would."

"Why would you not respect my mother's word and see Lady Tavia kept safe when given the chance?" Ingrid asked puzzled.

"Daughters are much like their mothers," Marta said, casting an accusing glance at Tavia. "

"I am pleased to hear that," Ingrid said, smiling.

"Not you," Marta corrected. "You are more like your father's mother… a hellion."

Ingrid grinned. "That is even better."

"You did not like my mum," Tavia said, having heard the disdain in the woman's voice.

"It was not for me to like or dislike her, though I will say when I saw you for the first time I thought you looked familiar," Marta said.

"And you took an instant dislike to me which means you disliked my mum. Why?" Tavia asked.

Marta clamped her mouth shut as if she would say no more but failed to do so. "You lie just as your mum did."

Tavia drew her head back feeling as if the woman had slapped her, her accusation was so unexpected.

Marta continued to accuse. "You tricked Lord Bhric into this marriage, tricked him into bed, and I would not be surprised if you carry another man's bairn."

Tavia's hand went instinctively to her stomach.

Marta's eyes spread wide with shock. "I knew it. I knew it. You were with child when he wed you. And you will get what you deserve just as your mum did."

The venom Marta spewed at her stung and

confused her as did the questioning look on Ingrid's face.

She turned to leave, run, cry, but something stopped her, and she drew her shoulders back and glared at Marta. "You are a vicious, bitter woman who knows nothing of the truth, and you are a blight on the Clan MacShane."

"I am of the Thrubolt Tribe and proud of it," Marta said.

"Aye, that you are and that is where you will return to," Tavia said, raising her chin with a tenacious lift, then turned and walked out the door. Tears stung her eyes as soon as she stepped outside and Fen, sensing her distress, hurried to her side. "We go to the keep, Fen."

The hound whined seeing Tavia upset, and he stayed close at her side.

***

Bhric did not think he saw the last of Ivan when he watched him depart and he suspected the man had no intentions of heading home. It was why he sent a troop of warriors to escort him off MacShane land. At least that would put some distance between them. He also had given orders to one of his tribe's trackers and a MacShane tracker, an exceptional one, to follow them once the troop left them. Ivan had come here for a reason, and it bothered Bhric that he had yet to discover what that reason was.

He was headed to Greta's cottage when he spotted her not far from it. He hurried his steps wanting to talk with her. He was worried about his wife. Seeing her ill each morning, so pale and weak after a bout of retching, had gotten him thinking about when her time came to deliver the bairn. Would she have the strength to deliver the bairn or meet her mum's fate?

"You look worried," Greta said and lowered her voice. "Give it time, her morning retching may stop."

Though her remark stunned him, he did not let it show. "How did you know?"

"Tavia has been pale the last few times I have seen her in the morning, and I noticed that she cringes at certain odors. The bairn plays havoc with her stomach. But what worries you more is her delivery time." She shook her head. "Sadly, I cannot help you with that. It will not be known until her time comes. She is strong and a fighter or she would have never survived her leg injury."

"Aye, that she is, and I regret misjudging her instead of seeing her worth."

"It is better you learned for yourself," Greta advised. "You will respect and admire her more for it and love her all the more for it."

"I had hoped in time I would come to love the wife chosen for me. Never though, did I imagine I would lose my heart completely to her," Bhric said amazed that he had.

Greta rested her hand on Bhric's arm. "Your strength gives her strength, keep her strong and perhaps fate will reward you."

Bhric caught sight of his wife and the way she swiped at her eyes as she walked. She was crying and it not only upset him, but it also angered him that someone or something had brought her to tears. He walked away from Greta without saying a word, though Greta smiled as she saw where he was headed and turned and entered her cottage.

"TAVIA!"

Bhric not only got his wife's attention with his powerful shout but those around them as well.

Tavia sniffled back her tears. She did not want her husband to see her crying.

"Who made you cry?" he demanded when he caught up with her.

"I did," she said truthfully, for she had allowed what Marta said to disturb her.

"I do not believe that for one minute," he said and took hold of her chin to turn her face up to look at him. "You will tell me whose words made you cry."

"I would prefer not to discuss it in front of the whole village," she said softly.

Bhric did not keep his voice low, though he did not shout. "Everyone should know I will not tolerate anyone who brings my wife to tears."

"Now that they will spread the word on that can we talk in private?" she asked and took his arm and began to walk, giving him no chance to deny her.

Bhric shouted for a hot brew in his solar before escorting his wife there and seeing her seated comfortably, Fen curled up beside her/

"Now you will tell me," he ordered.

"I had a thought after you mentioned how you recalled your mum being ill when with child that might shed some light on what my own mum may have suffered."

"Who here could possibly know anything about your mum?" he asked perplexed.

"Strange as it may seem… Marta."

Bhric's brow wrinkled for only a moment before it spread wide. "Of course, there would be a good chance that Marta would have accompanied my mother on a few visits to see your mother." Why hadn't he thought of that? A sudden thought hit him, and he grew worried. "Marta told you something that upset you. What is it?"

"Nothing to do with the bairn," she hurried to say, seeing his concern. "But I did find out why she dislikes me so much. She believes I am a liar like my mum and that she got what she deserved. She told me that I tricked you into marriage and she thinks I carry another man's bairn and I fear I added to her belief when my hand instantly went to my stomach as if I needed to protect our bairn." Her hand went there again.

Bhric squatted down in front of her, his hand covering hers. "I will see her sent home."

"As much as I would not mind that, I do not think it wise to do right now. People will blame me and believe Ingrid has been left vulnerable to my evil ways."

"I will not tolerate this from Marta. I will speak to her," Bhric said.

"So, you can find out more of what she refuses to tell me?"

"You are far too quick-witted, wife," he said since she was right. It was exactly what he intended to do.

Tavia shook her head. "Marta's words are so contrary to what I have heard others say of my mum. I cannot understand what lie she has imagined—"

"Tavia, what's wrong?" Bhric demanded concerned after his wife suddenly stopped speaking and had turned pale.

"It cannot be. I must be wrong," Tavia said, sitting forward in the chair shaking her head.

"Wrong about what?" Bhric helped his wife to her feet when she reached out and gripped his arm hurrying to stand.

"Marta believes that I am a liar like my mum, and she believes I carry another man's child. With that so, she must believe that my mum carried another man's child. If that holds any truth, it will mean I am not my da's daughter."

Chapter Twenty-seven

Sven rushed into the solar before Bhric could respond to his wife's remark.

"Ivan and our warriors are under attack," Sven said, breathing heavily. "One of our warriors returned for help and he's badly injured."

"Gather warriors and double the sentinels. We leave right after I speak with the warrior," Bhric ordered.

Sven gave a quick nod and left.

"You will remain in the keep and do not argue with me on this," Bhric ordered. "The matter with Marta can wait until I return."

Tavia would not add to his worry, though she did not know how patient she could be to find out what she believed might be true. "Be careful, husband."

Bhric eyed her skeptically. "And you will do as you are told, wife."

She leaned up on her toes to kiss him.

Bhric's arm circled her waist and lifted her to kiss her with an intensity that sent a shiver of fright through her, for she felt as if he kissed her for the last time.

"You best come home to me, husband," she said, her arms going around his neck to squeeze him tight, as if she could hold on to him forever.

"My love for you will allow nothing else," he said and kissed her again.

"You will take Fen with you," Tavia said when he placed her on her feet.

"Nay, he will remain with you."

Tavia shook her head. "Please, take him, Bhric. I know he will let nothing happen to you. Besides, he probably grows tired of doing nothing but follow me around. Let him do what he was trained to do… rush in at your side in battle."

Fen rushed to his feet upon hearing the word battle, his head up, his chest out, prepared to fight alongside his leader.

"We go to battle, Fen," Bhric said, and the hound barked.

Tavia entered the Great Hall with her husband to find Hertha waiting there.

"Your help is needed, my lady," Hertha said.

Bhric looked as if he was about to refuse her permission, then summoned a servant to fetch her a cloak. "Once done—"

"A warrior will escort me back here to the keep where I will wait for your return," she said.

"Finally, I have a wife who obeys," Bhric said and Tavia chuckled.

***

The warrior did his best not to moan in pain as Hume sliced away his blood-soaked shirt. The slashes on his chest bled but were not nearly as bad as the slash to his left arm.

"They came out of nowhere, my lord," the warrior said. "Riding down on us like demons from hell, screeching and brandishing their weapons… so many of them. When I lost the use of my fighting arm and took stock of how badly we were being beaten, I knew I had to go for help. Two men tried to stop me, thinking I was done for, more fools them. You must not delay, my lord. They need you."

The fury had risen fast in Bhric when he saw how badly his warrior had been wounded.

"You did well, Elug. I go now to save them, and you must rest and heal," Bhric said.

"And I will fight again, my lord," Elug said.

"That you will, Elug, that you will," Bhric assured him and looked to Greta and grew angrier when she shrugged, letting him know she did not know if Elug would survive.

Tavia squeezed her husband's arm seeing the exchange between him and Greta and whispered, "I will do all I can to help him."

Bhric could not explain why his wife's remark held promise, but it did, and he was grateful to hear it.

He kissed her quick again and she had barely enough time to remind in a whisper, "Come home to me, husband." Once he was gone, Tavia turned to Greta. "How may I help?"

It was an hour later when Elug was settled in a bed to rest, his arm stitched and one wound on his chest stitched as well, the other wounds needing none. Tavia had no idea if the man would survive, but then he had survived the ride back to the keep while badly injured. If anything, he was tenacious.

Tavia told herself to go straight to the keep as her husband had ordered. A light snow had started to fall, and she could use a hot brew and food, her stomach grumbling. But the need to know about her mum nagged at her, which had her turning to head to Ingrid's cottage.

"That is not the way to the keep, my lady," the warrior following her cautioned.

"A short visit to see how Ingrid does," she said and kept walking.

Ingrid turned worried eyes on Tavia when she entered and stopped her pacing, though she continued to rub low on her back.

"The pain will not stop," Ingrid said. "It is too soon for the bairn, or I am wrong about my birthing time. Or it is nothing but worry for my husband." She nodded as if that explanation satisfied her.

"Has Marta gone to fetch Greta?" Tavia asked, walking over to Ingrid to slip her arm around hers and walk her to the bed to sit. If so, why hadn't she passed the woman on the way here?

"Aye, but she should have returned by now." Ingrid grabbed at her stomach and cringed in pain. "It is time. I will lose the bairn and Sven as well this day." Tears began to roll down her cheeks.

"Nonsense," Tavia said curtly. "You are a strong Northwoman and will deliver a strong bairn for your husband to see when he returns home."

"I want Marta. I am sorry she treats you as poorly as she does, but she has always been there for me, please find her. I need her," Ingrid pleaded.

"I will send for Greta, then find Marta," Tavia said and went to the door and spoke with the warrior. "You must go get Greta. Ingrid's time has come."

"I cannot leave you," the warrior said.

"I am not going to leave Ingrid. I will remain here," she assured him. "It will not take long if you hurry."

The warrior took off running, quickly disappearing behind a cottage a short distance away. Relieved it would not take him long, she went to shut the door and see to Ingrid.

The door was shoved opened, and Marta stumbled in, William following quickly behind her, a dagger in his hand.

"Hurry, you all come with me," William ordered after kicking the door closed.

"I am not going anywhere with you. I am about to give birth," Ingrid said with an angry sneer.

"You come with me now or she dies," William threatened and held the blade to Marta's neck.

***

Bhric's warriors descended on the battle with roars and shouts and in little time the last of the mercenaries fell to them. He stood bloody on the battlefield, none of the blood his, and surveyed the results of his victory. The dead and dying lay scattered over the field.

"A few of our warriors are wounded but we lost none. Clan MacVannan did not fare as well," Sven said.

"Ivan?" Bhric asked, glancing about.

"Someone reported seeing him being dragged out of the battlefield but knows nothing more."

Bhric muttered an oath before saying, "Leave sufficient men here to clean up and get the wounded back home, MacVannan as well as MacShane. The rest will leave with us."

"What's wrong?" Sven asked anxiously.

"We have been tricked and I fear my wife is in danger," Bhric said and ran to his horse, Fen at his heels.

***

"You do not want to do this, William," Tavia said.

"Of course, I don't. You have been most kind to us, my lady, as have others. Life here is what it once was like at Clan MacVannan when Lord Bennett ruled. But no more. He has Glenna, and I fear what he may have already done to her," William said, tears pooling in his aged eyes.

"Lord Ivan has Glenna, doesn't he? You are part of Clan MacVannan, aren't you?" Tavia asked, her voice soft and gentle, all the pieces starting to fall into place.

William nodded. "Clan MacVannan was a decent clan when Lord Bennett ruled, but no more. Lord Ivan rules with brutal force. He starves and beats his people unmercifully. He cares for nothing or no one but himself and the power and wealth he can accumulate."

"He sent you here, didn't he?" Tavia asked, hoping to keep him talking and distracted long enough for the warrior to return.

"Lord Ivan forced me and Glenna to come here even gave us a sample of what awaited us if we did not obey him."

"That was why you were weak when you arrived here," Tavia said.

"Why didn't you just tell Lord Bhric? He would have protected you. You would have been free of Lord

Ivan," Marta said as if the solution was simple enough.

"My exact thought at one time, but then Lord Ivan stood two friends of ours we have known for many years in front of us and detailed what they would suffer if we did not succeed in our task. There was no freedom for Glenna and me if our friends were not free as well."

"You should fear more of what Lord Bhric will do to you than Lord Ivan," Marta warned.

"Either way, Glenna and I will not see tomorrow," William said, his stooped shoulders heavy with defeat.

Warnings was not what William needed if they or he and Glenna were to survive. "Where is Glenna?" Tavia asked, placing a gentle hand on William's arm.

Tears rolled down William's cheeks. "He has her and if I do not bring you to him, he will kill her."

"Give me the dagger, William, we will find a way to save Glenna," Tavia said and reached for it.

Marta moved quickly to shield Ingrid.

Tavia stilled William's arm as he went to raise it. "You have my word, William. We will get Glenna and bring her home safe, and you and she will live a fine life here."

Tears streamed down his cheeks. "We do not deserve it for what we have done to you, my lady. I am sorry that we planted and helped fuel the lies that were told about you and made others believe you evil." He looked to Ingrid. "My wife was ordered to see you dead from poison, but she could not do it. Instead, she gave you something to upset your stomach."

"The pouch," Tavia said, recalling what Hertha said about seeing one on the table In Ingrid's cottage.

"Glenna left it there by accident and returned to

retrieve it," William said.

"I laid doubled over in pain on the bed when I thought I heard someone enter the cottage. I assumed Hertha had returned, but when I turned to look no one was there," Ingrid said, shaking her head. "I believed I had imagined it."

"Glenna worried about being caught but she worried more what Lord Ivan would do to us since she failed to obey him," William said, his head dipping in defeat.

Tavia placed her hand over his and slipped the dagger easily out of his grasp. "The pouch. She did not get it from Hertha as she had me believe, did she?"

"Nay. She met with a person, the husband of the couple who was threatened. He pretended to be a traveler seeking shelter at Clan MacShane for the night. Glenna feared you might speak to Hertha and learn the truth, but I assured her that you would not give it thought that you had no reason to distrust us. That made Glenna feel worse, that you should trust us when we were not all trustworthy."

"More fool her," Marta said snidely.

"And more fool you for not recognizing her courage," William said, sadness filling his weary eyes as he shook his head.

"Why does Lord Ivan bother with me and Ingrid when he wants Lady Tavia?" Marta asked, no worry of him harming them now that he had no weapon and appeared completely defeated.

William dropped to a bench at the table, his legs no longer able to support him and tears gathering in his eyes. "He wants it shown how wrong Lord Bhric was about his wife being evil."

That made no sense to Tavia. There had to be more to Lord Ivan's reason for doing this, something that would benefit him.

"Lord Ivan expects me soon, my lady. If not..." He shook his head and wiped at his tears. "I fear what he will do to her, or what he may have already done to her."

The door opened and Greta entered. She cast a suspicious eye around at everyone, and when her glance fell on the dagger in Tavia's hand, she asked, "Is all well here?"

"It is," Tavia said quickly. "William and I will leave you and Marta to help Ingrid birth a strong bairn." She hurried William to the door.

Greta's hand went to her arm when she went to walk past her. "Are you sure all is well?"

"It will be soon," Tavia assured her and yanked open the door.

"You need to get word to Lord Bhric immediately," Tavia said to the warrior once outside. "Follow me to the keep and I will tell what needs to be done."

***

Bhric slowed his horse when he saw one of his warriors riding toward him and Sven and the warriors behind him did the same.

"My lord," the warrior said hurrying to deliver the message. "You must make haste, William, the elderly man who had sought shelter with us has confessed to all. He was sent by Lord Ivan on threat of death to spy on us and report to him what went on in our clan. His wife, Glenna, and he had planted and helped spread the lies about Lady Tavia. Glenna was the one who caused Ingrid to take ill, though she had been instructed to see her dead by poison and to make others ill as Lord Ivan saw done to Clan Strathearn. William has been ordered to bring not only Lady Tavia to Lord Ivan, but Marta and Ingrid as well, all to be found dead, the evil deed blamed on Lady Tavia."

"My Ingrid?" Sven asked with an anxious fear.

"She is safe though her birthing time is here," the warrior said. "But worry not, Greta and Hertha are with her.

"Lady Tavia?" Bhric asked, his stomach twisting tight.

"That's why you must hurry, my lord. Lady Tavia goes with William to meet Lord Ivan and save Glenna," the warrior urged.

Chapter Twenty-eight

"You finally made it here," Lord Ivan said a rumble of anger in his voice.

"Glenna!" William cried out when he spotted his wife sitting on the ground, her head slumped to the side. He hurried to her, dropping the dagger from his hand so shocked was he to see blood running from her bottom lip that was split wide while one eye was badly swollen shut.

"She got what she deserved for not doing as she was ordered to do. Ingrid should be dead and Lord Bhric's warriors too sick to fight," Lord Ivan said his face twisted in anger. "My plans had to be altered because of her failure. Now you fail me as well. Where are the other two women?"

"Ingrid is about to give birth and is attended by many women, Marta one of them," William said, tears falling as he lowered himself down next to his wife and took her gently in his arms.

Tavia saw the defeat on William's face as he sat there holding his wife, thinking death was certain this day. She hoped differently.

"I suppose Tavia, and the old couple will have to do," Lord Ivan said, disappointment mixing with his anger.

Tavia stepped forward, though kept a safe distance from Ivan. She had to gain enough time for her husband to reach them. She and William had not hurried their steps but with each step William had grown more anxious of what his wife might be suffering for his delay in reaching Ivan and he had been right to worry.

"If I am to die today, at least tell me why," Tavia said.

"If you think to keep me busy talking and give your husband time to rescue you, you are sadly mistaken. The mercenaries I sent to attack are no doubt keeping them busy right now. The three of you will be long dead by the time they discover your bodies."

"And how will you explain being a coward and fleeing the battle?" Tavia asked.

"I am no coward," Lord Ivan sneered. "I am more courageous and wiser than your fool of a husband. I will easily explain how I was wounded early in battle and two of my men hurried me away, and I will have a substantial wound to prove it."

"And will you kill the two men who now help you so they cannot speak the truth as easily as the mercenaries you hired slaughter your warriors as we speak?" Tavia asked and saw how the one man's eyes quickly darted to Ivan.

"I will see them rewarded for their loyalty," Ivan said.

"As you will see William and Glenna rewarded?" Tavia asked, seeking to put more doubt in the two warriors' minds.

"Enough," I will see this done," Ivan snapped.

"First," Tavia said, "assuage my curiosity. There must be a reason why you do this. Why you went through all this trouble to make me appear evil, to want me dead."

"I thought to wed you and see it done." He shook his head. "A plan that would have spared me coin and been much quicker."

"But my da refused your offer to wed me and then you made it seem as if you decided to withdraw your offer after discovering I had a limp and was not worthy to be your wife."

"You were never worthy to be my wife, but I must say your own foolishness in befriending the witch and your husband being disappointed in you made things much easier for me. Of course, you helped paint yourself evil as well. When Glenna sent word that you commanded not one but two war hounds and that you saved a warrior's leg from being cut off and how your husband had a change of heart and fell in love with you… it was all too perfect. Only a witch could make such remarkable things happen…. until, of course, she got angry and showed her true evil side. Unfortunately, Glenna failed to kill Ingrid with poison and sicken the others."

"You poisoned those at Clan Strathearn," Tavia said without question.

"I did, and I had everyone believing it was the evil witch who did it and sent her evil along with you to Clan MacShane. A brilliant plan that has worked well despite Glenna's failure. The dead animals I had killed in the forest, their hearts missing, helped add to the doubts and whispers."

"As well as the dead animals you profess you found along the way to Clan MacShane?" Tavia asked.

"A good tale that frightened my warriors enough to

keep them out of the forest, so they did not see what was not there to begin with," Ivan said. "But then the weak always follow without question."

"Again, why? Why want me dead?"

"I suppose it does not matter now since you will die shortly," Ivan said. "And it would be kind of me to tell you before you die for you would not want to live with the truth."

Tavia's stomach clinched, but she kept strong. Somehow she would survive this.

"Newlin is not your father," Lord Ivan announced with a bit of glee. "Lord Bennett was your father and once wed you became the rightful heir to Clan MacVannan since I am no relationship to Bennett at all. I heard a fellow speak of his heirless demise, and I seized the opportunity to make a claim. A few months after my arrival here, I began to hear whispers about the rightful heir to the clan. It took a bit of digging and torture, but it led me to the clan's old healer, Corlean, who confessed before she died. Healers do have a way of talking among themselves. She had learned the truth from your clan's healer, Eartha, I believe she was called. She thought it might benefit Clan MacVannan one day, of which, she was correct."

Tavia would not allow her shock to show. Instead, she smiled.

That turned Ivan angry. "You knew?"

"I knew something you did not which led me to investigate for myself," she said proudly.

"What was that?" Ivan demanded.

"That I am not evil. That I inherited the best of both my mum and da and had a da that raised me with love and understanding," Tavia said.

"Little good it does you now," Ivan snapped, then looked to one of his men. "Kill her! I grow tired of her questions.

Before the man could take a step, a booming voice was heard. "WILL YOU EVER OBEY ME, WIFE?"

Fen rushed out of the woods, planting himself in front of Tavia, his mouth drawn back in a vicious snarl, displaying fangs that had the two warriors stepping back.

Bhric followed after Fen, a claymore firm in his hand as he walked straight to his wife, paying little heed to Ivan. "You were ordered to remain in the keep."

"Circumstances warranted otherwise," she said with a slight smile.

"That was not for you to decide," Bhric said.

"ENOUGH!" Ivan shouted. "You think one warrior and a hound is enough to stop me from seeing this done?"

"You think I was foolish enough to come alone?" Bhric asked and he raised his hand and gave it a sharp snap, and a troop of warriors poured out of the woods surrounding the area.

Ivan laughed. "And you think I was foolish enough to not bring the vilest of warriors with me, if needed?" He let out a fierce roar.

"Stay behind me," Bhric ordered, stepping in front of her. "Guard her, Fen!"

Fen planted himself next to Tavia, turning his snarl more vicious.

Tavia turned and shooed at William, warning him to take Glenna and go. The warriors would not be concerned with the old couple, not yet at least.

William got his wife to her feet, and they disappeared into the woods as clashes of swords were heard in the distance.

Ivan turned his head at the sound, then turned a glare on Bhric. "You brought more than a troop with you."

"I brought Northmen and Scotsmen combined. Go join them," Bhric commanded his warriors surrounding them and they disappeared into the woods. "Your mercenaries do not have a chance against them. You no longer have a clan, land or coin. Hearing what you told my wife, Clan MacVannan rightfully became mine once Tavia became my wife, and you will pay with your life for the evil you have done."

"First, you will need to find me." Ivan mounted his horse with speed and took off, the two warriors staring after him in shock, not knowing what to do.

"Drop you weapons or die!" Bhric ordered.

The two men did not hesitate. They dropped their weapons.

"Go after Ivan," Tavia urged, stepping from behind him to stand at his side.

"And leave you?" Bhric shook his head. "Absolutely not. He will not get far."

Two mercenaries suddenly broke through the woods, grinning snarls on their grimy faces. Their appearance emboldened the two warriors who had dropped their weapons and they were quick to pick them up.

He shoved his wife behind him once again and ordered sternly, "Stay put until I say otherwise."

"Ivan ran off. He has no coin to pay you, but I do. Any one of you who brings him to me dead or alive will see good coin," Bhric ordered. "Fight me and I will see you taken alive to live your days out to serve a tribe of Northmen. Your choice."

The two men who had dropped their swords rushed to their horses, mounted and hurried off.

The larger of the mercenaries, broad and thick, stepped forward. "Glad we met up with you on the way here, Bhric."

Bhric laughed. "You mean you are glad my warriors discovered your presence before they turned their weapons on you, Finley."

"There is that," he said, his sizeable belly shaking as he laughed. "So, we get the money Ivan promised us if we catch him?"

"I should see you dead for accepting coin to attack me and my men," Bhric confirmed.

Finley laughed. "I had no intentions of attacking you, at least until you offered me more coin not to. A man does have to eat and feed his crew."

"You do bargain well, Finley, I will give you that and, aye, the coin is yours if you catch Ivan."

"We'll see to grabbing those two fools as well for no extra coin," Finley said.

"I imagine your men already have them, as for Ivan—"

"He's a slippery one," Finely said, "but we'll find him and bring him to you… alive he'll cost you more."

"I will spend no extra coin on him. Bring him back dead," Bhric said.

"Will do," Finley nodded. "So, the Clan

MacVannan is yours now? Your wife is the true daughter of Lord Bennett?"

"Did Ivan tell you that?" Bhric asked and swung his hand behind his back to keep his wife where she was when he felt her move to step from behind him.

"There's been whispers, tongues wagging among the common folk for years that Lord Bennett was seen sneaking around Clan Strathearn the night your wife was born. Naturally, people grow suspicious, and tales are born, or truths are buried in gossip." He laughed. "I have even heard ridiculous whispers that your wife's mum isn't her true mum. "But I guess the only one who can confirm the truth is your mum since all know she was good friends with Lady Margaret."

***

Tavia smiled as best as she could after returning to the keep. There was much excitement going on and tongues spreading the news rapidly. All were relieved to learn Lord Ivan was the evil that had invaded their clan and that he soon would be caught and punished. The most exciting news, however, was that Ingrid had given birth to a daughter. And while Tavia stood in Ingrid and Sven's cottage to welcome and rejoice over the little bairn, Tavia's mind was still in the woods, Finley's words echoing in her head.

Heard whispers that your wife's mum isn't her true mum.

How could that be? How could her mum not be her true mum? Her mum had been with child, her da had talked about how happy she was to carry Tavia. What happened to that child if she was not that bairn? And why had it all been kept from her? But most of all what she wished to know was… who truly was she?

"You will help me keep all men away from her, Bhric."

Tavia looked to see Sven and her husband staring down at the small-wrapped bundle in Sven's arms.

"I believe if she is anything like her mother it will be the men who need to watch out for her," Bhric said with a laugh.

Sven nodded. "That gives me hope."

"Thank you, Tavia, for seeing that William did not harm me," Ingrid said as Marta fussed over her.

"Aye," Sven said, taking his daughter to hand to his wife and sit next to them both on the bed. "We are grateful and proud that Lord Bhric has such a brave wife. You do him proud."

"That she does," Bhric said and though she smiled, he knew it was forced, her mind elsewhere and he could not blame her. "It has been a long day with much happening. We will take our leave so my sister can rest."

"But I want to know what punishment you have set for William and Glenna," Ingrid asked.

"They have suffered enough," Tavia said, thinking how they had found the elderly couple huddled in the woods together awaiting their fate. "They wish to return to Clan MacVannan once we are sure Ivan is dead. They want to help their clan that has been made to suffer under Ivan's brutal reign."

"But William must pay for what he did to Marta?" Ingrid argued.

"And what of Glenna and how she made Ingrid suffer?" Marta asked, her face pinched with annoyance.

"William was not the one who attacked Marta," Bhric said and continued to explain. "He told us it was one of Ivan's men who posed as a cleric and stopped here for food and drink. He was here to see Glenna and William and took advantage of the moment after learning that Marta disliked Tavia. And we are lucky that Glenna lied to the man and told him she had already poisoned the food and that a potion sat waiting for Ingrid to drink and succumb to. Otherwise, he intended to do it himself. Glenna was aware her lie would be discovered, and she would be made to suffer for it. And one look at her and you will see that she did suffer. Now rest, Ingrid, and enjoy the blessings of your newborn daughter."

Bhric took his wife's hand and walked with her to the door and when he opened it he found one of his warriors standing there.

"Chieftain Newlin is here, my lord. He waits at the keep." the warrior announced.

Tavia did not wait, she tugged her hand free of her husband's, pushed past the man, and hurried toward the keep. Fen was quick to keep pace with her and her husband was not far behind her.

"Tavia!" he called out, but she ignored him. Her leg would pain her for sure if she did not slow down. He caught up with her and grabbed hold of her arm to bring her to a halt. "Your leg," he warned.

"I do not care. I want to see my da. I want answers. After what Finley implied jokingly, I cannot help but wonder who I am. Or why I was lied to. I need to know,

Bhric." She let herself fall against him and sighed with relief when she felt his strong arms close around her. "I must know," she said not only hearing defeat in her own words but feeling it as well.

He hated to see her hurt like this and he could only imagine how she felt. Everything she believed true could very well be a lie. But why?

"I will make certain you get your answers, Tavia," Bhric said and kept her at a steady pace as they continued to walk to the keep.

"Tavia!" her da called out with joy throwing his arms wide when she and Bhric entered the Great Hall.

Tavia hurried into his arms, the arms of the man she had believed was her da. The man who had loved her, looked after her, cared for her since she was born.

"You are upset," Newlin said after hugging his daughter. "I can feel it."

"You came for a reason, Newlin?" Bhric asked, seeing his wife was far too upset to speak.

"I came with your warrior to warn you about Lord Ivan, and I wanted to see for myself how my daughter fared. We believe he is responsible for the poisoning of Clan Strathearn, one of his warriors confessing to the evil deed," Newlin said still holding on to his daughter, concerned for her.

"Sit," Bhric said, pointing to a nearby table. "There is much you need to hear."

Tavia sat beside her da and listened as her husband explained everything that had happened, though made no mention of Newlin not being her da. She knew he left that for her to ask.

Newlin stared speechless at Bhric for a moment

when he finished, then finally asked, "Why?"

Bhric looked to his wife, and she responded, turning to her da so their eyes would meet. "Lord Ivan claims that Lord Bennett is my da and that upon his death I inherited the clan and all its holdings the day I wed, and he feared losing everything since he is not truly related in any way to Lord Bennett." She was surprised to see her da's eyes widen in shock.

"What nonsense do you speak?" her da snapped. "I know not where Ivan heard such lies, but they are just that lies. Your mum loved me. She would have never cheated on me. Who told him such complete nonsense?"

Was that all it was? Complete nonsense? Had tales been told? But for what reason? And what of Finley's remark? Had he merely poked fun at the situation? Could it be all lies or had a dark secret been kept all these years?

Shea rushed into the Great Hall and yelled, "Fire outside the kitchen!"

They all got to their feet and rushed after Shea, Fen taking the lead and barking as he went. All knew a fire had to be contained immediately or a whole village could burn, and a keep destroyed.

Tavia's sore leg forced her to go slow so she lagged behind the others who quickly disappeared down the stone passageway. She was about to make her way down the enclosure that connected the keep to the kitchen when she was grabbed by her arm and viciously yanked back. Her eyes went wide when she was slammed against a thick body and looked up to see it was Ivan.

"Do not waste your breath asking me how I managed to enter the keep without being seen. I have snuck in and out of far more difficult places with ease. This was nothing, though sneaking out with you would be a different matter. That is why you will not be going with me."

Fright gripped Tavia tightening around her like an iron shackle when he raised a dagger to her throat.

"I wish I could stay and see your husband's look when he finds you dead on the floor, your throat cut," Ivan said. "And do not think you will delay me with talk this time. I will see this done quick."

Tavia shut her eyes her only thought her love for her husband and the pain he would suffer over finding her, then she heard the familiar growl. She opened her eyes to see two glowing eyes in the darkness of the passageway coming slowly toward them.

"Once you move that dagger, Fen will attack," she warned.

"It will be too late for you," he sneered.

"And you as well. Are you willing to die, or do you want to live to see another day perhaps even find another place to stake claim to?" The scent of burning wood suddenly grew heavy. "The fire has breached the keep."

"I set a good fire," Ivan said. "Your husband will lose more than you this night."

Ivan's hand was suddenly ripped away from her and she heard him gasp. She hurried and turned once free of his hold to see Ivan's eyes bulging wide, and his chest arched, and her husband standing behind him.

"As I told you when we first met… when my hand

goes to my weapon I never hesitate to use it. But then you can feel the truth of my words since my dagger is embedded deep in your back. Now let's see you finally use your weapon." Bhric's grip was strong on Ivan's hand that held his dagger. "Never will you bring harm to anyone again." It was a quick slash across Ivan's throat, his own blade ending his life.

Bhric released the man to drop to the floor lifeless, stepped over him, and took his wife in his arms to hurry her into the Great Hall, Fen following them.

She clung to him, the scent of burning wood thick upon him. "It was you I smelled. The fire did not breach the keep."

"Aye, it was me. I saw Fen look around once outside, then he began to sniff the ground until it took him to the kitchen, and he rushed inside. I realized then you were not with us. I cursed myself for not keeping you close to me. Fen entered the passageway before me and when I heard him growl, I knew you were in danger. I hurried to enter through another passageway that leads from the kitchen farther down by my solar which is probably the one Ivan used and found out about after his delayed departure from here."

"The reason he spoke with so many of the Clan MacShane people to find out all he could about this area and the keep," Tavia said, not letting go of her husband.

Bhric kept tight hold of her as she trembled in his arms.

"Why? Why did Ivan return when he could have run, disappeared, lived?" she asked more perplexed than ever.

"He knew I would never give up searching for him for what he had done to you and my clan and those I protect. It also would not have taken him long to realize that Finley was tracking him. He was a dead man no matter where he went." He hugged her tight. "It is over, Tavia."

She looked up at him. "Not truly, Bhric. I still do not know the truth about my birth."

Chapter Twenty-nine

Bhric stood on the top of the keep stairs with his wife waiting as the group of riders approached. "You are feeling well enough for this?"

Tavia placed her hand on her rounded stomach. "He is a bit of a devil tiring me out and playing havoc with my stomach, but I do well enough."

"You have three more months of his antics unless, of course, you carry a lass which means she does as she pleases just as you do." His hand went to rest on his wife's stomach, and he laughed when he felt a forceful kick in response.

"Will your mother be truthful with me?" Tavia asked.

"I will make sure of it."

"My da continues to believe it is nonsense and I hope the same. I do not think I could tell him otherwise. It would hurt him terribly," she said, thinking how upset he had been insisting Ivan had lied and that he was glad he was dead and could spread no more vicious lies.

She and Bhric decided to say nothing about it to anyone until they talked with his mother, but her visit had been delayed due to winter storms. Tavia had been upset with the delay, eager to discover the truth, but it mattered not after a while, the days spent with her husband too joyful to let anything disturb her.

His mother had certainly been right in seeing them wed… they were perfect for each other.

Tavia stood strong, her chin raised as his father and mother drew to a stop in front of the keep. One look and Tavia saw where her husband got his fine features. His da was a handsome man with light-colored hair like Bhric, and his mum's hair was pure white, long and artfully braided. Though she had white hair she had not a trace of a wrinkle to her beautiful face, and she was tall and slender standing nearly equal to her husband's height which was a bit shorter than Bhric.

"I am late to greet you," Ingrid said, rushing up to her mother who had dismounted with the help of her husband.

Ingrid proudly held her swaddled daughter out to her mother. "Your firstborn granddaughter, Astrid."

Orianna smiled with delight as she cuddled the sleeping lass to her chest. "She is beautiful, Ingrid."

"She looks like me," Sven said, coming up behind his wife.

"That is debatable," Rune said, looking down at his granddaughter and smiling.

They climbed the stairs after Orianna handed Astrid back to her daughter.

Bhric had refused to let his wife walk down the stairs to greet his parents, her leg having troubled her the last couple of days, and he worried it was the added weight of the bairn she carried that caused her leg to flare with pain.

"Tavia, how wonderful to see you all grown," Orianna said and reached out and hugged her.

Rune nodded after looking Tavia up and down.

"Your mother chose wisely for you, Bhric."

"Aye, the more fool me for not realizing it sooner," Bhric said. "Come, there is food and drink waiting for you."

It was a pleasant family visit even Marta joining in, though she kept her distance from Tavia. The woman had been too busy helping Ingrid with the bairn to cause her any problems and she was glad for it.

She listened and laughed along with stories the family shared and warnings were given to Tavia, in jest, to beware of one or two of Bhric's brothers and sisters. She envied the large family and the life they shared and hoped that she and Bhric would have a large family of their own.

But first, she needed to know about her parents.

It was as if Bhric read her thoughts. "Mother, a private moment with you, please."

"What do you mean a private moment?" Ingrid demanded. "You can say what you will in front of family."

"Let it be, Ingrid," Sven ordered.

She turned narrowed eyes on him. "Do you know something I don't?"

"Nay!" Sven snapped, "and I do not need to know unless Lord Bhric wishes to tell me."

Bhric led his wife and mother out of the Great Hall before Ingrid could say anymore, though it did not stop her from complaining to her husband and father.

They settled in Bhric's solar, the chairs grouped around the flaming hearth, the room holding a slight chill. Spring had settled in, but a chill wind blew now and again.

Fen, having followed them, not leaving Tavia's side since she had rounded with child, rested beside her chair.

"I will not make this any more difficult than it probably already is for you, Tavia. You both obviously heard something questionable about your birth," Orianna said.

"Aye, and I would very much like to know the truth," Tavia said.

Bhric reached out and took hold of her hand and looked to his mother. "The whole truth, *Màthair*."

Orianna was touched by her son calling her mother in the language of not only her birth but his as well. "You have to understand I gave my word, and this cannot be revealed to anyone, least of all to Newlin."

"He knows nothing of it?" Tavia asked, relieved to know her da had not kept the truth from her.

"Nothing," Orianna confirmed.

"Newlin is not Tavia's da?" Bhric asked.

Orianna shook her head. "Nay, he is not… and Margaret is not her mum."

Hearing Bhric's mum confirm not only that her da was not her da, but her mum was not her mum as well sent a shiver down so deep through Tavia that she was sure it touched her soul. "Who are my parents and why was I taken from them and given to my da?"

Tavia's hand went to rest on her stomach, thinking how she would never let her bairn be taken from her.

"Does the bairn trouble you?" Bhric asked concerned, his hand going to rest over hers.

"Nay," Tavia assured her husband. "I just cannot imagine a mum giving away her newborn bairn."

"Your true mother died in childbirth just as Margaret did, and Margaret's bairn died as well." Tears welled in Orianna's eyes. "Margaret and Newlin were thrilled when she got with child. They had lost two bairns before they even got to take shape, so when Margaret carried her bairn to full term they both were thrilled and excited. Unfortunately, her delivery did not go well.

"The same night a young servant lass at Clan MacVannan gave birth. She was a small one and weak from an ordeal she had suffered but had managed to escape. Lord Bennett treated her well while she was with him. Her delivery was not going well, and she was wise enough to realize she would not survive it. She begged Lord Bennett to keep her child safe. She had confessed all to him before she died, and he brought the bairn to me asking for help. I took the newborn to Margaret and told her the tale of the homeless bairn and how she needed protection. She took you in her dying arms and claimed you as her daughter and insisted I promise to never tell Newlin the truth. That he must never know that their child was lost that night. She feared he would never survive the news of losing both his wife and child. It helped that your mother had the same-colored hair as Margaret and was petite like Margaret. No one would ever suspect you were not her child."

"Someone must have suspected since Marta told me that my mum was a liar and cheated on my da and got what she deserved."

Orianna shook her head slowly. "I feared some of the people there that night had seen Bennett talking with me and assumed he was there wanting to see Margaret. He was grieving for the loss of your true mum, and Marta wrongly assumed it was Margaret he grieved for."

"What of the healers who helped deliver the bairn?" Tavia asked. "Ivan said the MacVannan healer confessed the truth that Lord Bennett was my da."

"Corlean and Eartha knew the danger in revealing the truth. Corlean probably confirmed whatever tale Ivan wished her to so that you continued to stay safe."

"Safe from whom and why would Lord Bennett bring the bairn to you? Why not simply have her raised by his clan?" Bhric asked.

"To explain any further, I need Marta here." Orianna saw the hesitancy in her son to grant her request and quickly said, "It is important she be here, Bhric."

Bhric nodded and went to get the woman.

Tavia had endless questions to ask the woman. but she sat silent, too shocked to know what to ask.

"Your parents loved each other very much," Orianna said.

"Which parents?" Tavia asked, her own question startling her since she did not know who was who, and that included herself.

"Your true parents."

"But they never got to meet me or get know me. How could they love me?"

"You were conceived of their love, and they sacrificed their lives to see you kept safe," Orianna said and turned quiet when Bhric returned with Marta.

Marta stood by Orianna, paying no heed to Tavia.

Orianna turned a soft smile on the woman. "You need to hear this, Marta, though what you learn will remain in this room."

"As you say," Marta said and stood rigid.

Orianna took a fortifying breath and said, "Tavia's true parents are part of our people, the Northmen tribes."

"She was born on this soil," Marta argued.

"Aye, but her parents are a Northman and Northwoman. Her mother was taken as a slave during a raid on a tribe. During her time there the tribe leader's son fell in love with her. When he learned she carried his child he wanted to wed her. His father refused his request and ordered the woman sold, wanting no future heir born to a slave. His son planned an escape for them both, but his father learned of it and tried to stop it. The son fought bravely and was able to set sail with the woman he loved. Unfortunately, he had been wounded and died in his love's arms before reaching Scottish soil. How the woman wound up at Clan MacVannan I do not know. She confessed all to Lord Bennett before she died begging him to keep her daughter safe. She knew the tribe leader would not give up his search for them, and she feared what he would do to their child if he found her, having sworn that no slave's child would claim heir to his tribe."

"I was born here on this soil," Tavia repeated what Marta had said, trying to make sense of who she always believed she was… a woman of Scottish blood.

"That may be, but the Northmen blood of two brave souls who loved each other dearly runs through you," Orianna said.

"Is there still reason to worry over my wife's safety from this tribe leader?" Bhric asked, knowing how vicious some North tribes could be.

"The leader recently died in battle and his tribe was conquered. There is no reason to worry any longer, though there is also no reason for it to be known since I intend to keep my promise to Margaret and never let Newlin know the truth."

"What leader and tribe?" Bhric asked and when she gave pause to her response, he worried what she would say.

"Asger of the Sturlung Tribe," Orianna said.

Marta's eyes turned wide, and she paled. "Asger is the one who killed my husband, sold me into slavery, destroyed our tribe and killed my daughter Eydis."

"Eydis did not die, Marta," Orianna said.

Marta shook her head. "Nay. Nay. I saw them drag her blood-covered body away."

"Eydis may have been bloody, but she was not dead. She survived. It was Eydis who fell in love with Asger's son, Brant… Tavia is your granddaughter."

Marta stared in shock at the woman. "It cannot be. I saw with my own eyes. I was sure she died."

Bhric looked to his wife, pale and staring at the flames in the hearth as shocked as Marta, though she remained silent, not uttering a word and that worried him.

Marta shook her head again. "If this is true and you knew this when you took the bairn that night why did you not tell me the lass was my granddaughter?"

"Think on what you say, Marta," Orianna cautioned. "If I had told you, you would have wanted to have kept her."

"Of course, I would have, she is my blood, my daughter's child," Marta said upset.

"Exactly. You would have wanted to bring her to live with you. Asger was relentless in his search for his son and your daughter. He had sent men to speak with Rune, believing your daughter would return to you."

"He kept the truth from him?" Marta asked.

"Rune spoke what truth he knew that your daughter was dead, killed in the attack on your tribe," Orianna said. "I was glad I had decided not to tell my husband what I knew and what I had done so you, and my family would have no secret to hide and nothing to fear. I only confessed all to my husband before we came here, and he was not at all happy with me." Orianna recalled his anger, but she had no regrets for what she had done."

"If Asger had found out you lied—" Marta shook her head.

"A lie was nothing to what may have happened if Tavia had been kept with us, Asger would have eventually discovered the truth and demanded her return and for what purpose? To kill his son's child, make her a slave? Your daughter begged with her dying breath for her daughter's safety, and I could not deny her that. I knew the only safe place for your granddaughter was with Newlin. No one would ever suspect she was not his daughter. She would be safe with him, and she has been all these years."

"Is that why you chose Tavia as my wife?" Bhric asked.

"I suppose part of it was, but it was Eydis' courage

that even with her last breath she pleaded for her daughter to be safe. She was a courageous woman, and I knew her daughter would be as well and that she would make my son the perfect wife. I also knew that he would be the perfect husband for her, always keeping her safe and that meant Eydis and Brant had not died in vain."

Tears ran down Marta's cheeks as she looked upon Tavia. "One of the servants saw how upset Lord Bennett was speaking with Orianna the night of your birth. Servants began to talk and when the whispers reached me I believed what I heard. That Lady Margaret had cheated on her husband and Lord Bennett was your true da."

Tavia simply stared at the woman as she explained, not knowing how to respond and feeling too numb to the unbelievable news to feel anything at all.

"When I learned you were to be Lord Bhric's wife, I requested to come here with him to make sure you did not do to him what I thought Lady Margaret had done to her husband. I believed you were just like your mother." She shook her head. "And you are, brave and strong like my Eydis." She shook her head again. "How did I not see my daughter in you? How could I have treated my own blood so poorly? Can you ever forgive me?"

Tavia stared at the woman only partially hearing her. It was all too much to take in, to believe, to accept. She wanted to forgive the woman—her grandmother—but she had known only hatred from her. How did she suddenly trust her? She did not know what to say and when she saw that Marta was still speaking but she could not hear her and that the room was dimming around her, she turned her head quickly to her husband and went to say his name… and was engulfed in darkness.

Bhric caught his wife before she slumped over in the chair, his heart beating wildly in his chest from fear. "Tavia! Tavia!"

"Get her to her bedchamber," Marta ordered. "I will send for Hertha."

Bhric did as Marta said, rushing through the Great Hall with his wife in his arms and hearing people shout to him. His mother stopped to explain to them. But what excuse she gave he did not know or care. His only thought was for his wife and his bairn.

Fen licked Tavia's face in between whines after Bhric laid her on the bed.

He let the hound be since it had helped wake her after the tree incident while he quickly dunked a cloth in the bucket of water and rinsed it. When he returned to sit beside his wife on the bed, he was relieved to see her eyes fluttering open.

"I am here, Tavia," he said softly, wiping her face with the wet cloth.

"Bhric," she whispered.

"Aye. I am here," he repeated and took her hand in his as he continued to wipe her face.

Hertha rushed in the room with Marta and Orianna.

"She's awake," Marta said with relief, her lower lip trembling, fighting back tears.

Hertha looked at Marta, finding it odd that the woman suddenly cared what happened to Tavia.

Tavia kept hold of Bhric's hand as she assured

everyone, "I fainted that's all."

"Have you eaten?" Hertha asked. "Or received upsetting news?"

"She has eaten little," Bhric said answering for his wife, then gave Hertha a slight nod in response to her second question.

Tavia went to protest then realized her husband was right. With the excitement of his parents visit and the wait to find out the truth about her parents, she had barely eaten.

"Food, drink," —Hertha looked directly at Bhric— "and rest should do it."

Bhric acknowledged with another slight nod that he understood that rest would help ease her upset.

"I will see it brought here," Marta said.

"Nay!" Tavia said and saw sadness wash over Marta's face. "Hertha, Please tell Shea to bring what is needed."

"Aye, my lady, and I will return to see how you fare after eating," Hertha said and left the room.

"Bhric, please take your mum and devise a good story to tell everyone, since I will see your mother's promise kept that my da never learns the truth," Tavia said and looked to Marta. "You and I need to talk."

"You need to eat first and you need rest," Bhric said, helping his wife sit up when she grabbed his arm to pull herself up.

"I will see that she eats and rests," Marta said.

Bhric worried over his wife and their bairn nestled inside her, but he also understood what finding out the truth meant to her. "Are you sure about this?"

"Aye, I am sure. We will talk later. "Tavia looked

past him to his mother. "As will you and I, Orianna."

"*Màthair*. Please call me mother," Orianna said.

Tavia smiled. "I never thought I would have so many mothers."

Bhric was glad to see her smile and her cheeks flush lightly and he could not help but kiss her soft pink cheek. "Send Fen if you need me."

Fen barked as if he understood.

Bhric stopped by Marta. "You are truly family now. Treat your granddaughter well."

"Of that there is no doubt, my lord," Marta said tears heavy in her eyes.

When the door closed, Tavia said, "Please tell me about my mother."

Chapter Thirty

Birthing time!

"Everyone does well together," Tavia said, her arm hooked on her husband's as they walked through the village.

"Aye, thanks to you," Bhric said.

"Me?" she questioned.

"Aye. Everyone is amazed how you forgave Marta and how she serves you and now lives in the keep. Shea cannot believe what a pleasant woman she is and how she requests things from her rather than demand since her sole task is your care.

"A task that requires her presence in the keep where she belongs," Tavia said. "Besides Shea is right. Marta is different now. Don't you Agree?"

"Very much so. I have never seen her so happy or smiling as much as she does. She is much more pleasant to be around. Even Fen has grown to like her and amazingly she has grown to like him." He looked at the hound that had kept close to Tavia the last couple of days and wondered if he sensed her time was near. "But I suppose it is because the hound protects you so well. I also like the way she looks after you and sees that you eat and rest and warns you to not overdo with your leg."

"You may have thought of her like family at one time, but she is truly family now. I share the same blood with her and another who soon will," Tavia said, resting her hand on her large-rounded stomach.

"You have grown very large in the last month," Bhric said with some worry. "He is going to be a big one."

"And I am determined to spit him out as quick as possible," Tavia said with a laugh.

Bhric wished he felt as confident. It had not made him feel any better knowing Margaret was not her true mother since her true mother also died in childbirth. But his mother believed Eydis had no desire to live after losing the man she loved. Lord Bennett had told her that the young woman seemed to wither away little by little, her heart broken in too many pieces to ever be put back together again.

"Aye, wife, take pity on me and do just that. I do not know if I can survive a long birthing time," he said, his stomach churning at the thought.

Tavia laughed again. "I will do my best." She hurried to change the subject seeing how upset her husband appeared with talk of her delivery time. "Have you heard any news about who will become the new Lord MacVannan?"

Bhric smiled. "Aye, I received word this morning and thought to surprise you with it."

"Then surprise me," Tavia said eagerly.

"Terence… Glenna and William's son, now Lord Terence," Bhric said.

Tavia smiled with delight. "How is it that their son is now lord of Clan MacVannan?"

"Terence made his fortune successfully serving the king and the king granted him lordship of Clan MacVannan as a reward. From what I hear he is a good man and a skilled warrior. It will be good that Clan

Strathearn has a strong neighbor and friend."

"Aye—OH!" Tavia cried out and stopped abruptly. She hoisted the hem of her garments some to see a wet puddle at her feet. "My water released."

Bhric stood staring at her.

"We need to get to the keep," she said when he did not move.

Bhric shook his head, scooped her up, and took off running, Fen racing ahead of him barking.

Tavia smiled when she heard cheers fill the air and shouts calling for a celebration, that an heir was about to be born.

"It's time! It's time!" Bhric yelled and Fen barked as they rushed into the Great Hall.

Marta turned wide-eyed and looked to Shea. "Get Hertha and Greta!" She rushed to follow Bhric up the stairs. "To my lady's bedchamber, where all the heirs of Clan MacShane were born," she ordered.

Marta needn't tell Bhric that. His grandfather had made it clear to him that Bhric's son would be born in the room where Bhric had been born, his mother had been born and Lord Donald himself had been born. Bhric was proud that he was able to keep his word to his grandfather and produce the first of several heirs who would see that Clan MacShane remained strong.

"Begone with you now," Marta ordered Bhric with a wave of her hand after he placed his wife on the bed. "I will see to my granddaughter."

Marta never failed to refer to Tavia as her granddaughter when in private. It was as if she had to reassure herself but then Tavia did the same as if she too needed reassurance.

"I am glad you are here with me, *Amma*," Tavia said.

Bhric saw tears tickle Marta's eyes. Tavia had asked Bhric the word for grandmother in Norse and called Marta by it whenever they were alone. It always brought tears to the older woman's eyes.

"I am blessed to be here with you and see my great-grandchild born. Now let's get you comfortable." Marta turned. "What are you still doing here? Go!" she ordered and shooed Bhric away.

"I do not want to leave her," Bhric said, fearful he would lose her.

Tavia stretched her hand out to him, and he hurried to her and took hold of it.

"A kiss for strength," she said and pressed her lips to his to linger for a moment. Then she whispered, "I love you always."

"Not as much as I love you," he whispered back.

"Now go!" Marta demanded, shooing him away again.

"You will keep me abreast of what goes on," Bhric ordered.

The powerful command in his voice had Marta responding with a bob of her head. "Aye, my lord."

"Do so as a grandmother who takes pity on her grandson-in-law who will worry himself senseless, Marta," Bhric said.

Marta smiled. "I will see you are kept informed."

Hertha rushed in, Ingrid behind her, then Greta entered shortly after her. Shea was the last to enter and waited to the side for instructions.

Bhric walked to the door and cast one last look at

his wife and saw courage but also a bit of fear on her lovely face, and he wished he did not have to leave her. She sent him a brief wave and he returned it with a smile, then reluctantly walked out the door closing it behind him.

***

"You are going to wear your boots out if you do not stop pacing," Sven warned him.

"It has been hours and not a single word from any of them," Bhric said with a glance at a Fen who kept anxious eyes on him.

"Not true. Ingrid said all was going well the two times she came and took Astrid to feed."

"That tells me nothing," Bhric argued.

"It tells you that your wife does well. Sit, have a drink, and tell me what happened that has changed how Marta feels about your wife and your wife feels about her," Sven said.

"I cannot. I have given my word," Bhric said. "Maybe one day in the future. For now, know all is well."

"That suits me, but you are not going to get away with that response with your sister. She is determined to find out," Sven warned.

"I already know," Ingrid said with a smile and handed a content Astrid to her da after entering the solar. "But like my brother, I am sworn to secrecy."

Sven's mouth hung open as his wife waltzed out of the room. He shook his head. "How does she do that? Find things out. You have got to tell me now. She will torment me with it. You must tell me."

"Does she know or does Ingrid make it appear that way so I will now discuss it with her, and she will find out?" Bhric said with a laugh.

"You are right. It is good you remind me how devious your sister can be."

"Something you should remember yourself," Bhric warned with another laugh and finally dropped down in a chair. "I prefer battle to this endless wait."

Sven grinned. "I was relieved I had a battle to fight while Ingrid was birthing our bairn. It was much easier returning home to find it over and done, my daughter born. A good battle takes your mind off everything."

About an hour later, Shea appeared with food for the two men. "Marta says to tell you that Lady Tavia is doing well, and it should not be long now."

"How long is not long?" Bhric asked.

"Marta did not say, my lord," Shea said and hurried out of the room.

An hour later Bhric started pacing again, then stopped when he saw Marta standing in the open doorway. He stared, his heart hammering in his chest and was relieved when Marta smiled.

"Your wife has given you a fine son."

"A son and an heir to the Clan MacShane," Sven shouted in joy and his sleeping daughter woke with a cry.

Bhric felt an intense pride in hearing he had a son.

Marta's smile grew. "Your wife also gave you a daughter."

"Twins?" Sven yelled and his daughter he got to stop crying from his last outburst began to cry again.

Bhric had to sit, he was so shocked, though he was

quick to ask, "Tavia?"

"She is a strong woman and did well. She asks for you," Marta said.

Bhric was quick to follow Marta out of the room, Fen hurrying out with him, though he stopped her when they reached the stairs. "All is truly well, Marta."

"It is. My granddaughter is much like her mum, strong and courageous. I am so proud of her," Marta said.

Bhric hugged the woman to her surprise. "Congratulations, *Amma*."

"And you as well, Da," Marta said with a huge smile as Bhric flew up the stairs, Fen keeping pace behind him.

Hertha was holding one bairn and his sister Ingrid the other when Bhric entered the room, but Bhric glanced at them both fleetingly. First, he wanted to go to his wife as did Fen, reaching her before Bhric did and getting a generous ear rub.

"Two. I delivered two," Tavia said proudly.

Bhric leaned over her to place a kiss on her brow. She was sitting up in bed, dressed in a fresh nightdress, her cheeks flushed lightly and a brightness in her eyes that brought a smile to his face.

"You did well, wife, actually, more than well," Bhric said prouder of his wife than he ever imagined he could be.

"I was right," Ingrid called out. "My brother is a potent man to plant two bairns inside you."

"Ingrid,!" Bhric warned and all the women laughed.

Ingrid walked over to him and handed him the

swaddled bairn. "Your son. He was born first."

Bhric took the small bundle and stared at his son as he let loose with a wide yawn, then returned to sleep. He had a thatch of hair the same light color as Bhric's and fine features.

Tavia stretched her arms out to him. "I will take him so you may hold your daughter." Fen sniffed at the small bundle as she took her son. "Family, Fen, he is family."

Hertha placed the little bundle in Bhric's arms, and he stared at her amazed of how beautiful she was, dark hair like her mum's and the most beautiful blue eyes.

Marta came to stand next him and whispered, "She is the picture of my daughter when she was born."

"She is beautiful," Bhric said for all to hear.

"Between Astrid and your daughter, you and Sven are going to be busy fighting off the men," Ingrid said.

Bhric cringed. "I do not want to think of that now."

"Why? Because you know what is on a man's mind all the time?" Ingrid teased.

"Ingrid, go to your husband and daughter," Bhric commanded.

"It is time for all of us to leave the new parents with their newborn bairns," Greta said.

"I would return to see how you do," Hertha said, "but Marta assures me she will look after you and fetch me if I am needed."

"Aye, Marta will take good care of me and the bairns," Tavia said.

"Of course, she will, she's family," Ingrid said with a grin and walked out the door. All but Marta following her.

"I should send my sister back home," Bhric said, now wondering if she had actually discovered the truth.

"And lose all entertainment?" Tavia said with feigned shock.

Bhric laughed glad to see that his wife teased and looked so well.

Marta approached them after Bhric went and sat on the bed beside his wife. "I will leave you now and return to help you when it is time to feed the bairns."

"Before you go, *Amma*," Tavia said, "Bhric and I would like you to know the names we have chosen. We had discussed it and had a name chosen for a son and a daughter and now we can use both." Tavia smiled softly. "Our daughter will be named, Eydis, after my mum and our son will be named Brant after my da."

Marta could not stop her tears from falling. "I believe your mum and da would be immensely proud of you just as I am, as well as the da who raised you to be a strong woman."

Tavia smiled, pleased that she acknowledged Newlin, the only da she had ever known.

Marta quickly wiped her tears away. "You should rest. Let me put the bairns in the cradles. You can rest while they sleep for once they wake they will be hungry and keep you busy."

Marta took the lad from Tavia, but Bhric stood and placed his daughter in the second cradle, seeing it was the one Astrid had outgrown.

"Rest," Marta ordered before closing the door behind her.

Fen went and sniffed at both bairns in the two cradles, then stretched out in front of both to sleep.

Bhric slipped his boots off and got in bed to sit beside his wife and tucked her in his arms and contentment washed over him when she settled herself comfortably against him.

Tavia draped her arm over him, rested her head on his chest, and looked up at him. "I never expected to find such happiness with you, Bhric, and never did I expect to find such a binding love with you."

He cupped her chin and ran his thumb slowly over her bottom lip. "I had hoped for both and yet I got so much more with you. You are my heart, Tavia, it beats strong because of you and would wither without you, and in my heart is where you will always be, now and beyond this earthly plane."

He brought his lips to hers and sealed his declaration of love with a tender kiss and while she slept in his arms, he thanked the heavens that this mother had been wise and courageous enough to rescue and keep safe a tiny bairn that would one day be his wife.

Bhric rested his head on top of his wife's head and smiled, the familiar scent of mint drifting off her hair and closed his eyes. He did not know how he made it through the delivery. It had absolutely exhausted him and so he joined his wife in sleep.

The end… but don't miss Flora and Fia's stories!
The Highland Warlord's Kiss and The Legendary Highlander
Find out more about Donna and her books at
www.donnafletcher.com

Printed in Great Britain
by Amazon

27268088R00212